## Advance Praise for
# *Kennedy's Goodbye*

"Kati Rose's wise-cracking narrator in *Kennedy's Goodbye* is absolutely irresistible, as she grapples with the contradictions and mixed messages of her staunchly Catholic upbringing. Funny, wise, entertaining, and heartbreaking, the novel is filled with memorable characters, moral dilemmas, and the full-throttle exuberance of youth."

—**Helen Fremont**, author of the national bestseller
*After Long Silence* and *The Escape Artist*

"Kati Rose writes with wit, candor, and endearing intimacy. Her *Kennedy's Goodbye* is replete with the heartache and hope of growing up in a culture awash in confusion."

—**David Ritz**, author of *Respect: The Life of Aretha Franklin*

"Kati Rose grabs your gut from the get-go with her quick, fresh prose and a simply complex protagonist you'll root for in this compelling, coming-of-age debut novel."

—**Laurie Graff**, author of *You Have to Kiss a Lot of Frogs*
and *The Shiksa Syndrome*

"Kati Rose's Kennedy takes readers on a hilarious, heartbreaking, and deeply reflective ride through the confusing days of the end of childhood and the beginning of adulthood. Kennedy's funny, sarcastic, and poignant voice guides readers through her coming of age as a confused Catholic and avowed rock fan. This book will take you back!"

—**Paul Young**, Associate Professor, Georgetown University,
author of *Seducing the Eighteenth-Century French Reader*

# KENNEDY'S
# GOODBYE

## Kati Rose

**Post Hill Press**
New York • Nashville
posthillpress.com

Published in the United States of America
1 2 3 4 5 6 7 8 9 10

*For Keith.*
*We did it for real.*

# Goodbye to Innocence

**May 1971**

There is an 8mm film titled *Goodbye to Innocence*. In it, I am wearing my first Holy Communion dress—white chiffon with sheer long sleeves, a belt that ties in a bow in the back, and satin tails that dangle like bicycle streamers. I am barefoot.

I am wrapped like a snake around one of the thinner trunks of a large six-trunked tree that shadows our house. I dance around the trunk, twirling, showing off, flinging my hair. I look free.

In this cameo, no one tells me what to do. No one cries. No one steals. No one ignores me or tells me to leave Mom alone. No one feels sad or lonely. There is no fear. There is no pain. No one leaves.

The film ends with a scotch-taped paper towel inscribed with the film's title blowing away from the six-trunked tree, me running to catch it, me waving goodbye.

It is goodbye to a lot of things.

I am seven.

1

## CHAPTER 1

# D.O.A.

**April 1975**

Rog and I were driving down Sand Creek Road the way that we always did: on one of our so-called joyrides, testing Roger's brand-new rear speakers.

"Listen, Boss," he told me, his thumb and index finger wrapped around the volume knob on his car's dash.

But I never had time to hear.

Instead there was a screaming screech and a crashing boom, like cracking thunder. And then everything was in slow motion and fast and standing still or maybe a combination of them all. There was an eerie silence despite the noise.

"Jesus Christ! Shit! Fuck!" Roger yelled.

*Thou shalt not take the name of the Lord thy God in vain.*

I was half on and half off of the passenger seat, my copilot seat, as if crouched on the floor of the car. My hand was wedged sideways between the dashboard and the windshield.

Rog was lying down on the driver's side, the pilot side, his bucket seat a bed instead of a seat. He didn't look like Rog at all. He looked like the Joker from *Batman*. His eyeballs looked crazy. His lips looked purple-red and stretched too far.

"Boss, you OK?" Rog said.

He reached out for me like a blind person, groping the air while struggling to sit up.

"Goddamn it," Rog said.

*Thou shalt not take the name of the Lord thy God in vain. Again.*

I heard voices, maybe yelling. The car was making a hissing sound, like steam from a tea kettle. I heard jingles like falling glass, and loud static playing from the rear speakers.

"Boss, are you hurt?" Rog said.

"Maybe my hand," I said.

My hands were shaking when Roger took them into his. He held them, bent my wrists and fingers, then turned my hands back and forth like he was inspecting them—like it was the first time that he had ever seen them. He found a red mark along the edge of my right hand and ran his finger along it.

*No one ever touches me.*

"I'm going to kill whoever is the son of a bitch that just rear-ended us!" he said.

*Thou shalt not kill. Mortal sin.*

Roger's hands were hard like a worker's but soft like someone who cared all at the same time. Some of his fingernails were yellow. Dad said that was from the cigarettes.

"Boss, we've had an accident," Rog said.

And that, right there, was the beginning of the end. Or maybe it was the other way around.

Rog and I had been joyriding for as long as I could remember: he the pilot, me the copilot. Besides being my brother, Rog was my best friend. I was ten and Rog was hours away from turning twenty-one.

Rog struggled to push his car door open using his shoulder, and finally, both of his feet, kicking it open wide enough to escape.

"Goddamn it. Sit tight," he said.

If Roger didn't stop swearing, he'd end up going to hell in a hand basket. He was already sinning his way right into it—he swore, he sped, he smoked. He was on his way to being a hoodlum, according to Dad. And Dooley.

Dooley was our brother. The oldest. Roger called him Super Dooley. Before he was a police officer, Dooley was an Eagle Scout and a volunteer-everything. Dad said that volunteering was even more special than having a job. According to Dad, Dooley had a vocation, a job that God Himself asked you to do for Him. Dooley was Dad's favorite. Dad never yelled at him the way that he yelled at Roger. In fact, Dad listened to Dooley all the time, and even answered him back. Even when Dooley was at work being a cop, Dad listened to him on the police scanner that Dooley bought for him. Dooley was heard. Our brother Dooley was special.

*Super Dooley.*

I looked around.

People walked along the car, stepping over metal and broken glass.

Rog talked to some guy holding his neck.

I ran my finger along a crack in the windshield, a lightning bolt.

I heard sirens in the distance.

"Don't be afraid, Boss, the police are coming," Rog said.

He lit a cigarette and opened the copilot door, reaching into his glove compartment. He fumbled through some papers and hid a hash pipe behind them before closing the compartment's door.

"Rog, smoking is a fast way of getting into hell according to God and Dad. Plus, the surgeon general said that it's bad for your health," I said. "Your rearview mirror is on the floor and your windshield has a lightning bolt in it."

"My fucking car is fucking wrecked. Goddamn it. I can't fucking believe this is happening," he said.

I watched Roger's cigarette dance up and down, balanced between his lips, as smoke and all of his sin words fell out of his mouth.

"Do you need an ambulance, Boss?"

*An ambulance?*

"No," I said.

I knew from the sounds of the sirens that the police were getting closer.

"Is Dooley coming?" I asked the smoke that sat in my lap. It smelled kind of good. It smelled like, *I don't know*, like Rog.

My hand hurt.

Rog stood in the road, smoking, passing papers back and forth with strangers. He was so pale, almost see-through, except for his lips, which were still purple-red.

I felt sad in my heart for him but didn't know how to tell him. I wanted to throw up, but I did as I was told. I sat tight.

The sirens grew louder until their silence sounded Dooley's presence.

I was never, and never have been since, as happy, or happy at all, to see Dooley as I was at that moment. But even at that, watching Dooley walk toward the scene of the accident was more like watching Reed from *Adam-12* on TV than it was like watching a real-life brother coming to help. One hand rested on his holster. The other tugged the brim of his hat that rested over his wavy black hair.

He stuck his head into Rog's car and inspected me through the open window where Roger's empty bucket seat laid alongside me.

"Minor Caucasian female," Dooley told his walkie-talkie. Then he asked me, "Kennedy, what happened? Was Roger driving too fast? Was he being reckless?"

Dooley was always volunteering to find things that Roger did wrong, like it was his job in our family. Like it was his vocation.

"We weren't even moving!" I said.

Dooley did not hear me. Dooley wasn't even listening. He never did.

"That's a negative," he said, when they asked him in their cop code words if I needed an ambulance.

*Whew. I hate ambulances.*

Dooley walked to Roger. They talked, argued, like they always did.

"We were stopped dead. We got sandwiched. My car is wrecked. Please just take Kennedy home. Make sure she's OK," Rog said.

Rog blew his cigarette smoke right into Dooley's face and bit his lip as if he was going to cry. That was the face he made when he was getting yelled at by Dad or lying about something.

I could always tell when Roger was upset. That was part of my job as Boss and copilot. That's what Rog said.

Dooley backed away and approached our crumpled car.

"C'mon, I'll give you a ride in my police car," he said, opening my copilot door, which made a loud cranking noise that wasn't there before.

I didn't want to ride in the police car and I didn't want to leave Rog.

"What about Rog? We can't leave him alone!" I said.

But Dooley kept walking toward his police car.

"Hey! My hand hurts!" I said.

But only the police car's lights answered me with their click swirl tick-tock.

I wondered why God chose Dooley to do His work if he couldn't even be nice to Rog or answer me? *Volunteering is a vocation.* He could be nice to strangers, and to Dad and his fiancée Bea, but he couldn't be nice to Rog or me.

We got into the police car and Dooley talked into his walkie-talkie. He turned to me.

"Were you two on one of your joyrides?" he said.

I didn't want to answer him. I didn't want Rog to get into trouble for smoking or speeding, when in fact, he wasn't doing either when the car ran into us.

"We were testing his new speakers," I said.

But Dooley was too busy listening to his police radio to even hear me, or maybe even remember that he had asked.

*Whew.*

I continued.

"There was an enormous bang and then Rog was lying down instead of driving and his face looked just like the Joker from *Batman*. My hand hit the dash or maybe the windshield and I was crouched and then there was glass everywhere and Roger's windshield got a lightning bolt in it."

*Come in, Adam-12. I mean, even Malloy answers Reed sometimes.*

I stared at Dooley. He really was as handsome as a movie star. He was always dropping to the floor to do push ups, and spent a lot of his time combing his thick moustache and brushing his teeth so that he could kiss Bea.

*Gross.*

As we turned our corner, I saw Mom standing in the doorway like she did when I got off of the school bus.

7

Dooley sounded his siren as we slid into the driveway.

Mom approached Dooley's side of the police car. The pilot side.

"Go inside, Kennedy," Dooley said.

"But Dool—" I said.

"Go!"

So I did.

I sat next to the police scanner listening for cop code words about Rog. I traced the red streak along the side of my hand and watched Mom walk back into the house.

Silence.

"Mom, is Roger OK?"

"Think of Easter," Mom said.

"Think of Easter" was what Mom told me to do whenever I felt anything.

"Like dead Jesus on the cross?" I had asked, when she first suggested this.

"No, like jelly beans and pastels and bunnies," she had said.

It seemed reasonable that jelly beans and pastels and bunnies were better things to think about than dead Jesus, but even dead Jesus didn't seem as bad as the thought of having left Roger all alone with his new car crumpled and looking so pale I thought he'd fade right away.

Over and over I heard the screech and felt the bang, felt the stillness and the slow motion, *Boss, you OK?* the sound of the siren, the sound of Dooley's silence.

*Think of Easter...*

Finally, the dispatcher said in cop code that the police were leaving the scene of the accident.

"Mom! Roger is coming home!" I said.

But Mom simply stood still by the front screen door, waiting.

Silence.

8

*Honor thy father and thy mother. Thou shalt not kill. Which commandment am I breaking by wanting Mom to answer me?*

I'd learned all about the commandments from Sister Mary Ruth, or Ruthless, as Roger called her. Rog was good at giving people names like Sister Mary Ruthless and Super Dooley.

Being disrespectful to a nun was definitely a sin against the second commandment, but I couldn't blame Rog for naming her that. She was the meanest nun ever. Her favorite commandment was the first one that said you were not allowed to worship any gods before God Himself. So, Sister Mary Ruthless walked around all day telling kids that there was no Santa Claus.

"Boys and girls, there is no such thing as Santa Claus. Go home and admonish your parents for being pagans. Believing in Santa Claus is a sin against the first, God's ultimate, commandment," she said.

That nun swung at the air all day long, just hoping to hit someone, connecting at least half of the time.

"It's hit or miss, Boss," Roger warned.

That's how mean she was.

I thought about Easter and prayed Hail Marys because they were easier to figure out than commandments.

"Say Hail Marys when you're scared, Boss. She's nice. She's a mom and a girl. And girls are nice. Like you," Roger told me.

Roger's Hail Marys were like Mom's think of Easter.

"It can't hurt, Boss," Roger always said.

After a gazillion years or maybe five minutes, Dad and Roger turned our corner together, but in their separate cars. Roger's car looked barely like his car at all, but rather, a maroon cartoon accordion on wheels. It trudged toward our house, its trunk bouncing up and down like Roger's cigarette did when he talked, banging and puffing. Smoke seeped out of Roger's pilot window, but I couldn't tell if Roger was smoking or if his accordion cartoon car was smoking.

*Is Roger's bucket seat back to being a seat instead of a bed?*

Roger rolled his crumpled car as far into the driveway as was possible, and it became clear—both Roger *and* his car were smoking.

*Roger is smoking and Dad isn't yelling.*

Dad circled Roger's car, shaking his head back and forth.

I rushed past Mom through the front screen door to Roger. I wanted to hug him but didn't know how.

Roger finished his cigarette and put it out against the bottom of his Converse, stashing the butt into his back pocket. He knew that Dad would have had a conniption if he left it on the ground. According to Roger, Dad was good at conniptions.

"Stand back, Boss, the creases are sharp," Rog warned.

Roger's accordion cartoon car looked sharp and scary. Roger looked like he was going to throw up.

Dad looked at Mom, who, at that point, was standing on the cement front steps.

"He's OK," Dad told her.

She nodded.

I did the only thing that I could think of to help Rog. I ran across the street to get Valerie, our neighbor and Roger's girlfriend. Rog promised that one day he would make Valerie my sister.

I told Valerie everything—about testing the speakers and the screech and the boom and the way that Roger was lying down and the crumpled cars both in front of us and behind us and the rearview mirror on the floor and the lightning bolt windshield and my hand and the dash and the sirens and Dooley and the sound of the lights on the police car and the silence and she listened.

"Are you OK? Is Roger OK?" she asked.

Valerie teared up, which made her green eyes sparkle even more. Valerie was the prettiest girl I had ever seen.

I showed her my hand where the red mark was already turning purplish *like Roger's lips* and she told me to go get Marcus.

I was Chicken Little. I ran next door and knocked on Marcus's door.

Roger's best friend, Marcus, gave me a funny feeling somewhere inside of me below my navel. Mom said that saying belly button was crass, so we said navel.

Marcus was very skinny and had a lot of muscles on his abdomen (we weren't allowed to say tummy or belly, also crass, according to Mom) that you could count if you wanted to. He had a scar running along them like the crack in Roger's windshield from driving his car into a pole after drinking way too much alcohol. He looked just like Robert Plant, the Led Zeppelin dude, but I didn't think that there was any redemption for Marcus even on a stairway, especially according to Dad. Marcus drank and smoked and cussed and used crass words like pussy and boner and weed and almost never wore a shirt.

"What the fuck are you doing here, Boss?" Marcus asked me as he opened his front door.

*And there are his muscles, all six of them, staring right at me.*

I told him everything that I told Valerie.

He stared at me without answering, but it was a different kind of silence than Dooley's, than Mom's. He ran to our driveway, to Roger's car, where neighbors were already circling like scavengers.

"Holy fuck, Rog! What the hell happened to your car?" Marcus said.

*Hail Mary full of grace...*

All I could do was pray to the Blessed Mother, what with Roger's cigarette and the circling neighbors and the cussing and the crumpled car. And the muscles.

I looked at Dad because I was afraid that he might yell at Roger, or Marcus, or anyone. But Dad just stood next to Roger, sad birds amongst vultures.

I watched from the sidelines until I got too sad to stand, and went inside where Mom stood over a griddle waiting for it to heat up. I smelled the electricity.

*No meat on Fridays during Lent.*

I didn't know how Mom expected anyone to be able to eat. I wondered how she could even stand. My knees hadn't stopped shaking.

Mom poured pancake batter while I prayed on crystal rosary beads until Dad and Roger came inside. We sat at the kitchen table pushing pancakes on our plates and listening to Dooley describe someone else's tragedy on the police scanner.

Roger stood.

"Thanks," he said, and left the table without permission.

Dad didn't yell.

I knew from the way that Rog was biting his lip that he wanted to cry.

He grabbed his suede fringed jacket and swung it over his shoulders. He was leaving. He was going to the fence, where all of the neighborhood's hoodlums hung out to make nothing of their lives. That's what Dad said. To me, it looked like the place where cool people smoked cigarettes together.

Gina walked through the front screen door as Rog was leaving.

Gina was Roger's twin, his *Irish* twin. That meant that they were born as close as possible to each other without actually being twins. That made them special.

Not me. I was born a whole lot of years later, right on Dad's birthday, but seemed to be a pain in the neck to everyone. Except Roger.

"What happened to your car?" she asked.

"It's fucked," Rog said.

Gina looked at me and I shrugged my shoulders because I didn't know what else to do.

I looked at Dad because Rog had said the F word in front of him and God and everyone else. But no one, except me, and maybe God, seemed to notice.

Roger waved at me as he left through the front screen door like he always did. His suede fringe swayed goodbye. His cigarette was lit by the time he reached the bottom of the driveway.

"Is this supper?" Gina asked, grabbing a pancake and walking to her room.

Gina never went to the fence. She was too busy trying to find a husband.

I grabbed a pancake, like Gina, left the table without permission, and went to my room.

All of the rules were out the window that day, apparently.

*Why do adults make and break all of the rules but kids have to follow them? How come Sister Mary Ruthless can be so mean? How come Roger can smoke and Dooley can bully and Marcus can say pussy? How come I'm the one in the velvet confessional box telling Father my sins and getting punished with his penance?*

Gina tapped on my door and asked me what had happened. I told her everything—the screech, the boom, my hand into the dashboard, the silence.

"Was Dooley there?" she asked.

"Of course," I said.

"Tell Mom about your hand," she said.

I wouldn't. I had been trying not to bother Mom ever since the ambulance took her away and she had her lady parts removed.

Thou shalt not bother Mom was the commandment.

So I didn't.

I prayed the rosary.

*It can't hurt, Boss…*

*Hail Mary full of grace please help Dad yell less at Roger, make Rog less sad…*

In between beads, I thought about Gina, how pretty she was, like Valerie, but more in a Marcia Brady kind of way. Gina was lucky because she got to be Roger's Irish twin.

*I want to be Roger's twin.*

I thought about the way that Marcus asked Gina out on dates, not in a usual way, but in a Marcus way, by singing a song or lying on the ground howling or crawling after her like a dog. Marcus was weird that way.

"Why do you always say no to Marcus?" I had asked Gina.

"He's not husband material, Kennedy," Gina said.

I wondered which sins I had committed when I felt happy that Valerie had listened to me, and how good it had felt when Roger held my hands in our crumpled car.

*Hail Mary full of grace please keep Mom healthy even though she is missing her lady parts…I promise to try to leave her alone, just as I was told…*

I thanked God Himself for Gilbert O'Sullivan, because when I played his 45, "Alone Again, Naturally," we were not alone anymore, but alone together.

*Hail Mary full of grace, please help make Roger's birthday OK, because even though I am Roger's Boss and copilot, I'm not sure that I can fix him alone, maybe you can help, cuz you're nice, like Roger said…please help…*

I kissed my rosary's crucifix because that was what you were supposed to do when you were finished with the gazillion prayers.

I sat awake in silence listening for the sound of the front screen door, the sound of Roger coming home, but fell asleep hearing only the screech and the boom the screech and the boom.

*Boss, you OK?*

The next day, Mom made a yellow cake that she let me frost with homemade chocolate frosting.

"Roger is sad," I said to Mom as I was spreading, making sure not to pull up the top layer of the cake with the knife. Mom would have had a fit if I wrecked the cake. A conniption.

She handed me a tube of writing gel.

Maybe she hadn't heard me, or maybe she just didn't feel like answering. Maybe missing your lady parts made you answer more like silent God and less like Mom. Maybe I was too much of a big pain in the neck.

"Mom, Sister Mary Ruthless said that if we don't bring in flowers for the Blessed Mother then She will whisper into God's ear that we are damnable sinners," I said.

I was allowed to say damnable because it was within proper context.

I squeezed the tube of gel and began writing in perfect cursive on Roger's cake, even though my purply hand hurt from when it decided to smash into the dashboard of Rog's car.

"So, can I pick lilacs to bring into school? Mom? Once they bloom? Mom?"

"Take all you want," she said.

Well, that was easier than I thought. Maybe Mom understood all about lilacs, maybe because she was a mom like the Blessed Mother.

I knew better than to ask Mom to explain to me why the Mother of God would think that we were sinners if we didn't bring in flowers for Her, even if that was what Sister Mary Ruthless said. And even though I was afraid of the Blessed Mother whispering damnations into God's ear, I was more worried about Roger's sadness. And Mom.

*Think of Easter…*

"Mom? Can I use the whole tube?"

I took Mom's silence as a yes and drew smiley faces on Roger's cake until the tube was empty. I hoped that they would make him feel a little less sad.

Rog worked a double shift that day, and in between, we celebrated his birthday. He held his neck as he blew out his candles. His eyes watered with tears.

"Do you really have to go back to work?" I said.

"It's OK, Boss, I need all the money I can get now that my car is a Goddamn mess," he said.

*Thou shalt not take the name of the Lord thy God in vain.*

## CHAPTER 2

# Wish You Were Here

**May 1975**

As if Dad, Dooley, God, and the surgeon general weren't already on Roger's back for smoking cigarettes, now the crumpled car was in question.

"Have you heard from the insurance company?"

"Are you going to tie down that trunk?"

"Why haven't you secured that mirror with duct-tape?"

"Don't you think you should wire that seat in place?"

"When are you going to replace that windshield?"

"And by the way, what the hell are you going to do with the rest of your life?"

KAPOW! KLONK! SOCK! ZOWIE! BONK! BOOM!

Dad and Dooley fired questions at Roger like punches from *Batman*.

Rog continued to look as crumpled as his car, biting his lip as if he was lying or trying not to cry all the time.

I did what I could. I asked Rog if he wanted to play rummy. I made his bed, I poured his coffee. I said Hail Marys. I dusted his dashboard and washed his crumpled car, hoping if it was clean, then somehow it would be better.

"Boss, what the fuck did you do to the car?" Marcus asked.

"I washed it with Fab," I said, "with lemon-freshened Borax."

"It looks like shit," Marcus said.

He was right. As I had sponged along and in between the jagged metal, sudsy tears ran down and washed away in a stream of pink. The Fab took the finish right off.

*Stand back, Boss, the creases are sharp…*

Roger didn't even notice.

"What the heck is Roger going to do with the rest of his life?" I asked Marcus Dad's question.

"Oh no, oh no, oh no, don't you ever go, oh no…" he Robert Plant-ed me.

He played the air with his greasy fingers, messing up the words the way he always did.

"Marcus. I'm serious. Can't you fix his car or help him figure out what he's going to do with the rest of his life?"

"Boss, he's got you. He's got Valerie. What more does a guy need? Go home. Rog will be fine. He'll figure it out," he said.

And he did. Sort of.

Rog duct-taped the rearview mirror and wired his bucket seat into a permanent sitting position. Only the copilot door worked, so Rog had to climb through my side to drive. The tied-down trunk clanked as we drove. The windshield's bolt of lightning grew. Our joyrides, although shorter and slower, were smoky and loud with music from speakers that dangled by wire threads.

"Jesus fucking Christ, now what?" Rog said.

*Thou shalt not take the name of the Lord thy God in vain.*

I reached into Roger's glove compartment and stuffed the hash pipe down my shirt.

Roger needed buckets of lilacs to save his soul.

Dooley approached the car, the pilot side, his police car's red lights click swirl tick-tocking behind us.

"Fuck off," Rog said.

"It's my duty as an officer of the law and as a citizen to protect a minor. You're endangering her welfare." Dooley head-nodded toward me.

Roger exercised his right to remain silent.

"You know I can issue you a ticket for that windshield. The vehicle is no longer safe to be on the road," Dooley said.

"Bullshit," said Rog.

"Take her home," Dooley said, "or I will."

We drove home after Rog smoked three more cigarettes.

"Rog, you're going to go to hell in a hand basket. Have you been to confession?" I asked.

"Don't worry about me, Boss," he said.

But I did.

Dad stood waiting in the doorway. No doubt the police scanner told him what had happened.

"What the hell is the matter with you? Have you no sense about you? Is this what you intend to do with the rest of your life? Smoke cigarettes and hang around with a bunch of Goddamn hooligans? Endanger the welfare of a minor?" Dad said.

*Um, Dad, for the record, thou shalt not take the name of the Lord thy God in vain. I'll have to go to confession for ALL of us…*

Rog stood twirling a button's loose thread, answering like God—not at all.

"Answer me! What the hell is the matter with you?" Dad yelled.

19

Rog and Dad stood in silence staring at each other for a gazillion years, or maybe seven-Mississippi.

"I don't know," Rog said, bit his lip, turned, and left for the fence.

We never drove in the crumpled car again.

Rog rode his bike to work, and if I could, I rode alongside him until I had to turn back alone.

Besides praying to the Blessed Mother, I didn't know how to help Rog figure out what the hell was the matter with him, or what the hell he was going to do for the rest of his life.

*Forgive me, Father, for I have sinned.*

## Never-Ending May 1975

"Aren't you worried about your nipples?" I asked Gina, after she slid off her bra from beneath her shirt seconds before Wayne, her newest boyfriend, arrived for their date.

"No. Hide it," she said.

"What if Mom finds out you're not wearing it?" I said.

"Mom's lucky I don't burn it," Gina said.

I didn't understand why she would rather burn her bra than wear it, but I didn't ask. Gina was on a mission. Maybe it was part of her husband hunt.

I was on a bra hunt.

Bea, Dooley's fiancée, was on a color hunt. She was at our house all the time showing Mom stupid little pieces of material stapled to squares of cardboard she called swatches. Somehow those tiny colored swatches turned into dresses for the wedding. Her swatches looked awfully thin to me, and I was worried about my nipple situation, which was budding faster than Mom's lilac bushes.

*Doesn't Bea understand that we are supposed to be leaving Mom alone? Why is she allowed to bother her? Didn't Dooley tell her the commandment?*

"We aren't supposed to bother Mom," I said.

Bea held cardboard to my face.

*Turn the other cheek…*

Stupid Bea wasn't even there when the ambulance took Mom away. The night that I heard our address come across the police scanner. *Caucasian female, late forties, possible cardiac.* The night that Dad and Dooley led Mom down the hallway holding her up by the elbows like a prom queen. When they put Mom on a stretcher and wrapped her up like a mummy and slid her into the ambulance's monster-mouthed tailgate. The night that Dooley locked her in—Dooley—good at everything, like vocations and locking moms into monster's mouths.

I would have told Bea all about it, how Mom wasn't a possible cardiac at all, but that she had to have an operation to take away her lady parts, and that was why we had to leave her alone. So she could rest. Recover. Be back to the old Mom in no time. Be back to the Mom that used to be. But Roger told me that what happened to Mom was her own private business, so that was why all I said to Bea was that we were supposed to leave Mom alone.

"PINK!" Bea screeched, "EVERYONE loves PINK!"

I stared at her.

Bea had huge blonde hair, the bright kind that Mom called bleached, not the natural kind like Marcia Brady or Gina or me, which she wore in a bouffant that made her even taller than she already was. Her white eye shadow and thick, black, fake eyelashes made her look just like the wolf in sheep's clothing I feared she was.

"Don't you like PINK?" she screeched.

"Leave Mom alone," I said, "let her rest."

But Bea never could help herself. She was always so very Bea.

21

I didn't want to wear pink or be in their wedding at all because I thought that it was mean the way that Dooley didn't ask Roger to be his best man, or at least an usher.

"It's OK, Boss," Roger said, "he'll ask one of his cop brothers."

And he did, making Dad very proud, once again.

"He's a fine choice, son," Dad said to Dooley.

*Is Dooley perfect at everything?*

I wondered if they would wear their cop costumes.

As for me? I would be a giant budding flower girl in the color of Fab-faded maroon.

*Think of Easter...*

I tried to look on the bright side of Bea. Marrying Dooley meant that he'd be moved out of the house by fall, and maybe he would stop bullying Rog. Maybe then Dad would stop yelling. Maybe then Rog would stop biting his lip like he was lying or trying not to cry all the time.

Rog sat on my bed.

"Boss, we need to talk," Rog said.

"We always talk."

"No, we need to *have* a talk. I need to tell you something important."

"Are you asking Valerie to marry you? Are you buying a new car? Did you figure out what the heck is the matter with you?"

"Boss: Shut up. I'm leaving," he said.

Roger stared at the floor and twirled the fringe on his suede jacket, except he wasn't even wearing it.

"Are you going to work?" I asked.

"No! Jesus Christ, Boss, just shut the fuck up and let me talk."

*Thou shalt not take the name of the Lord thy God in vain, for the gazillionth time, but OK...go ahead...talk...*

"I enlisted. Air Force. I'm leaving on an airplane to go to Texas for basic training for six weeks. And then probably to Nebraska," Rog said.

My stomach fell.

*Think of Easter...*

"For six whole weeks?" I asked.

"No. For forever. I mean, for now. I don't fucking know for how long. It's what I need to do. The Air Force, Boss, they have these big machines called computers, and I'm going to learn how to program them. I'm getting the fuck out of this prison. I'm breaking this joint."

My shirt was wet with tears.

"Like Peter, Paul, and Mary?" I asked.

"What?"

"Like Peter, Paul, and Mary, the song, 'Leaving on a Jet Plane'?"

"Yeah. Sure. Like the song, I guess," Rog said.

"You can't leave me, Rog. I'm your Boss. When are you coming back home?"

"Boss, I already told you I don't know when I'm coming back," Rog said.

I stared at the floor.

"Boss. I have to go. I have to do this. You're making this really hard for me. You're killing me..."

"Killing you softly?" I asked.

"Stop talking to me as if you're a Goddamn lyricist, Boss. Jesus Christ. I'll miss you so much. I don't want to leave you, but I have to go. Please understand. I have no choice. It's going to be good. I'm getting the hell out of here, making something of myself, just like the old man wants."

"But who will be my pilot?" I said.

I twirled the invisible fringe on my invisible suede jacket, twisted invisible button threads on my button-less shirt.

The silence grew fangs.

"Boss, it's the only way out of here. Can't you just be happy?" Roger yelled. Just like Dad.

*Happy?*

"But what about us? You're just leaving me here? You're leaving without me?" I yelled back.

"What's all the yelling about down there?" Dad yelled.

Roger left my bedroom and left the house. I watched him walk to the fence. His cigarette glowed in the night as he pulled Valerie into him and just held her there. I wondered if that was the last time that I'd ever see him at the fence. Or if it was the last time that I'd ever see him hold Valerie beneath that street light.

*It's all my fault. Roger's leaving all because of me. If I wasn't his Boss and copilot and if we weren't joyriding like Dooley said we never would have had that accident and Roger's car never would have become a crumpled accordion. If I wasn't a minor none of this would have even mattered. It's all my fault. Me and my endangered welfare forced Roger to join the Air Force and move away. God, please don't make him leave. I'll never drive with him again. Hail Mary full of grace help us, I'll always pick lilacs for You. I'll never stash his hash pipe down my shirt again. I'll be nicer to Dooley even if Roger says to ignore him. I'll leave Mom alone and never ask that she returns to the regular Mom, the way she was before her lady parts got taken away. I promise I'll be perfect...*

I lay in bed holding my rosary beads because they were all I had to hold. I prayed on them for Rog and Valerie, and Mom and Dad, and even Dooley and Gina, because after all, we were all losing. Maybe if God wouldn't answer or help me, somehow, somehow, maybe the Blessed Mother would.

But nothing changed Roger's mind. Not me. Not God. Not the Blessed Mother.

"We're in the home stretch, Boss," Roger said.

We made construction paper countdowns together. Rog's counted down single digit days until he left for the service, and mine counted down the many days of the remaining reign of Sister Mary Ruthless.

We drove to the airport in silence and watched Roger get locked into a giant silver bird. We watched him fly away. We didn't even say goodbye. We waved. I watched Roger's hard but soft hand *Boss, we've had an accident* move back and forth, *are you OK?* seeming to grow as it rocked, getting closer and closer to my face, *do you need an ambulance?* slow motion calloused pillows enveloping me like some distorted cartoon hand.

When we got home from the airport that day, on my bed were two things—the keys to his crumpled car and Baby Crissy.

She was life-sized, a twenty-four-inch nine-month-old. I'd wanted her for years, but I guess that Fake Santa thought that I was too old to play with dolls, and maybe I was. But Roger knew that she was all that would be left of us. We needed someone.

I played Gilbert O'Sullivan's 45 over and over and over, watching the circle go round and round. He felt so alone in his lurch that he'd even jump off a tower if things didn't get better.

**lurch |lərCH|**
NOUN (in phrase leave someone in the lurch)
: leave an associate or friend abruptly and without assistance
  or support in a difficult situation
: where Gilbert O'Sullivan was left at a church in his song
: where I was left at the airport

I cried until I had no more tears, or maybe until Dad told me to turn off the record player and go to sleep.

I found my rosary beads, but my prayers were hollow, so I threw them on the floor without apologizing.

I held onto Baby Crissy the only way I knew how—the way I wished that I was held.

I whispered into her life-sized ear.

*Roger was the pilot, the big brother. He took me everywhere and taught me everything. We picked blueberries and caught bullfrogs and blew whistles through crabgrass. We smoked cigarettes and hid hash pipes and drove fast and listened to loud music until we crashed our car. Then one of us joined the Air Force and flew away. The end.*

## CHAPTER 3

# Last Child

**Everlasting May 1975**

"Dad, does Roger's trunk still count?"

"Roger's trunk?" Dad said.

"The tree—his trunk of the tree," I said.

I hugged the trunk that I had chosen as Roger's. Dooley said that the tree that shadowed our house was just a big useless weed, but Dad said that it was symbolic of our history there, our roots.

"You said that each of our tree's trunks stood for the six of us. Now that Roger is gone, does it still stand for Roger?"

"The tree!" Dad said with recognition. "Yes, of course. Always, Kennedy."

*Whew.*

I carved Rog's initials into one of the six trunks. The thickest trunk. I slithered around it like a snake.

The tree remained the same, but things changed. The house became quieter after Roger left. Dad stopped yelling. Dooley stopped bullying. The front screen door slammed less. The smell of cigarettes faded. The hooligans gathered less. The lilacs bloomed silently and died.

I played solitaire till my fingers were sore and tore off a numbered construction paper square each day from my count-down, each one closer to summer.

I wrote a haiku as a gift for Dad for our shared birthday, and made the mistake of showing it to Sister Mary Ruthless, who told me it didn't evoke enough sense of the natural world.

"But Sister, the stars are of the natural world," I said.

She swung at me, and missed. The air rustled.

*Turn the other cheek...*

"Mary Kennedy, I am the Lord thy God, thou shalt not have strange gods before Me. Go to confession. Astrology is the devil's science," she said.

Had Sister called herself God or was she simply quoting God? Or Moses? I wasn't sure.

I painted a picture on shirt cardboard of the tree that shadowed our house, and at its roots I wrote the haiku:

*Dad and Kennedy*
*Gemini twins born today*
*Making us special.*

Dad had thought it was only right to name me Mary Kennedy, after both the Blessed Mother and the first catholic president who was shot just months before She decided that it was a good time to give me to Mom and Dad. Even though we weren't Irish twins like Roger and Gina, and even though I wasn't a superhero like Dooley, didn't it mean something that Dad and I were born on the same day? Didn't that make us special twins too...even if the Gemini twins were just pagans in the sky?

Unfortunately for me, everyone came bearing gifts that year, and mine paled in comparison.

Gina brought her newest and steadiest boyfriend, Wayne, to our birthday celebration. I looked him over but couldn't really figure out if he was husband material or not.

Bea brought binders for Mom and Gina to look at filled with invitations inviting no one to everything.

But Dooley? He came bearing a gift for Dad greater than that of any of the three wise men. It was a plaque for Policeman of the Year, and he presented it to Dad as if it were his.

"This belongs to you, sir. Without you, I wouldn't be where I am today," Dooley said.

Dad was so proud. Everyone was proud. Our birthday had become all about Dooley and his award.

Bea gushed and hugged him.

*Why is Bea allowed to make her own rules? Touching Dooley. Bothering Mom.*

The only happy part about that birthday was when Dad broke out our birthday beer—mine in a shot glass, his the remainder of a 40-ounce bottle.

"Happy Birthday, Schnapps!"

Schnapps was Dad's nickname for me when he wasn't calling me after the Blessed Mother or the dead president.

"Happy Birthday, Dad!" I said, calling him Dad, because that was the only name that I had for him.

I was eleven and Dad was forty-nine.

The glass clinked.

I threw our haiku away.

## CHAPTER 4

# You Ain't Seen Nothin' Yet

**August 1975**

Marcus let me hold the light for him while he tinkered with his engine. Together, we spent the summer watching Gina leave in Wayne's car. It was my job to catch her bra as she threw it out the window on their way by.

"Why won't your sister let me take her out, Boss?" he asked.

"Cuz you're not husband material," I said.

Marcus looked up from the engine and stared at me. His long, curly, dirty-blond hair covered one eye and his fingers were black with grease. Something beneath my belly button—I mean *navel*—squirmed.

"When do you think I can get a bra of my own?" I asked him, feeling the lace of Gina's bra between my fingers.

Marcus shrugged.

"Wear Gina's," he said.

He plunged his fingers back into the grease.

No thanks to Marcus, by the end of the summer, I got a bra. It was what they called luck o' the Irish.

It was all because of Aunt Aileen, Dad's sister, who dropped by the house that summer, *unannounced*. This was a grave sin according to Mom. Mom hated Aunt Aileen—a pagan who sent her kids to public school and dropped by houses unannounced.

I couldn't understand how anyone could hate Aunt Aileen. She wore eye shadow and cool clothes and had a whole bunch of kids and drove a station wagon just like Mrs. Brady from *The Brady Bunch*.

Aunt Aileen had a big house with rooms that had special names—like dining room, parlor, piano gallery, breakfast nook, and screened-in porch. Plus, it had at least three powder rooms, which are bathrooms, in case you don't know.

Dad and Aunt Aileen were Irish twins just like Roger and Gina, and they were very close. She and Dad liked to drink together: she her wine, and Dad his beer. (That was what Mom called it, *"his beer,"* in a slow, weird, French-accented kind of voice, her lips pursed and her words pronounced as if they were in italics.) They laughed and joked and acted like a couple of Irish drunks instead of Irish twins, according to Mom.

But that one particular day, Aunt Aileen dropped by to show Mom the dress that she had bought to wear to Dooley's wedding.

"Mint green! For Ireland!" she said, in what she called her Irish brogue.

She held up her dress, and I could see clear through it to Valerie's house. It was made of the same see-through crepe that my ugly, pink, giant flower girl dress was made of.

*Isn't Aunt Aileen worried about her nipple situation?*

"Of course I'll need proper coverage, or all of the boys will be chasing after me...right, Kennedy?" she said.

"Like me!" I said.

"Oh, but of course, darling! We women need to be modest about ourselves, don't we?" She paused, then added with a laugh, "Or did you mean that all of the boys are already chasing you?" She elbowed me, as if I was in on her joke or her club or something. Mom stared at me, her mouth puckered in as if she were sucking a lemon.

"The coverage part," I said.

"Mom will make sure that you get the proper coverage, just like me! Don't you worry!" Aunt Aileen said.

*Whew.*

I didn't have any boys chasing me, but I liked the way that Aunt Aileen made me feel as if I was in her club. Plus, she seemed to understand that I needed a bra. But I was still worried.

After that, Mom told me to leave Aunt Aileen alone, so I did.

I prayed my rosary and asked the Blessed Mother and the silent God for a bra. I prayed that Mom would talk. I prayed that Roger was safe and that I might see him again. I prayed for his soul and Marcus's soul. I thanked God for finding Wayne, who seemed more and more like husband material. And finally, I thanked them both for Baby Crissy, and draped my beads around her neck like a holy necklace.

And it worked.

By the weekend, Dad drove Mom and me to Sears where a thin woman in a snuggly fit shirt dress approached me with a fabric yardstick. She wrapped it around my nipples and wrote down a number. Then she wrapped it below my nipples and wrote down another number.

She wasn't mean, necessarily, but silent and soft-yardstick wielding, a potential wolf in sheep's clothing. Mom said nothing as they both ushered me into a fitting room and shoved a box through the gaping drape.

It was just like being in a confessional, minus Father minus velvet plus lace and a box claiming to provide a downy foundation for my heavenly shape.

*Blasphemy.*

My bra was smaller and softer than Gina's, but did a good job hiding whatever was going on with my out-of-control nipple situation.

*Stand back, Boss, the creases are sharp...*

The next time that I held the light for Marcus as he fingered his engine, he didn't even notice that I had become a bra-wearing woman like Gina.

So, I went to Valerie's.

"I got a bra," I said to Valerie as she opened her door.

"Congratulations! You're a woman now!" she said, inviting me in.

Valerie was all shiny and glittery amongst strewn newspapers and yellowed stained walls, Marilyn amongst the Munsters. She sat down in a heap of skeins of yarn, rolling one into a ball.

Valerie handed me a skein.

"Here. Roll," she said.

So I did.

"Have you written to Roger?" she asked.

"I didn't know I could," I said.

*Why didn't Mom tell me this?*

Valerie picked up an envelope that lay next to her and tore off the top left corner, a return address written in Rog's chicken scratch.

"Here! Get writing!" she bubbled.

I held the torn address, rubbing it back and forth until the writing was nearly smudged. It felt almost as good as holding Baby Crissy.

Finally, I had a way to talk to Rog. I wrote till my fingers were sore.

## CHAPTER 5

# Go All the Way

### September 1975

Sixth grade began with a lay. She was six feet tall and had a neck so long it looked like a giraffe's. She wore her hair in one of those short, round, modern hairstyles called a perm. She did not wear a habit. She wore turtlenecks religiously through which I could not see her nipples or her bras, or her breasts, for that matter.

And as far as *my* heavenly foundation, I was relieved to be wearing a bra, and equally as relieved that all of the other girls in the sixth grade were wearing bras too, including my best friend Clarissa.

"Thank God you're wearing a bra, Kennedy. It would have been so gauche if you came to school in an undershirt," Clarissa said.

Clarissa knew everything about everything. And everybody, for that matter.

Miss Turtleneck cared a lot about mathematics and how evil entered the world. (Through human acts, by the way, and we all suffer because of two bad apples, Adam and Eve, she said.) She taught church history, which was boring, but much easier to understand than all of the rules and commandments that she never mentioned directly.

She taught us all about proof and confidence, trust and consistency.

"Every time your mathematics works, people, it is a reminder that God is faithfully holding all things together consistently," she said over and over, teaching us how to prove everything.

At each day's end, she said, "This is why we all suffer each and every day, but Jesus brings us hope." Her eyes filled with tears nearly every time she said it. She sure was passionate about mathematics and turtlenecks and hope.

I didn't mind. I liked math and I liked her confidence. I liked how she showed us how to solve all of the math problems perfectly. Mathematics did seem next to Godliness. This was much more comforting than the nuns and their commandments, their rules and rulers.

"Math is true! God is true!" she proclaimed.

*But can she prove that hope is true?*

By Dooley's wedding, I was so full of confidence and Godliness and mathematical proof that I forgot that Bea was a wolf in sheep's clothing. I forgot that I was a giant flower girl in a new bra beneath a nearly transparent pink dress made from a swatch stapled to cardboard.

And right in the back of the church, where I was left standing alone like Gilbert O'Sullivan, right before the ceremony was about to begin, right where the echo was utmost, Bea couldn't help herself.

"Kennedy is wearing a BRAAAAAAAAAA!" Bea's resounding was greater than that of a choir of angels. "You can see it right through your dress! Aren't you *darling?!*"

*Is that a question?*

I didn't want to be *darling*; I wanted to be normal and grown up like Gina and Valerie and Marcus and Rog. I wanted to feel confident like mathematics. Perfect like proofs. Next to Godliness.

I tried to be cool and collected, like The Fonz, like Clarissa and Miss Turtleneck, but I wanted to cry. All that I could think about was all of the people who were going to laugh at me—the two sides of the church, the one side filled with the people that we knew, and the other side filled with the people that Bea knew. Fellow wolves.

*Jelly beans and pastels and bunnies. Pastels like pink. Stupid ugly pink giant flower girl dress. Pink streams of Fab-faded paint running like the tears that our crumpled accordion car cried.*

"Every time your mathematics works, people, it is a reminder that God is faithfully holding all things together consistently," I heard Miss Turtleneck say, as I stood faithfully holding my budding breasts together, consistently, beneath the sheer fabric.

*Think of Easter...*

Chin up, I processed down the church's aisle, following Gina who looked like Marcia Brady, a real-life angel, in her yellow chiffon gown and button mums dangling from ribbons in her long, dark-blonde hair. I went bra first, a giant flower girl, dropping broken pink roses onto the church floor so that a prettier girl, a girl with proper coverage, a bride, Bea, could walk all over them because she was more special, a superhero's wife-to-be, covering my heavenly shape with a basket of broken roses and oversized mums.

As Dooley and Bea received the Sacrament of Holy Matrimony, Dad's face grew proud once again. I tried to focus on the fact that it was a special covenant, an agreement between Dooley and Bea and God and all, but I could not help but wonder what it would be like to marry someone, or to have a boyfriend like Gina had, *husband material*, someone to care for, and someone who cared back. I missed Roger. Gina wiped tears from her eyes. Maybe she was happy for Dooley, or maybe she missed Roger too.

As we exited the church, everyone threw rice at us from the satchels I had watched Bea and Mom make—nylon net tied with satin ribbons. *Why does Bea get to do things with Mom?* It was supposed to be good luck for Bea and Dooley—*luck o' the Irish?*—but flung rice felt like frozen raindrops.

"Isn't this AMAZING?" Bea said, slipping on the rice.

But Dad didn't seem too pleased about getting hit with rice, and stood, shaking it out of his tuxedo. Maybe Dad and I *did* have something in common, like true Gemini twins. We both hated getting pelted in the face with frozen raindrop rice.

I didn't dance at their reception on account of my see-through dress. Plus, I had no one to dance with. I wasn't half of a couple like Mom and Dad, Dooley and Bea, or Gina and Wayne. Even Valerie and Marcus had each other to dance with.

"How come you brought Marcus as your date?" I asked Valerie.

"Because he's lonely too. We both miss Roger," she said.

Marcus didn't look lonely to me, but rather, very un-lonely in the way that he danced with Valerie at the reception, holding her close to his abdomen with his lips up next to her ear like he was whispering. Only he wasn't.

I wrote to Roger about everything: Miss Turtleneck and math, Godliness and perfection, proof and confidence, rice and covenants. But I didn't mention my heavenly foundation or my see-through dress, or the part about Marcus's abdomen and Valerie's ear. Roger would have killed Marcus if he ever knew that.

*Thou shalt not kill.*

## October 1975

The house was even quieter after Dooley moved out—plus he became a detective, so he wasn't talking on the police scanner any more. He drove an unmarked car instead of a real cop car and almost never came down our street. I thought that maybe it was because Roger wasn't around to yell at through his cop microphone, but Valerie said that it was because he was paying attention to his new bride, Bea, and working a different beat.

Gina kept her bra on more and cried more.

Mom sucked on lemons more and slammed everything more.

Everything was exponential, a math term for more and more.

"God loves us more and more as we grow closer and closer to Him, it's exponential, people," Miss Turtleneck said. "Even your hope, the more you believe, the more it grows."

To me, hope was just another Santa Claus-something you believed in and waited for that turned out to be a big fat lie.

Dad remained silent until he became exponential, yelling more and more, but in a strange whispery way as if he were holding in diarrhea while trying to sing ventriloquist-style.

Instead of going out every night, Gina and Wayne stayed in and talked to Mom and Dad more and more. It didn't take long for Dad's whispery ventriloquist act to turn into a full-blown yell-at-Roger voice.

"What the hell is the matter with you?"

"What about college?"

"How are you going to afford a mortgage? Doctor's bills?"

The more Dad yelled, the more Gina cried.

"And what are *you* going to do about her mortal soul?" Dad asked Wayne.

*Well, this is different.*

The more Gina cried, the more she paced. The more she paced, the more Wayne followed her mumbling, "Relax," while touching her back with the palm of his hand. I watched from the sidelines, trying to figure what it was all about. No one was smoking. No one was a hoodlum. This time, Gina was in trouble.

*Hail Mary full of grace...*

The lemon sucking, slamming, crying, and pacing continued. Dad spurted small bursts of diarrhea whispers at Mom's slamming back.

Baby Crissy and I spent most of our time in our room, trying to add up what sucking plus slamming plus diarrhea whispers equaled.

Something weird was going on.

"Gina, what's wrong?" I asked.

"Relax," Wayne said to me.

I became a detective like Dooley, or Columbo.

"How come Gina cries all the time?" I asked Marcus.

"Boss. Cuz she's in trouble, man. Ya dig?" Marcus said.

*I dig. But I still don't know what's wrong with Gina.*

When I went to Valerie's to get to the bottom of it all, she was pinning pattern paper to an oatmeal colored fabric that was covering her kitchen table. The girl on the pattern package was about my age.

"She looks like Laura Ingalls from *Little House on the Prairie*," I said.

Every girl wanted a prairie dress. Clarissa had one, naturally.

"It's for you! For the wedding!" Valerie said.

"What wedding?" I asked.

"Gina's, silly!"

*Huh?*

"To Wayne? Wayne is husband material? Gina's getting married to Wayne? How come no one told me?" I asked.

Valerie looked like she had just given away a big surprise. Like she had just told me that there was no Santa Claus. A tiny wrinkle ran between her green eyes.

"Oh, Kennedy, I thought you knew," she said.

*As if. This is Santa all over again. More and more lies. Exponential.*

"Don't be upset," Valerie said. "Look how pretty we are going to be!"

Valerie held up another pattern package, picturing a similar dress on an older girl. She showed me the material for hers, and for the blue and pink aprons that slid over our necks, over our nipple situations, and tied in the back.

"What about Rog?" I asked.

"I'm not making a dress for him!"

Valerie thought that she was so funny, so I smiled.

*Has anyone bothered to tell Rog? Is Rog really going to miss another wedding? Does Rog know that Gina is in some kind of trouble? Will Valerie and Marcus dance too closely again?*

I watched Valerie cut the fabric for our dresses, kind of like the way I watched Marcus fix his car engine, but without the car, the abdomen, and the funny feeling somewhere below my navel.

From that point on, Baby Crissy and I listened like mad, ears to walls. If I had a tape recorder, I would have set it up to record all of the whispery conversations that I was missing out on, like Peter Brady from *The Brady Bunch*. But that was a serious offense, according to Mr. Brady, and I didn't need more ways of getting into hell or more sins to confess to Father. I already had to confess my anger and envy about being excluded, even though it seemed to me that the offenses really belonged to others.

*Turn the other cheek…*

But Baby Crissy and I heard Mom and Dad when they yelled outright.

"How will we explain this to people?" Dad said.

"It's sheer blasphemy for them to be married on All Saint's Day!" said Mom.

"Father said it's the earliest possible date! What the hell do you want me to do about it, for Christ's sake?" Dad said, at his yell-at-Roger volume.

*Thou shalt not take the name of the Lord thy God in vain.*

Valerie must have told Gina that she had slipped up, because soon after, Gina came to me to ask me to be in her wedding.

"A giant flower girl?" I asked.

*Aren't you darling?*

"No, a real bridesmaid, a junior bridesmaid. Valerie is making dresses. She's going to be my maid of honor, and once Wayne and I get married everything will be OK," Gina cried.

This explained everything.

*As if.*

I didn't tell Gina that I already knew about the Laura Ingalls dress on account of her tears. I wanted to touch Gina on the back with my palm to make her feel better the way that Wayne did, but I didn't know how.

*Hail Mary full of grace…*

I told Clarissa all about my Laura Ingalls dress, and she said that *Little House on the Prairie* was for babies.

"But you have a prairie dress," I said.

"Why blue and pink? That's so gauche," Clarissa said.

*Like jelly beans and pastels and bunnies.*

Aunt Aileen came to the house in her Mrs. Brady station wagon and drove Mom, Gina, Valerie, and me to a bridal store where Gina got to try on all kinds of beautiful bridal gowns. Mom sucked on lemons, and even Aunt Aileen seemed less Mrs. Brady than usual.

I ignored them the way that Roger told me to ignore Dooley and Bea, and helped Gina zip the dresses while she wiped away tears.

Gina stood sideways, looking at herself.

"Do I look fat?" she asked.

"No!" I said, but no one else answered her.

Valerie just rubbed her back, like Wayne.

"It's OK, it's OK," Valerie said.

*Relax...relax...*

Baby Crissy and I calculated the addends: Gina crying plus Wayne repeating "relax" plus Mom slamming plus Dad yelling plus blue and pink dresses plus a wedding was equal to something. We just didn't know what.

There was some reason why Gina was sad, why Wayne wanted her to relax, and why they had to get married. Why Gina was in trouble. Baby Crissy and I came up with only one sum, one solution: Gina was pregnant.

*Thou shalt not commit adultery.*

It was not possible. Premarital sex was a grave sin. Mortal.

But if me and Baby Crissy were right, then Gina and Wayne were going straight to hell in a hand basket.

*So why are Mom and Dad giving them a wedding? In a church? With Father? And why is Valerie making dresses for us? How is everyone OK with all of this? Is God OK with this?*

Everyone was in a state of sin. Mortal sin. Not only for committing their sins, but for being accomplices in the sins of others.

*Is it OK for me to be in the wedding? To stand up with sinners?*

I would have asked God, but He never answered.

It all continued—Gina cried, Dad yelled, and Mom slammed right up until the morning of the wedding, when a photographer showed up at the house and told everyone to smile. So we did.

Gina and Wayne's wedding was a quiet repeat of Dooley and Bea's—even the guests spoke in whispers. But, to me, their wedding seemed more holy, more sacred, more Godly. Something about Gina and Wayne's wedding felt like math: safe, abounding, even holy in the face of damnation.

"Math is abounding. God is abounding. Exponentially, people," Miss Turtleneck had said.

No one made fun of me that All Saint's Day, not even Bea. Both my heavenly foundation and the velvet apron that Valerie made to cover my oatmeal Laura Ingalls gown hid the mystery of my budding bosom, hallelujah.

During the catch-the-bouquet game, Mom said, "Sit. You're too young to play. You'll ruin it for everyone." So I watched from the sidelines along with the other married women, like Bea and Mom and Aunt Aileen. When Valerie caught the bouquet, everyone oohed and cheered and laughed, but it didn't seem like much of a contest to me—everyone let her catch it.

Marcus fought to catch the garter and took a very long time walking his fingers up Valerie's leg to place it beneath her velvet apron. Everyone laughed and cheered, but to me, it was strange watching Marcus touch Valerie in such a way.

*Thou shalt not commit adultery.*

I glanced at Mom, who was not only lemon sucking, but looking very angry. For once I was grateful for lemons.

Valerie and Marcus sure had a weird way of missing Rog.

"You're the most beautiful bride I have ever seen," Wayne said to Gina as they were leaving the reception. And he was right— Gina shimmered, her tears finally gone.

## CHAPTER 6

# Only the Lonely

**November 1975**

Dad wore a lonely face after Dooley's police scanner silence and Gina's All Saint's Day wedding.

Mom's slamming carried on. I started wondering if the secret operation took out a lot more than just her lady parts.

We were a triangle. Three blind mice. Mom, Dad, Kennedy. A trinity.

After twenty-five days of almost total silence, the time between All Saint's Day and Thanksgiving eve, the house finally spoke. It was as if Lent had ended, and Jesus had risen from the dead, pilgrim-style.

*Is this Miss Turtleneck's Jesus-hope? The exponential kind?*

Sounds of a particular Mom-slamming, the slow smell of bacon frying, and Dad and Mom's bickering over the particulars of *Dad's Production* signaled life. That's what Mom called it—*Dad's Production (Dahd's Praw-duck-shawn)*—in her French way, her italicized way of speaking that was sharper than her silence.

I ran to the kitchen to take my assigned seat alongside Dad to watch him make his biannual (a word for twice a year, according to Miss Turtleneck) turkey dressing.

I almost had to agree with Mom's exasperated slamming during *Dad's Production*. Everything had to be perfect, just like being Catholic and the commandments. Or math, for that matter. But equating math to Catholicism was blasphemy—yardstick and hell-worthy. But Dad was big on all three: perfection, Catholicism, and math. His own personal trinity.

Dad's giant cutting board was laid in front of him along with his sharpened carving knife. Only Dad was allowed to touch his knife, except Mom when she was allowed to wash it.

"Where's my fork?" Dad asked.

And so it began.

With her particular slam, Mom banged Dad's carving fork onto his cutting board. Mom stood over the thinly sliced bacon that had been simmering in the frying pan. The gas flame was set not too high, not too low, but just right.

*Like Goldilocks and her bear trinity.*

"Paper thin, Schnapps," Dad said, slicing celery first, and then onion.

"Here," Dad said to Mom, which meant that she was supposed to come over and remove from the board the celery and onions and add them to the bacon.

"Tenderly!" Dad said.

There was nothing tender about the way Mom transferred those vegetables, but we all knew that they had to be cooked gently until nearly translucent. *Like a giant flower girl dress.* That was the rule. The commandment.

"How's the bread?" Dad asked, staring at Mom as she fried tenderly.

This question, above all others, really got Mom slamming.

Mom was in charge of freezing the bread for Dad so that he could cut it, but Dad insisted that the bread was just the right amount of frozen—not too much, not too little.

Mom was pretty darn good at this job, if you asked me, and usually, the bread was the proper amount of frozen. If not, Mom slammed the freezer door frequently, checking the bread often, while Dad and I drank beer (which Mom slammed onto his cutting board after Dad said simply, "Beer").

That particular year, it was one of those beer times since Mom just couldn't get her frozen right. Dad's lonely face seemed to soften a bit as we drank, melting into an almost non-yelling-yet-also-non-silent Dad face.

Once the bread was perfectly frozen, Dad cut it up into little cubes. He said that if the cubes were not all the same size, and essentially perfect, then the dressing would not taste good.

I told Dad everything that I learned about cubes from Miss Turtleneck.

He answered the way God did—not at all.

Dad stirred all of the other ingredients into the cubes with his special fork until the big moment arrived—The Moment of Truth. That was when Dad said, "Spoons!" and Mom slammed two spoons onto his cutting board, and he and I got to taste test the raw dressing.

"Perfect!" Dad said.

And then, when Mom was not looking, he added more salt.

I was eleven and Dad was forty-nine and I loved being on the sidelines of *Dad's Production*. I knew that I wasn't Dooley and I wasn't a superhero, but Dad and I were both in the same lurch. We were each missing someone—he Dooley, and me Roger. Maybe we could be lonely together, like me and Baby Crissy, like me and

Gilbert O'Sullivan, naturally. Maybe since I was the only kid left at home, and maybe since we were Gemini twins, we could be special together. We could be friends.

## December 1975

Valerie promised that after Thanksgiving she would teach me how to crochet.

"Wrap it around, put it through the hole, grab it, bring it back..."

Over and over she directed me until I caught on. If you crocheted enough around a center, you could make squares. And squares made gifts like scarves and blankets.

Crocheting was just like *Dad's Production*: if you followed all of the rules, and did exactly as you were told, then you ended up with something good, something safe and warm.

I thought about how this was the way it was supposed to be with God. If you followed all of the commandments, then you got into heaven. But I had a really hard time imagining something safe and warm like God in heaven when hell was lurking everywhere and adults were lying left and right.

*Think of Easter...*

Valerie gave me a garbage bag full of hand-me-down balls of yarn and a crochet needle.

"Get going!" she said. "You're running out of time!"

I wrapped around and pushed and pulled over and over ball after ball until I had a square that I thought was large enough to wrap around Roger's entire body. And then I kept going, made it even bigger, just to make sure that it made him feel safe and warm.

I finished Roger's blanket in the nick of time. I wrapped it up in Christmas wrapping and a brown paper bag and sent it along with the longest letter ever. I even asked him if others besides

Mary, the Blessed Mother, could conceive without sexual relations. I made no mention of Gina.

Right before Christmas, I heard back from Roger. He loved the blanket and all the work I put into it. He said that it kept him warm on cold Nebraskan nights, and that it made him think of me all the time. I hoped, Miss Turtleneck's Jesus-hope, that he meant that he felt safe and warm.

Roger made no mention of chaste conceptions.

*Thou shalt not commit adultery.*

He sent me my first album, the Carpenters, with a pretty brown cover. Karen and Richard Carpenter were sister and brother, just like me and Rog. Karen Carpenter seemed like a nice girl, confident like Miss Turtleneck, but also, she seemed sad. I wondered if she could be both.

Christmas day came, and it should have been fun like it always was, but it produced a special kind of lemon sucking from Mom, and it was all my fault.

Everyone but Rog was at the house—Bea and Dooley, Gina and Wayne, and of course, Mom and Dad and me.

We opened presents. My favorite (besides the album from Rog) was a large radio, like a transistor, only much bigger, with an antennae, and FM and AM radio stations.

We ate supper, complete with *Dad's Production: Christmas Edition.* All was calm, all was bright.

Gina stood sideways in front of me like she had while trying on wedding gowns.

*Do I look fat?*

She looked like a movie star in a deep green plushy velvet jumpsuit. A grown-up Marcia Brady. A real-life disco queen. Beneath her bell bottoms, she wore the strappy crisscross knee-high sandals that Wayne had bought for her as a wedding gift. Dad said that they were inappropriate for a bride, and indecent even for Pocahontas, but she wore them anyway.

*Honor thy father and thy mother.*

But there was something different about Gina. She didn't look fat, but her abdomen was sticking out in a way that it never had before—convex, as Miss Turtleneck would say—and not at all like Marcus's countable muscles.

*I knew it! Gina is having a baby, and they think that I am too stupid to put two and two together. They think that I am some dumb little kid who doesn't matter, not perfect like Dooley, not special like the Irish twins.*

And then I did the worse thing that anyone could ever do—I touched her. I don't know why I did it. I was just so happy about how beautiful Gina looked, so soft and touchable, like a blanket made of yarn. I reached out and put the palm of my hand on the part of her abdomen that was sticking out. *Over her baby.* I said the only thing that I could think of, or maybe it was just the only thing that I wanted to say.

"You are so beautiful," I said.

*Stand back, Boss, the creases are sharp...*

"KENNEDY!" Mom yelled in a Bea-screech type of French, her mouth opened wider than I'd ever seen it opened.

Dad grunted.

Bea gasped.

Dooley stood and held out his hand, holding up an invisible someone.

Wayne smiled, a type of smile that I did not recognize.

But then Gina did something almost as bad as I had, almost as forbidden—she held my hand under both of hers and pressed them into her abdomen.

"I'm having a baby!" she announced.

Mom made a noise like Julia Child, real French, Dad reached for an invisible cigarette, Dooley comforted a visibly stricken Bea, and Wayne stood next to Gina looking as if he had a secret, like the cat who swallowed the canary, as Dad would say.

But me and Gina? We just stood there, touching. It was weird, but it felt nice to have my hand beneath both of Gina's, on top of her soft, creamy velvet, on top of her baby, safe and warm.

"We are like a fuzzy flesh sandwich," I said.

Gina cried.

"Who do you think you are? Get your hands off of her!" Mom yelled.

*Boss, we've had an accident...*

"Mom, it's fine," Gina said.

"She's being fresh!" Mom said. "I repeat. Get your hands off of her. Apologize now!"

I felt terrible for making Gina cry again.

"Relax...relax..." Wayne said.

He was back to his old trick: rubbing Gina's back.

Dooley shook his head as if he were God Himself on judgment day.

"Kennedy, apologize!" Bea reiterated.

*Huh? Are you my mother? First you hog my mom and then you become my mom? What the heck, Bea? What is so wrong with me touching Gina?*

I didn't know what was so wrong with what I did, but some grave sin had occurred. I feared retribution I feared hell in a hand basket I feared swinging yardsticks and open palmed nuns. But the only open palm was mine.

"Maybe *you* guys are going to hell in a hand basket this time! For all of your lies! For all of your sins! You think me and Baby

Crissy are so stupid! We knew all about the sin baby! We know how to do math!" I yelled.

Silence.

I went to my room.

"Who's Crissy?" I heard Bea ask.

She never could help herself.

I cradled my new radio in one arm and Baby Crissy in the other. I hoped, Jesus-hoped, that she, at least, felt safe and warm.

From the new radio, a pretty sounding lady named Diana Ross sang a song asking me a whole bunch of questions, even one about hope.

America sang a song for people who seemed lonely.

The Raspberries wanted to go all the way because I guess that felt good.

Captain & Tennille said that love will keep us together.

*Love?*

## CHAPTER 7

# Have a Cigar

**December 1975**

A reading from the book of sexual relations according to Mom circa 1972:

"Where do babies come from?"

"God."

"No. How do they get inside the mom? Does the Holy Spirit put them in there like He put Jesus into The Blessed Mother?"

"Blasphemy. This is the man."

Mom holds up right index finger.

"This is the woman."

Mom makes lying down peace sign with index and middle finger of left hand.

Mom slides right index finger into left-handed peace sign.

"During sexual relations, a man's penis deposits sperm inside the woman, which fertilizes the woman's egg. And that's where babies come from."

This is the word of the mom,
Thanks be to God.

A letter to St. Roger according to Kennedy circa 1975:

Rog,

Is it true that Wayne figured out Mom's human hand peace sign puzzle? Is it true that Gina and Wayne had sexual relations out of wedlock in order to make a baby? Is it true that they are going to hell in a hand basket for having premarital sex, a sin against at least the fourth, fifth, sixth, and ninth commandments, and nearly all of the seven deadly sins?

Boss

. . .

Boss,

Gina and Wayne did the deed—they had sex—if that's what you're asking. That's how you make a baby, at least the last time I checked. Not sure what Mom's puzzle is all about. No one is going to hell. Wayne loved on Gina a little too much a little too soon, and that's alright with God.

Rog

# CHAPTER 8

# Walk This Way

## January 1976

Rainy days and Mondays always got Karen Carpenter down, and if I worked really hard I could crochet a whole row of a granny square for Gina's baby's blanket by the time the stereo's arm touched back down on "We've Only Just Begun."

Miss Turtleneck helped me to figure out the dimensions and how many baby granny squares I needed to crochet and sew together. The baby was too small for one big square blanket.

"Kennedy's sister is a Jezebel," Clarissa announced during the dimension discussion.

"Who's that?" I asked.

"From the Bible, dummy! Everyone knows who Jezebel is." Clarissa laughed.

"Hey," Miss Turtleneck said, snapping her fingers twice, an action that, for her, meant to stop. "Remember that God forgave Adam and Eve, the original sinners. And this is why we all suffer each and every day, but Jesus brings us hope."

*Here we go again...*

I intended to ask Mom who Jezebel was and maybe even what hope was all about. *If Bea can bother her, I can bother her.*

I got off the bus, crossed the street, and saw Mom standing in the front screen doorway the way she always did. But something was wrong. Something was different. The house looked lonely.

*Like Dad?*

"MOM!" I yelled, running.

Our car was gone—our crumpled accordion car was missing.

"Mom! Where's our car?"

"Kennedy, that was not your car, it was Roger's. Marcus had it towed away, thank goodness, and got a little cash for it. Stop being selfish. You should be happy for Roger," Mom said.

"Where is it? Does Marcus get to keep the money? Roger needs money! Doesn't anyone care about him?" I Bea-screeched questions at Mom.

"Stop being ridiculous. Stop being selfish. Be happy for Roger. You'll be punished," Mom said.

*Oh. Great. The "you'll be punished" line. Mom finally finds her voice and this is how she chooses to use it? Threatening me with Mom-God punishment? This line of punishment is much worse than a nun's yardstick or open palm, worse than the Blessed Mother whispering that I had sinned into God's ear. "You'll be punished" was Mom and God getting together, a marriage, combined to make a punishment in hell worse than any other—Satan, fire, eternal shame—forever and ever, amen.*

*But what about our car? Who said Marcus could take it for money? Thou shalt not steal!*

"Why wouldn't Rog tell us about the car? Or Marcus? Or anyone?" I asked Baby Crissy, who only stared back.

I grabbed the beads from her neck and began to pray to the Blessed Mother. Maybe She could help me *save me* from the spiritually married Mom and silent God with their angry eyeballs on me for eternity.

*Think of Easter...*

First Friday confession couldn't have come soon enough. I knew I was in a state of sin, if only venial.

I fell to my knees in the velvet box just as the screen slid open, filling the dark closet with tiny bits of priest light.

Me: "Bless me Father for I have sinned, it's been one week since my last confession. And these are my sins."

Father: "Yes?"

Me: "I pouted and acted ridiculous and selfish when our car got stolen."

Father: "What car?"

Me: "Our car."

Father: "Have you discussed this with your parents?"

Me: "Sort of."

*Of course not.*

Father: "Did you steal the car?"

Me: "No, Father, it was mine!"

*How could I steal my own car?*

Father: "Do you know who stole the car?"

Me: "No, Father, not exactly."

I didn't want to rat out Marcus, and maybe Roger knew all about this scheme, but my portion of the car was taken without my permission, and that's called stealing. If the car hadn't belonged to me too, why would Roger have left the keys for me? After all, I was the one who washed it and faded it to pink and sat in the copilot's seat trying to remember joyrides and Roger.

Father: "Mary Kennedy?"

*Um, wait a second. Sister Mary Ruthless said that God erased all knowledge of recognition in the confessional. "God graces the confessor anonymity," she said, and that means that the priest isn't supposed to know who you are. Does the priest always know who you are? Is this another adult cheat? Well, great, I know who you are TOO Father Aloysius.*

But even though I knew who Father was, it didn't make me feel any better that he knew who I was.

Me: "Yes, Father."

Father: "If there has been a vehicle stolen, then you and I need to speak with the proper authorities. Have you spoken with your brother?"

Me: "Roger?"

Father: "No, not that no-good Roger. I am speaking of Dooley."

*Oh. Naturally. Perfect, movie star Super Dooley.*

Me: "Um. No, Father."

*Why the heck would I involve him?*

Father: "Speak with your brother, please, Mary Kennedy."

Me: "Yes, Father."

*Not a chance.*

Father: "What else?"

Me: "What else what, Father?"

Father: "Sins, Mary Kennedy. Stop wasting my time, and God's time."

Me: "Oh. I disrespected my mother by crying and pouting about our stolen car."

Father: "Mary Kennedy. This is ridiculous."

*The ridiculous word. Again.*

Me: "Father. I simply don't want to be Mom-God punished. So I came to confession."

Father: "Surely you *will* be punished if you don't stop this nonsense and disrespect. Speak with your brother. And say three rosaries in honor of your poor mother who has to deal with your foolishness."

Me: "Yes, Father. Thank you, Father."

You always had to thank Father even if you didn't want to, or even if you hated what he said or the penance that he gave you. It was another one of the rules.

I said the rosary five times as soon as I got home that day: three for Mom like Father told me to, one because I believed that it was Father who was ridiculous, and one because I never spoke with Dooley.

I prayed that Rog got some of the money that Marcus stole. Maybe it would help him buy a plane ticket or a diamond ring for Valerie.

I never did ask Mom about Jezebel, or hope, for that matter.

**hope** |hōp|
NOUN
: a feeling of expectation and desire for a certain thing to happen
: a person or thing that may help or save someone
: grounds for believing that something good may happen
: *archaic* a feeling of trust
: something that I didn't understand

Hope sounded good, by definition. Truth.

I mean, if Adam and Eve, the worse sinners ever, ate from the tree of knowledge and caused the whole universe to have original sin, and still God loved them, then surely there was hope left for me.

It was because of hope that I took a calculated risk.

*Go all the way...*

"Mom, I'll need a ride after school tomorrow. Can you ask Dad if he will pick me up? Please?" I said.

Mom looked at me for two-Mississippi, long enough for me to feel obligated to explain.

"I'm going out for spring cheerleading," I said.

"What would you want to do *that* for?" Mom said.

I ducked, the air around me swirling as if a nun swung. But there was no nun. Just Mom and that French way that she had about her.

*What would I want to do that for? To make something of myself, like Dooley. To make me popular, like Clarissa. Maybe being a cheerleader will make Dad proud.*

I answered like God, with silence.

I took Mom's shaking of her head back and forth while sucking like a gazillion lemons as a yes.

*Mom, don't you know that even Adam and Eve were redeemed? God gave them Miss Turtleneck's Jesus-hope...*

So I took all of Miss Turtleneck's confidence and assuredness of math and even the vague promise of Jesus-hope with me to try outs. I wore my gym uniform because that was what we were supposed to wear. That was the rule.

"Why are you wearing *THAT*?" Clarissa asked, with a tone somewhere between Mom's French and Bea's screech.

All of the fake Marcia Brady girls, including Clarissa, were wearing cute shorts and tops, the kind that pretty girls like Marcia Brady and Gina and Valerie wore. The kind that I didn't even own.

The cheer coach, a fake Marcia Brady mom, Coach Mom, stood before us in the same adolescent outfit as the fake Marcia Bradys.

"Line up, cheerleaders. Arms length between you. When the music starts, begin the tryout cheer. Oh! This song is perfect, isn't it, cheerleaders? Good luck!" she said.

*I mean, I guess if you like the Bay City Rollers and their "Saturday Night" song, then yeah, it's perfect.*

And so it began.

It wouldn't shut up. The Marcia Bradys kept Bea-screeching letters and words and numbers at me, pushing their pom-poms and lifting their arms and legs just like they were supposed to. Each letter or number a different move. Every word a different gyration.

I couldn't do anything. If my feet moved, my arms didn't. If my arms moved, my feet didn't. It was all clapping and snapping and lifting and spinning and I wasn't anything but clumsy.

"Why don't you know the cheer? Haven't you practiced?" Clarissa asked, once the music stopped.

I ducked before her nun-swung question.

Over and over I'd practiced in front of Baby Crissy, just like Miss Turtleneck advised in math.

"Practice makes perfect, people," she said.

*But does practice make perfect people?*

"I did practice," I said to Clarissa, who was already chatting with the other girls.

I wanted to quit then, before the second round of tryouts, the solo auditions. I couldn't even remember the solo cheer, and I knew that my chances of making Dad proud or being popular by becoming a cheerleader were headed down the drain.

*Turn the other cheek...*

"Mary Kennedy, you're up first," Coach Mom said.

So I did what I knew how to do—my best. I tried to cheer just like Marcia Brady did when she tried out for cheerleading. I chanted our tryout cheer like a last prayer.

"One, two, how do you do? The Angels!"

I marched in place and swung my borrowed pom-poms.

"Three, four, guess who's gonna score? The Angels!"

But then I couldn't remember what the Angels did for five, six, so I stopped altogether after a couple more jumping jacks and a toss to the floor of my pom-poms.

Silence.

Everyone stared at me except Clarissa, who was hidden within a huddle of fake Marcia Bradys. And then the huddle began to shake with laughter. At first quiet, and then loud with taunting and pointed fingers.

"Cheerleaders. Shhh. Shhh," Coach Mom said.

Each of the fake Marcia Bradys performed their solo audition cheers perfectly, like math, like Dad's frozen cubes.

"I'm sorry, Mary Kennedy, you didn't quite make the team," she said.

*Quite?*

And then, "Congratulations, cheerleaders! The rest of you have made the team!"

The fake Marcia Bradys, including Clarissa, screamed and jumped in their circle, skipping out of the gymnasium without breaking their huddle.

Coach Mom gathered her equipment and skipped behind them.

I sat tight.

*One, two, think of Easter; three, four, jelly beans and pastels; five, six, bunnies and Hail Mary full of grace and stand back, Boss, the creases are sharp...*

Once the coast was clear, I stood and watched them pile into Coach Mom's station wagon. Even Clarissa.

I walked to the lavatory. *Hail Mary, full of grace...it can't hurt, Boss,* feeling so lonely that I was the only one not chosen. I felt ugly *Kennedy is wearing a braaaaa!!!!!* and so alone again, naturally. I was ashamed. So ashamed. Too ashamed to even tell Roger. I wondered if Karen Carpenter was ever a cheerleader. I hated that Mom was right. I hated that I wasn't going to make Dad proud. I hated that I trusted myself and took a calculated risk. I hated God for not warning me. God never ever helped.

I changed back into my school uniform, never wanting to wear that gym uniform ever again. Or go to gym, for that matter.

Dad picked me up, and when he asked me why I needed to stay after school, I told him that I stayed for extra credit in gym, because I needed all the help that I could get. I was hopeless.

I thought Dad almost smiled.

Mom never asked about the tryout.

Sometimes silence was golden.

As for hope? Well, in the word according to Marcus—suck it. I just wasn't sure what "it" was.

*Bless me, Father, for I have sinned. Like Marcus.*

## May 1976

Spring brought forth lilacs.

"For the Blessed Mother," I said.

Miss Turtleneck dug into her untapped art closet for her blessed statue while I stood at her desk holding a bouquet of lilacs.

I was pretty sure that stashing a statue of Mary behind a bunch of stuff in a closet was a sin against almost every commandment, so I prayed for Miss Turtleneck.

*It can't hurt, Boss...*

"Full of hope!" Miss Turtleneck said, stuffing the stems into a dusty vase.

I wondered if the Blessed Mother gave up whispering damnations into God's ear.

May brought forth a modest baby shower for Gina that Mom slammed together. We ate cake and drank punch while Gina opened up a whole bunch of pastel wrapped presents.

*Think of Easter...*

Gina cried when she opened up my granny square baby blanket—happy tears for a change. I printed in pink pastel marker the Hail Mary on an index card and hid it in the blanket's folds just in case Gina had forgotten how to pray.

## June 1976

June and Gina brought forth her defiled conception, her sin baby, a girl, Maryanne.

"Name her after both the Blessed Mother *and* her mother," Dad said. "Give that baby some hope."

*Jesus-hope?*

And finally, Miss Turtleneck brought forth her final goodbye to the sixth grade.

"And so, people, remember, math is abounding, God is abounding. And this is why we all suffer each and every day, but Jesus brings us hope."

I was like Bea, I couldn't help myself. I raised my hand.

"How does Jesus bring us hope?" I asked.

"Through His DEATH, Kennedy!" Miss Turtleneck screeched in a Bea-voice, laughing as if the joke was on me.

*Like the Joker from Batman?*

It wasn't funny. How could death bring hope to anybody?

*Stand back, Boss, the creases are sharp...*

## REPRISE

# Goodbye to Innocence

### June 1976

There is an 8mm film entitled *Goodbye to Innocence* in which I starred.

"Hey Dad, wanna watch the filmstrip with me?"

Dad answered like God. Not at all.

Even though I could not make Dad proud by being a cheerleader, I continued to be determined to be his friend. But Dad made that difficult when he didn't answer.

I set the projector on top of a TV table pointing to a semi-blank wall.

In *Roger's Production, Goodbye to Innocence,* I wore my first Holy Communion dress, white chiffon with sheer long sleeves, with a belt that tied in a bow in the back, and satin tails that dangled like bicycle streamers.

"Why do I have to wear *this* dress?" I had asked Rog.

"It needs to be white, that's why."

"What kind of a movie are we making?"

"A goodbye movie. Once the camera starts, don't make a sound."

"But Rog, if it doesn't have words then how will people know what it's about?"

Roger huffed like he was blowing cigarette smoke into Dooley's face.

"From the music—and my term paper—now can you just shut up?"

It didn't make sense to me, but I did what Roger told me to do. I loved being a movie star for Roger. I didn't even mind that he told me to shut up, because he didn't really mean it that way.

"OK, now, when the camera starts, you're going to slither like a snake around the tree trunks. Tilt your head back, swing your hair and dance," Roger had directed.

So I did.

"Ready. Set. Twirl!"

I loved the sound that the camera made—a fuzzy *tick tick*. It sounded safe.

Dad's newspaper made a sharp snap, and I knew that meant that he had curled down the top corner to look over at me, at *Roger's Production, My Production.*

"Turn that off," Dad said, "you look like a stripper."

I turned off the projector and smiled, because I knew that at least over the snapped newspaper corner, for a few seconds, Dad had been paying attention to me.

"Can I watch it in my room?" I asked my new friend Dad.

I took his continued God-silence as a yes.

I played the film over and over.

*Why did Roger think that saying goodbye was a celebration like first Holy Communion, one where he wanted me to dance and swirl and act like a stripper? Thou shalt not kill, or maybe thou shalt not commit adultery. Commandments are confusing.*

Over and over I watched that Kennedy. Pretty like a bride Kennedy. Roger's boss and copilot Kennedy. Happy Kennedy. Dancing Kennedy—free and barefoot—before sin and hell in a hand basket, before Roger left and then everything. And then nothing.

I was still there, real-time Kennedy, but everything was different. Even the family tree I twirled around was different. It was taller, thicker, older.

I put the projector away because it made me miss Roger. It made me miss cigarette smoke and Santa Claus, blueberries and bullfrogs. It made me miss everything. Even Baby Crissy didn't make me feel better; that night, she answered the way that God and Dad answered. With silence.

"Who is Innocence?" I remembered asking Rog, referring to the title of his production.

"Someone you will say goodbye to someday."

*I Jesus-hope not. I hate goodbyes.*

## CHAPTER 9

# Born in the USA

**July 1976**

While Jesus was busy bringing hope through death somehow, America was busy having her two-hundredth birthday—her Bicentennial. Everyone was celebrating.

"Kennedy." Dad was holding his newspaper, one section, folded in quarters. "In honor of the Bicentennial, the village is allowing residents to paint the fire hydrants in their neighborhoods." He sort of pointed to what I assumed was an article—as if I could see it. "They can be painted any way you want—they just have to be red, white, and blue. What do you think?"

*I mean, what do I think about what? The idea of painting our hydrant or the idea of celebrating by painting any hydrant? The village allowing us to paint at all? Is Dad actually asking my opinion about something? Is Dad asking me if I want to paint our hydrant with him?*

Instead of answering, I just kept looking in the direction of Dad and his folded paper, and answered the way God and he did—not at all.

"We can go to Western Auto and get some paints and paint the hydrant out front," Dad said.

*We? Does Dad mean the real we, as in he and me, we? Or does Dad mean he will go to Western Auto and I can wait in the window for him to come home? Does he mean that we will paint the hydrant together, or is just Dad going to paint the hydrant while I watch from the sidelines? Or me? Am I going to paint the hydrant?*

So many questions.

"Us?" I asked.

"Why not?"

I didn't know why not, nor did I know if that question was a real one that needed an answer.

"Now?" I said.

"Let's go," Dad said, jingling his keys.

So we went.

*Is Dad trying to be my friend too?*

Dad picked out all of the supplies that we needed for our hydrant project—primer, paints, painter's tape, brushes—while I watched, so excited to be a part of something with my friend Dad.

When we got home, I watched from the sidelines.

Dad hosed down the hydrant, the sun drying the water almost as soon as it ran off the hot iron. Then he primed it.

"A blank slate, Schnapps," Dad said, "now it's your turn."

"To do what?" I asked, lost.

"To make America proud."

*Oh boy. Ask not what your country can do for you, ask what you can do for your country. OK, Kennedy, you can do it.*

The thing was, I wanted to make *Dad* proud—not America. But if painting was the way to do that, then I would paint.

"Easy does it, Schnapps," Dad said as he walked toward the house, leaving me to decide what America might want, or even what Dad would think that America might want.

And it was then, while I was painting the hydrant into a waving flag, masking tape defining the stripes, thinking about how to make a star stencil, that a Pontiac GTO Judge in midnight green drove up and parked alongside me, right next to the hydrant.

"You can't park here. It's illegal. Fifteen feet," I said to the driver.

The driver, a man wearing pilot sunglasses, blew a steady stream of smoke out of his pilot window and laughed.

"Still following all the rules, huh, Boss?"

Roger got out of his car—a man, with short hair and a uniform, like Dooley's, but different.

"*Rog!*"

"You like my blues?"

"*Rog!*" I yelled again, disbelieving.

I wanted to hug him, but I didn't know how.

"Your hair!"

I'd never seen Roger with short hair. I'd never seen Roger in a uniform. I'd never seen Roger be a man.

"Kennedy—you're all grown up!"

I was twelve and Rog was twenty-two.

"Nice aviators! I got a bra!"

"I see that!" Roger laughed. He waved at me the way that he did. I punched Rog in the arm like Marcus did. I didn't know why. It was what I knew to do. It felt like something between a wave and a hug.

"Does Mom know you're coming? Where'd you get the car? Do you have to wear those clothes all the time? Dad's going to love that. Did you come for the Fourth of July? Do you want to help me paint the hydrant? Did you see baby Maryanne yet? Are you staying home for good now?"

I fired Kennedy-questions galore at him.

Roger put his cigarette out against the bottom of a black dress shoe and flicked the butt into the road and answered like God.

"You littered."

"Is Valerie home?" he asked.

We both looked in the direction of Valerie's house and said nothing.

"Boss, you're doing a great job on that hydrant. Does Dad know you're doing that?"

"It was Dad's idea, he even bought me the paint for it. We're friends now."

"That'll be the day. Keep painting, Boss, I'm going to deal with the rents," he said.

Roger meant Mom and Dad. He had cool words for everything.

*Who could paint?*

I followed Rog into the house.

Mom was as surprised as I was, and squeezed out a Julia Child noise. Real French.

Dad shook Roger's hand, called him "son," and showed him Dooley's milestone police plaque.

"What brings you here?" said Dad.

"Wanted to show you the uniform, sir," Rog said.

Dad answered like God.

Rog bit his lip and was back into his ripped jeans in no time.

We walked across the street to surprise Valerie.

"Baby!" Valerie squealed, her eyes sparkling in the sun.

She hopped on Rog like a monkey, and Rog backed her into the house.

"Get lost!" he said, and slammed the door in my face.

I painted the fire hydrant for a gazillion years, until Roger and Valerie finally came out of the house.

"Stencils," she said, handing me star cut-outs.

I wished that Roger could live at home forever, and it was nice to have the old Valerie back, the one not attached to Marcus. They helped with the hydrant for a little while and then went out in Roger's GTO. I finished up just as dusk was turning into dark and Jesus-hoped that it was good enough for America, and good enough for Dad.

Dooley blocked off our whole street with horses that he got from the police station for a special Bicentennial picnic called a block party.

The fence was full with all of Roger's hoodlum friends.

"Kennedy," Marcus asked, "what did one flag say to the other flag?"

I shrugged.

"Nothing! It just waved!"

Marcus's muscles danced as he laughed at his own joke.

I looked away. I didn't want to remember the way that Marcus had danced with Valerie at Dooley's and Gina's weddings, and the way that he had walked his fingers up Valerie's leg to put Gina's garter on her, and the way that his mouth fake-whispered into Valerie's ear. Plus, I wasn't in the mood for the weird feeling below my navel from Marcus's six pack.

*Turn the other cheek...*

It was the best Fourth of July ever. Everyone laughed and talked and ate. The neighborhood moms doted on the sin baby.

No one yelled. No one cried. Dooley and his best man shot off fireworks that they had confiscated from civilians.

*Thou shalt not steal.*

Even the sky smiled.

It all seemed too good to be true.

*What does Dad always say? If it seems too good to be true, it probably is...*

The best part of it all was having Roger home. It felt like old times, safe and warm. We spent days together playing cards and joyriding in Rog's new GTO. We spent time with Gina and the sin baby. We talked about math and the military. Roger smoked.

Nights were reserved for Valerie. I didn't mind—I liked seeing them all wrapped up together like a human pretzel, kissing and giggling, Valerie's eyes shining like diamonds. I waved as they drove off in the GTO.

"That's too loud for this neighborhood," Dad said, as Roger's taillights and the sounds of his speakers and dual mufflers faded.

"At least he's here, Dad," I said.

Dad stared at me for a long time. Maybe he heard me.

When Roger's Air Force leave was up, I pretended that he was driving to work, not to Nebraska for a long time, and this helped with our goodbye. I reasoned with Baby Crissy that since Roger had a car, it would not be too long before he returned again. Plus, didn't he have to come back to marry Valerie someday soon, especially since she caught the bouquet at Gina's wedding? When I asked her that question, she answered me like God.

I drove my bike alongside Roger's GTO, waving frantically for as long and far as I could, but then Rog said, "Gotta book, Boss!" and screeched away, leaving smoky dust just like in the movies.

I cried all the way to Marcus's house, the wind pushing my tears back into my hair as I pedaled. I couldn't wait to hold Baby Crissy. I knocked.

"Boss?" Marcus said.

"Thou shalt not covet thy neighbor's wife, and that means stay away from Valerie or I'll tell Roger," I said.

"Boss. What are you talking about?"

I didn't answer him or his muscles.

I pedaled home, held Baby Crissy, listened to my radio, and prayed the rosary for Rog, that he would return to Nebraska safely.

*It can't hurt, Boss.*

Dad was right. It was all too good to be true.

## August 1976

In honor of America's birthday, our town opened a brand-new colossal library with a gazillion books. There were sixteen card catalogues and two floors, and sections for all of the different kinds of books.

Dad and I got new library cards, plastic ones, which Dad called laminated. The only bad thing about our new laminated library cards was that you could take out only three books at a time with them.

"It's OK, Schnapps; when we're done reading, we'll get more," Dad said.

*Huh. Heard again.*

Because we were on a big reading binge, and because the mosquitos were terrible that year—even the fog truck couldn't get rid of them—Dad decided that it was a good idea to build his very own luxury screened-in porch. I even helped Dad build it, holding the fabric as Dad hammered huge stakes into the ground.

"Just like Double A's!" Dad said, referring to Aunt Aileen and her luxury screened-in porch.

Except our porch was in our backyard, not attached to our house, and without Aunt Aileen's indoor-outdoor carpeting and wicker furniture.

"It's a camping tent," Mom said.

"It's a luxury screened-in porch. Isn't Dad brilliant?" I said.

I took Mom's silence as a no.

Dad and I read book after book in luxury. Even though we were silent, it felt as if we were spending real time together, like friends.

On the second of only two nights that Mom joined us with her knitting, she spoke.

Mom: "Why do you let her take out books that are over her head?"

Dad: "Because she has read nearly everything in the young adult section."

Mom: "So?"

Dad: "So, I told her that since she has read nearly everything in the young adult section, she can take out any book she wants from any section."

Mom: *Silent lemon-sucking face and a stare that lasted two-Mississippi.*

Dad again: "There's nothing wrong with her reading above her current reading level. Anything over her head will stay over her head."

Mom: *Silent again, but left tent for good with yarn and needles.*

Dad: "Good riddance, Old Lemonsucker!"

Dad laughed.

*What? Dad thinks that Mom sucks on lemons too?*

Dad never said anything fresh to Mom. It felt like me and Dad won something...I just wasn't sure what.

Me: "Yeah, Old Lemonsucker!" I said, and laughed.

Dad: "Hey, watch that mouth."

*Honor thy father and thy mother.*

I could read over my head, but I could not understand the rules or the commandments for the life of me.

The sounds of that summer: Roger's GTO's dual mufflers, the fireworks, the mosquitos buzzing outside of our luxury screened-in porch, the jiggling of ice cubes in the glasses of lemonade that I brought to Dad, the sound of our pages turning, and the sound of our silence as Dad and I sat added up to something abounding and big.

*Math is abounding...God is abounding...*

Could it have been Jesus-hope?

## September 1976

Summer ended with Mom laying three new white uniform blouses and a box of New Freedom sanitary napkins on my bed.

"Let me know if you have any questions," she said.

*Why are you closing my bedroom door and leaving?*

I held the box as if it had answers.

*How is new freedom different from old freedom?*

I read its words to Baby Crissy:

"Beltless! Pinless! Fussless!"

It seemed as if some colossal complication had been cured and suddenly women were able to wear their best white outfits anytime, ride a bike while waving and smiling, even cheer! All you had to do was wear these freedom pads.

*What are me and America free from, really?*

I held a pad and smelled it. *Gauze.* I poured my lemonade onto it and watched it dribble around the edges and onto my bed. So much for the protective shield.

*What do I always tell you, Schnapps?*

But somehow these prepared me, even with their leaky protective sides and adhesive strips, beltless to boot, to face the world fussless into new freedom.

*Thanks, Lemonsucker.*

## CHAPTER 10

# Come, O Creator
# Spirit Blest

**October 1976**

Miss Kinstler, our second lay, was a frosted lady with a fanny so big that it didn't fit between the rows of desks. This made whacking anyone off-guard an impossibility. She was pretty, with a wide, open, homey face and thinly plucked eyebrows. She wore a lot of shimmery makeup and shiny clothes like a movie star. She was moody.

She had a knack for using words ending with a "*shun*" sound, words like damnation and confirmation. She didn't give a hoot about mathematics like Miss Turtleneck did, except for the God triangle, wherein were three Gods in one. To me, it was more like science than math: the air, the solid, and the fire.

*Like Earth, Wind & Fire? No, like wind, earth, and fire—God the Father, God the Son, and God the Holy Spirit.*

I was like Bea, I couldn't help myself. I raised my hand.

"Miss Kinstler, in what mathematical scenario does three equal one?"

Miss Turtleneck had me well trained. Plus, I was genuinely curious and confused. I wasn't trying to be disrespectful or fresh.

But she answered like God—not at all—and hated me from that question forward.

The cool part about the God triangle was that the Holy Spirit Guy, the Invisible One, was like a superhero. Not only did He figure out how Mary could give birth to Jesus without constructing Mom's human hand peace sign puzzle—or without having sex out of wedlock like Jezebel, or Gina—but He made the Body and Blood of Christ turn into bread and wine so that it was easier for us to swallow Him.

"All of this will come to fruition for you, girls and boys, as you embark upon the Sacrament of Confirmation," Miss Kinstler assured us.

Fruition, which she pronounced while making quotation marks in the air, means that it will happen. It took the Jesus-hope right out of the equation for you.

Clarissa was Miss Kinstler's favorite, but then again, Clarissa was everyone's favorite. Boys stuck to her like magnets. She became fall cheer captain. She was chosen to be the partridge in the pear tree, the star of the big finale song in our school's Christmas musical, before it was even Halloween. Her hair and her breasts grew exponentially to her popularity. Or maybe it was the other way around.

Even though Clarissa was busy with boys and cheerleading, she continued to doodle "BEST FRIEND" on my notebooks and book covers. It was as if she didn't want me to forget. Or maybe it was the other way around.

Clarissa gained even more popularity by circulating a paperback to the fake Marcia Bradys, and especially to the boys. It had been banned by our principal because it was about menstruation. Plus, Margaret, the main character, was a particular kind of pagan called Jewish.

Naturally, I had read *Are You There God? It's Me, Margaret.* from our colossal library back when it may or may not have been over my head.

Miss Kinstler turned the other cheek when it came to Clarissa and her contraband.

## December 1976

By December, both Clarissa and I had gained our new freedom, just like Margaret, but there was no freedom in the fruition of womanhood.

"What can you make out of this?" Clarissa asked, handing me a skein of yarn, variegated with silvery shimmer.

*Crocheting plus mathematics equals fruition. A sure thing.*

"A few squares. Maybe a scarf or two?" I said.

"That's it," she said, "a scarf! Yes!"

So while Clarissa blossomed, I crocheted her shimmery skein into a sparkly scarf.

"Perfect," Clarissa said of the scarf. "Now, can you wrap it in Christmas wrap for me?"

So I did.

I brought the package back to school and handed it to Clarissa, who immediately handed it to Miss Kinstler.

"Merry Christmas!" Clarissa said.

The frosted teacher loved the shimmery scarf and wrapped it between her glossy face and satiny blouse. It *was* pretty, if I said so myself.

"I made it myself," Clarissa said.

*Thou shalt not lie.*

"Oh, you are perfection! My partridge! My Jesus!" she said to Clarissa.

*I am the Lord your God, thou shalt not have strange gods before Me. The favorite commandment of Sister Mary Ruthless.*

And so I, one of eight milking maids, stood behind Clarissa, the perfect partridge in a pear tree, air pumping invisible udders, over and over and over, until at last, the Christmas musical's finale came to fruition.

I did my best to forgive Clarissa for lying about the scarf because that was what best friends did. Plus, Miss Kinstler loved the scarf, so that made me feel good about my creation.

"This is so gauche, Kennedy," Clarissa said as she opened my Christmas gift to her, a silvery change purse I crocheted.

"What did you do? Use all of the leftover scraps of yarn from the scarf to make this?" she laughed.

In fact, I had.

"Kennedy, sometimes you worry me."

Sometimes I worried me too.

## January 1977

Christmas was uneventful. The sin baby and I were both too young and too old to believe.

Upon returning to school after Christmas break, the loudspeaker spoke.

"Students and faculty," said our principal, "let us pray for Clarissa and Clarence MacLeod and their family. Let us pray for Mr. MacLeod. Eternal rest grant to him, O Lord; and let perpetual light shine upon him. May his soul, and the souls of all the faithful departed, through the mercy of God, rest in peace. Amen."

*Boss, we've had an accident...*

I stared at Clarissa's empty desk chair, awaiting its explanation.

I looked to Miss Kinstler for answers as she negotiated her fanny to Clarissa's desk, placing on it an empty mayonnaise jar wrapped in red construction paper. In felt tip bubble letters, the paper read, "Donations for the MacLeod Family."

*Clarissa's dad is dead?*

Classmates lined up and dropped coins into the jar, small change sympathy, tokens found in couch cushions or on tops of dryers.

I was like Bea, I couldn't help myself. I raised my hand.

"Miss Kinstler, what happened?"

"Have you not drawn the conclusion?" Miss Kinstler asked.

*One, two, how do you do? The Angels!* I mean, I understood from the announcement that Clarissa's dad is dead. *I guess I mean is Clarissa OK? Why didn't she tell me?*

The hot-face nausea of being told that there was no Santa Claus in that very building by that Sister Mary Ruthless filled me.

"Have you no compassion for my confusion?" I said, in air quotes, trying to copy Miss Kinstler's way of using words ending in "*shun.*"

The whole class gasped.

I was banished to the hallway.

I pressed my ear to the door, trying to hear her explanation of his expiration.

I couldn't stop "*shun-ing.*"

*Three, four, guess who's gonna score...The Angels!*

*How can coins make death better? How did he die? What happened?*

*Five, six,* and then I remembered what the Angels did on five, six—*we're here for kicks, the Angels!*

And so I did. I kicked the classroom door, and Miss Kinstler let me in.

"What kind of a best friend are you, anyway?" she asked.

*Stand back, Boss, the creases are sharp...*

After school, I knelt beside the week-old stack of Dad's beloved newspapers, and one at a time, I began to read. I wasn't even sure what I was looking for, but there it was: "Man Plunges to Death in Hudson."

I brought the headline to my room and read to Baby Crissy:

"MacLeod, forty-two, of Albany, plunges to his death Thursday just shortly after 11 p.m."

*Do you need an ambulance, Boss?*

Clarissa's dad was just like the guy in Gilbert O'Sullivan's song, except he hurled himself right off a bridge instead of a tower.

*What made Clarissa's dad so sad that he had to go and jump off a bridge?*

I tried to call Clarissa over and over until a mean sounding man told me to stop harrassing them. So I did. I couldn't pray for Mr. MacLeod because suicide was a grave and mortal sin against everything on earth, so Baby Crissy and I listened to Gilbert's 45 instead. I prayed Hail Marys for Clarissa and Clarence and Mrs. MacLeod, and I thought a lot about death and how it would be for Clarissa without a dad, and about how sad she must be.

*Where is Miss Turtleneck's Jesus-hope? What is God even thinking?*

I listened to the new Aerosmith album that Roger had sent to me for Christmas. I looked at the boys on the front of the album cover until I got that weird feeling below my navel that I got from looking at Marcus's abdomen. I switched albums, played KC and his Sunshine Band, and looked at them instead, cuz he liked it that way, and wondered.

I never did put anything into that death jar.

Clarissa returned to school within the week with a tub of Vaseline, a hairbrush, and not a word about her plunging father.

"I got Frampton for Christmas," she said to the swarm of boys surrounding her.

She smeared her lips shiny and brushed her dark hair straight.

I was twelve and Clarissa's dead dad was forty-two for eternity, but someone named Frampton had come alive.

It all was pretty Godless and hopeless to me, which was not good, because confirmation was coming fast and hard and so was the Holy Spirit.

*Aw, shit...*

## March 1977

Father and Miss Kinstler seemed to be in disagreement about the exact definition of confirmation; therefore, we had to learn them both word for word. It was all Vatican II's fault.

My interpretation of the definitions was that they were the same. One sounded nicer than the other, more of a wolf in sheep's clothing instead of just a wolf. They were exponential—be perfect, or be more perfect. If not, eternal damnation was guaranteed.

Miss Kinstler and Father told us that if we couldn't be perfect, then we shouldn't receive our confirmation. This confused me. It was mandatory.

Miss Kinstler gave us blue stapled booklets with questions in them, a gazillion at least. We had to memorize each question's answer word for word. Recess and religion class were combined and spent in church with Miss Kinstler, Father, a pointer, and us being quizzed on the blue booklet. It was a fiery kind of *Jeopardy*.

The Holy Spirit, in simplest terms, was supposed to be a blessing from God. But He had a lot of baggage: seven gifts, twelve fruits, sixteen acts committed against His fruits, and six sins against Him. There was a lot of math involved.

Father said that if we hadn't memorized the answers to all of the questions in the blue booklet *verbatim* (in Bea-screech), then the bishop would smack us hard across the face, in front of everyone in the church. That would be an embarrassment not only to ourselves, our families, the bishop, and our principal, but to God, the Holy Spirit, and worst of all, him and Miss Kinstler.

Father said that if we got the answers perfectly correct, the bishop would smack us softly anyway.

My interpretation? Either way, you got hit.

*Turn the other cheek...*

"Class: I 'caution' you to answer the 'questions' correctly. If not, it will be a 'reflection' on me, and you will receive 'incompletions' as 'examination' grades. Therefore, no 'confirmation.' 'Damnation,' and 'cessation' of God's gift of the Holy Spirit will come to 'fruition,'" Miss Kinstler said.

Her and her Goddamn *"shun"* words, all in air quotes.

*Thou shalt not take the name of the Lord thy God in vain.*

She really outdid herself that time.

I was terrified. The thoughts of zeros as examination grades and imperfection and corporal correction by the bishop and damnation, and worse yet—being an abomination to Mom and Dad and God and Jesus and Mary and the Holy Spirit and everyone in the whole universe made me want the only person who I thought could help save my soul.

Rog.

I found the piece of paper tacked to the bulletin board in our kitchen inscribed with the name and address of the air force base where he was. Underneath the information, Mom had written, "in case of emergency," and after that, a phone number. I un-stabbed it and ran across the street to Valerie.

"Kennedy, we can't use this number unless someone died," Valerie said.

"My soul *is* dead!" I cried. "It's an emergency!"

I told Valerie everything, about the booklet and the perfection and the air quotes and the slap across the face and hell, and she listened.

And then she helped.

Valerie slid her finger into the hole marked with the number one, and spun the rotary dial ten more times from memory.

"My secret number," she whispered, handing me the phone.

It rang and rang and rang, a gazillion times, maybe more, until finally, someone answered.

"Yeah?" we heard a man say.

"Hello, may I please speak with Roger?" I said.

There was banging and shuffling and yelling in the background. Then Rog.

"Valerie?"

"No, Rog, it's Boss."

"Kennedy—what the fuck?"

"Rog, that's a sin. We are all going to hell. Eternal damnation."

"What the hell is wrong?"

"I don't know if I can commit to being perfect every second of every day for eternity! I don't know how!"

"I thought someone was dead. What the fuck are you talking about?"

*Why is Rog being so mean?*

I cried.

"Confirmation, Rog, I have to promise to be a perfect Christian and soldier of Jesus Christ through the power of the Holy

86

Spirit which is the third part of the God triangle and I don't think that I can do it. There are so many things to memorize, and there are gifts and fruits and sins—more sins, Rog! More than the ten commandments and the seven deadly ones!"

"Jesus Christ, Boss. Calm down. Just do it for Mom and Dad. And duck when the bishop swings like you did for Sister Mary Ruthless. Put Valerie on," Rog said.

Valerie said a couple of "uh-huhs" and one "I will" and then turned all giggly and flush. And then she hung up.

*What the hell? They hung up on me!*

"Rog will call you when he can," Valerie said, "just relax."

*Great. Like Wayne told Gina? Look where it got her...*

Rog had been my last Jesus-hope.

## April 1977

So I did what I knew to do—my best. I memorized and memorized and memorized, reciting every answer to Baby Crissy, for whom I made a red construction paper miter, *blasphemy*, even though I knew it was a sin I'd have to confess somehow. I was prepared to be perfect. Maybe the bishop would hit me softly, and maybe Dad would be proud.

I prayed a gazillion Hail Marys even though She wasn't a part of the God triangle, the Trinity, Jesus-hoping that She would help me anyway.

"Gina will be your sponsor. She's your only sister, and her feelings will be hurt if you don't ask her. So ask her," Lemonsucker said.

A sponsor was the person you chose to guide you on earth for the rest of your life, but not in a real way—just in the religious, spiritual way. I wasn't sure that Gina was a good choice on account of her sin baby and all. But I did as I was told, hell already lurking as it was.

"And I suppose I'll pick her name as my confirmation name?" I said.

I took Mom's God-silence as a yes.

And so it was: Mary Kennedy Regina.

*A Blessed Mother sandwich.*

I wore a pretty peach-colored dress with long angel sleeves beneath my white robe, and a red beanie held on by two bobby pins distributed by the frosted teacher.

"It would be an 'abomination' if your headwear fell," she said, attempting air quotes while dispensing the pins.

"Your sleeves are never going to fit under your robe, and your dress should be white like mine," Clarissa said, "for your re-Baptism in Christ."

"They're angel sleeves," I said, "like our cheer team, the Angels. Are you nervous?"

"Huh? About what?"

*Where is Clarissa's soul? Isn't she nervous about the bishop and the questions? Isn't she worried about getting the answers wrong in front of God and Father and Miss Kinstler and Mom and Dad and Gina and Wayne and Sin Baby and Bea and Dooley, a superhero? Isn't she afraid of eternal damnation like I am? Hell in a hand basket?*

"You're so gauche, Kennedy," Clarissa said.

*Turn the other cheek...*

I practically held my breath throughout the entire confirmation ceremony, but the bishop did not even ask any questions like Father and Miss Kinstler threatened, but rather he spoke to us in a soft, gentle voice about being soldiers in Christ's war. I wasn't sure where the war was, but the bishop talked all about accepting God into our lives and showing Him that we are His warriors by being destroyers of Satan with our greatest weapon, our gift from God—love.

*Love?*

I was shocked that this young, red-headed man spoke so kindly to us. He didn't smack anyone across the face, but rather, placed his open palm along our cheeks in a protective way, which I found both comforting and creepy all at the same time. But it was much better than being hit or going to hell.

I was pretty mad at everyone for lying to us about what the bishop was going to do, but it seemed to me that that was the way that adults told their truths—by lying.

I had a party and a cake trimmed in red for the Holy Spirit, with a large white dove drawn on it made out of gazillions of mini frosting rosettes.

Dad and Lemonsucker gave me a birthstone ring, representing my new birth, or re-Baptism in Christ, and Gina gave me a cross pendant. Dooley, Bea, and Roger chipped in together and gave me a card with twenty-five dollars cash in it, which was enough money to buy at least four, maybe five, record albums.

I prayed for the feeling of being filled with the fire of the Holy Spirit, but mostly, I became filled exponentially with the weird feeling I got from looking at Marcus's muscles. So I stuck with praying the rosary a gazillion times.

## May 1977

Despite my decades of prayer, the fiery feeling was everywhere—in my Andy Gibb poster, in Joe Perry's album covers, in The Fonz and his motorcycle, even as I stood outside of Clarissa's boy huddle.

It was lust.

*Thou shalt not commit adultery.*

It was boy-huddle envy.

*Thou shalt not covet thy neighbor's wife, and maybe even their boy-huddle goods.*

I'd be filled with fire, alright, the eternal flame of Mom-God hell somewhere below my navel. Forever.

When May brought lilacs, I stood before the frosted teacher with a bunch.

"What am I supposed to do with those?" she asked.

"Put them in a vase with water and give thanks and praise to the Blessed Mother even though She's not the fiery Holy Spirit," I said, but she had no appreciation for my explanation, and threatened me with detention if I continued to act with such insubordination.

The frosted teacher had taught me the art of "*shun*-ing."

I dodged detention by gaining possession of a vase from the principal's office.

For our birthday, Dad and I had our standard lasagna and lemon cake, and Dad and I shared an entire bottle of beer.

"Cheers to the teen years!" Dad said.

I was thirteen and Dad was fifty-one and it sure seemed as if Dad wanted to be my friend too.

I saved a little bit of beer and drank it in my room after Lemonsucker and Dad went to bed.

"Cheers!" I said to Baby Crissy.

She was two, and besides Rog, she was the best friend anyone could ever ask for, even Clarissa, and thus far, even Dad.

"Cheers!" I said to the Blessed Mother.

I thanked Her for Dad and our forming friendship, and I asked Her for help finding the love weapon of which the bishop spoke so softly.

I prayed that hope, even Jesus-hope, wasn't Jesus-dead after all.

## CHAPTER 11

# Seasons in the Sun

**August 1977**

"I told you it was going to do that," Lemonsucker said to Dad, when our luxury screened-in porch collapsed from a minor wind. Dad responded with Lemonsucker's two-Mississippi silence; he answered her like God.

The collapsed tent and Mom's sour attitude couldn't stop me and Dad and our forging friendship.

I filled in the muddy holes where the stakes once held the tent in place and watched Dad drag the dirty walls to the garbage can.

"We still have books, Dad," I said, "we can always read inside."

We continued to go to the library and watched TV together all summer, even Lemonsucker. We watched *Happy Days* and *The Bob Newhart Show*, *M\*A\*S\*H*, *60 Minutes*, and *All in the Family*, and it felt like family. A trinity.

On Fridays, Dad pushed Lemonsucker through the grocery store to get us home in time for *The ABC Friday Night Movie*.

He'd give me a list of things to get while she shopped, "to expedite the misery, Schnapps," he said, so that we were home in time for the movie.

Dad discovered mill shopping that summer, and on Saturdays, we traveled to Troy to shop. The mills were huge abandoned warehouses where they sold brand-new stuff with imperfections for a cheaper price. Dad loved going to the mills because finding bargains and imperfections were hobbies for him.

Just like when he found imperfections on my report cards.

Dad was like God—he expected perfection across the board.

"Only one-hundreds are one-hundreds, Schnapps. Grades in the nineties are grades in the nineties," he'd say.

He had me there. Numbers were numbers. Math was math.

*Math is abounding! God is abounding!*

Old Lemonsucker just stood in the mills with her arms crossed, waiting for Dad to be done.

Not me. I looked at all of the bargains just like Dad, forgiving their imperfections. I wandered off, admiring the huge open warehouse space and thought about what it might be like to live in such a space, with windows from the floor to the part that should have been a ceiling, but it wasn't. Steel continued into an A frame, beams criss-crossed like tic-tac-toe boards.

I thought about what it would be like to have my own apartment like Bob and Emily Hartley from *The Bob Newhart Show*, Baby Crissy perched in a rocking chair that I painted just for her.

I looked at the bedding and thought about what it would feel like to have a person next to me in my bed, like Gina and Dooley had. Someone to kiss like Rog and Valerie had.

What if I cooked my own supper, called up friends, and invited them to my vaulted-warehouse-Bob-and-Emily-Hartley apartment? I would drink Aunt Aileen's wine from pretty glasses with long stems, and maybe even smoke cigarettes if I felt like it.

I would invite all the people who sang their feelings like Karen Carpenter and Gilbert O'Sullivan, and maybe even Roger could fly home and bring Valerie. I'd invite Aunt Aileen, and even Clarissa, if it all wasn't too gauche for her.

*What if Baby Crissy and I live happily ever after? The end?*

And then a new show launched on TV, *The Love Boat*. My friend Dad was particularly excited as he had read the book, *The Love Boats*.

It was the greatest show. All of these strangers went on a cruise ship and ended up falling in love.

*Love?*

Dad commented on all of the pretty girls, and I stared at all of their kisses, especially the kiss between Kristy McNichol and Scott Baio, wondering what it was like to be in love. To be kissed.

Lemonsucker said that *The Love Boat* was unrealistic and kitschy.

Clarissa thought that it was gauche and had better things to do on a Saturday night.

But me and Dad? We didn't care what anyone thought.

That season—of books and TV and mills and a boat just for love—was like living inside somewhere or someone else, even if for just a little while.

It felt too good to be true.

*What do I always tell you, Schnapps?*

## October 1977

Eighth grade was not much of a grade at all, but more like an island TV show hosted by a Hawaiian nun—specifically, the swaying sister, Sister Mary Evangeline.

We had no structure, no subjects, no time slots. Instead, Sister Mary Evangeline spoke before us, all the while her hips moving in a hula, encouraging us to join alongside her in Hawaiian dance.

"Join me! Join me! Love God through your body, let Him flow through you like a trade wind," Sister said, as her hips swayed in a most unnatural way for a nun in a habit.

She spoke about Pearl Harbor and how it affected her people. The Law of the Splintered Paddle was about leadership, hierarchy, and human rights, Sister said.

We learned about the whaling industry and endangered species, and the threat to the Hawaiian monk seal. Sister told us about cultivating crops and exporting goods like coffee, cocoa, pineapple, sugarcane, and honey.

We learned about archipelagos and volcanoes and mountains, and the different kinds of flowers indigenous to Hawaii, and which island they represented.

Mornings, after the Pledge of Allegiance from the loudspeaker, we recited the motto of Hawaii instead of prayers.

"The life of the land is perpetuated in righteousness." And then we said, "Aloha."

Aloha means hello, welcome, best wishes, goodbye, or even love. *Love?*

"Aloha is the greatest prayer of all, and when said with love, could mean everything to someone someday," Sister said. "All the religion you need is within your aloha, my little flowers. Besides, Jesus has only two commandments: love the Lord your God with all your heart, and with all your soul, and with all your mind; and love your neighbor as yourself."

Sister fluttered her hands around her heart, like the wings of a bird.

*Blasphemy.*

These two Jesus commandments seemed pretty easy in comparison to the rest of Catholicism, but I was pretty new to this whole love thing.

Sister Mary Evangeline told us about her life growing up in Hawaii—her brothers and sisters and mother and father, and how much she missed them. She described her long black hair, and how she still remembered the day that they cut it off when she became a nun.

Whenever Sister spoke about her life or family back in her homeland, she cried.

I hated seeing the swaying sister cry, and tried to talk to Clarissa about it, but she didn't have quite the same interpretation as I.

"Sister Mary Evangeline is nuts," Clarissa said.

So I did as Sister encouraged. I stood next to her. Everyone stared as she taught me to hula.

*One, two, how do you do? The Angels!*

Sister moved her feet as if they were on satin pillows, what was left of her long jet black hair peeking through the tight white band that surrounded her face like a picture frame. Her fingers fluttered like butterflies and her eyes closed, as if she had been taken away to another place. Her hips swayed, making her black below-the-knee habit ripple. This was how she told me to move, as if I'd been lifted away by a Hawaiian breeze, or taken on the wings of God Himself in the form of a white dove. In other words, the Holy Spirit.

*Thou shalt not commit adultery.*

I wondered why Sister was allowed to move in such a way— eyes closed and hips swaying.

"Gently move your feet as if you are tiptoeing and sinking into warm Hawaiian sand," she said.

Sister Mary Evangeline showed me how to move my feet, my hands, my hips.

"Sway! Sway!"

"Yes, Sister Mary Evangeline. Thank you."

*Practice makes perfect, people!*

I practiced and practiced and practiced, Baby Crissy an affirming audience.

*Three, four, guess who's gonna score! The Angels!*

Eventually, some of the fake Marcia Bradys joined in, but I was the only one who danced Sister's special hula—"I Am Hawaii"—thus earning Sister's nickname for me: Hawaii.

Clarissa had the partridge in the pear tree; I had the state of Hawaii.

Maybe being a state would make Dad proud.

## December 1977

In December, Sister brought in a fake palm tree and strung Christmas lights around the trunk.

Throughout Advent, the season awaiting the arrival of Jesus at Christmas, as Sister spoke, we made paper birds called origami cranes. Her goal was to make one-thousand cranes for our lighted palm tree, because she believed that if one-thousand cranes were folded and a wish was made, then that wish would come true.

Sister's wish? To travel back to the homeland to see her family.

Every time someone finished folding a crane, Sister strung it and hung it on the tree. Each time she hung, we recited, "O flock of heavenly cranes, cover my child with your wings."

Sister seemed to be practicing some kind of voodoo, but I liked it. "Anything that goes to or leaves Hawaii does so on wind, waves, or wings," Sister said, and cried.

Over Christmas break, I shuffled back and forth between WPTR and WTRY, listening to each radio station's year-end countdowns and trying to win albums. Finally, I won an album by Debby Boone. Turned out she was all lit up and filled with a whole bunch of Jesus-hope.

I played Debby Boone's Bea-screech song over and over like a prayer, Jesus-hoping that God would light up Sister's life and send her home to Hawaii.

*Hail Mary, full of grace, by wind, waves, or wings. Amen.*

## January 1978

When we returned from Christmas break, there was no swaying sister.

"Where's Sister?" I asked no one in particular.

"Hawaii," I heard someone say.

My heart smiled. It was a Christmas miracle. Sister's wish had come true. By wind, waves, or wings, she had traveled home. Sister's cranes worked. Maybe my Debby Boone prayers and rosaries helped.

*It can't hurt, Boss...*

Whatever it was, I was so happy for Sister that her wish had come true.

*O flock of heavenly cranes, cover my child with your wings. Thank you, Blessed Mother.*

"Sister's crane wish worked!" I said to Clarissa.

Clarissa rolled her eyes.

"What the hell are you talking about *now*, Kennedy? Sister's mother died, that's why she's in Hawaii. Don't you know anything?"

*No. Over and over again, no.*

I'd never had my heart soar *like wings* and sink *like waves* so suddenly. It had been too good to be true.

97

*What do I always tell you, Schnapps?*

How could God have been so mean as to have allowed Sister's crane wish to come true and then kill her mother? Or was it the other way around? It didn't matter. It made no sense.

I stared at Baby Crissy, willing her alive.

"Be careful what you wish for," I whispered.

"Shut up, Debby Boone!" I yelled.

*I am Hawaii and I can't fix Sister.*

*Do you need an ambulance, Boss?*

When Sister returned from Hawaii, I had no idea what to do for her. I wanted to say or do something to make her feel better. I was at a loss for words, so I did what I thought that Sister might like.

I stood before her.

"Aloha," I offered.

Sister cried and hugged me.

No one had ever hugged me before. Ever.

"Hawaii! You've heard me! Aloha!"

Sister cried some more.

*She hugged me.*

"Alcatraz! Stop making Sister cry!" Clarissa said.

"They're happy tears, I think. Right, Sister?"

But all Sister did was cry. Exponentially.

*Alcatraz?*

Sister and I danced her pain away; at least that's what she called it.

Boys smiled at me. The better I got at the hula, the more Sister said to let the songs flow through me. The more those songs flowed through me, the more the boys smiled.

"Why Alcatraz?" I asked Clarissa.

"Because you're Hawaii, dummy, a stupid island all by yourself having to do Sister's stupid hula dance," said Clarissa.

*Stand back, Boss, the creases are sharp...*
I let the flow flow.

## April 1978

Finally, I Jesus-hoped, I made Dad proud.

"Look, Dad, all one-hundreds!" I said of my third report card of the year.

Dad scanned.

"See?" Dad said. "I told you that you could be perfect."

I hadn't really earned the grades the old-fashioned way, but I could have. It wasn't my fault that Sister wrote in a whole bunch of one-hundreds in her grade book for me every time I practiced being Hawaii! But I guess when you're Hawaii, you're as close to perfect as you can get. Plus, if it made Dad proud, it was alright with me.

When May brought blooming lilacs, we had no traditional Crowning of the Blessed Mother. Instead, Sister allowed us to bring in records to play to rejoice in song and spirit as tribute to Mary, and her own mother, who had loved music.

I brought in the Debby Boone album for Sister, who had fallen in love with her hope song. I never took it home. I hoped that hope knew its place.

All of May we listened to songs and folded origami flowers from perfect squares of bright colors and scraps of old wrapping paper we all brought from home.

"Your old wrapping paper will become our treasure, my little flowers," Sister said.

And it did.

## June 1978

By June we had boxes and boxes of colorful origami roses and lilies and orchids.

Eighth grade was a dream, an episode of *The Love Boat*. It flew by like a trade wind.

As graduation approached, I grew anxious. It felt just like when Roger left. Plus, Clarissa and I were attending different high schools. I made a countdown from leftover scraps of someone else's old wrapping paper that Sister let me take home, folding each piece into an origami number.

"Alcatraz, you're so gauche. No one but you would be sad about leaving grade school," Clarissa said.

Maybe she was right. But I loved Sister and her swaying hips and her alohas and her Hawaiian hug.

As June flew, Sister became more and more like a teacher and less and less like a Hawaiian television host.

We cleaned out our desks, wiped their surfaces with dirty sponges, washed the windows, and turned the blackboard back to black.

For graduation, I wore a pretty mint green dress *for Ireland* and an origami flower over my right ear, the way that, according to Sister, girls in Hawaii did when they were looking for love.

*It can't hurt, Boss...*

Maybe it was voodoo, but I needed all the help that I could get finding that greatest weapon—love.

At the end of our graduation mass, Sister presented to each of us a lei, a sign of friendship, honor, celebration, and love.

*Love?*

It was aloha in flower form.

"Aloha, Hawaii," Sister said to me, "thank you for your friendship."

Sister pressed her forehead against mine and breathed out a Hawaiian breath, "ha," and wrapped me with a lei she had strung from the origami flowers that we had made.

"Aloha...aloha..." was all I could say.

And just like that, like the flutter of Sister's dancing fingers, eighth grade was over. To celebrate my graduation, we had a fancy dinner at the restaurant where Roger worked before he moved away, and cake and punch back at the house.

And it was there that I realized exactly how I could make Dad proud, exactly how I could prove to him that I was as special as Dooley.

I took the lei from around my neck and presented it to Dad.

I spoke Dooley's policeman plaque words.

"This belongs to you, sir, without you I wouldn't be where I am today," I said.

Dad looked at me. Blank. Confused.

"Why would DAD want your STUPID paper roses?" Bea screeched.

Bea was a wolf. There was nothing sheepish about her.

I wanted to say that they weren't paper, but they were. I wanted to say that they weren't roses, but some of them were. I wanted to ask Bea why Dad would want Dooley's stupid Policeman of the Year plaque, but he did.

*Boss, we've had an accident...*

"Aloha. Aloha to all of you," I said, and went to my room.

I placed the origami lei over Baby Crissy's head in exchange for my Catholic lei of crystal beads, and prayed that paper roses weren't really just fake folded love.

*What do I always tell you, Schnapps? If it seems too good to be true, it probably is.*

## CHAPTER 12

# A Whiter Shade of Pale

**July 1978**

Summer turned from leis of aloha to a laying to rest, beginning
with an announcement from the pulpit of Father's death. He'd
suffered a massive heart attack and died just hours before the
morning's first Sunday mass. Sister Mary Evangeline found him.

I felt worse about not feeling worse about Father dying than I
did about Father dying. I thought about how mean he had been
all those years, like when he didn't care that our crumpled car got
stolen. I thought about how he made me do all those penances for
being ridiculous, when it was he who was ridiculous, or the scary
way he taught us about confirmation with a blue booklet and a
pointer, or how he threatened us with that nice bishop. I thought
about how he began every Sunday's mass saying that we weren't
worthy enough to be in his presence—or maybe he was speaking
of *His* Presence, but either way, he deemed us all unworthy. I
hated the way that he drank all of the Jesus blood at the end of

Communion as if he were at a bar, like he was enjoying it, not like he was swallowing Jesus at all.

I wasn't sad. I was relieved. One less wolf.

Parishioners cried, some sobbed.

I wanted to laugh. I stole a look across the aisle at Clarissa, and she looked like she wanted to laugh too. For once, I felt that we were real best friends—like we were interpreting things the same way like best friends do.

Lemonsucker was sucking.

Dad was stoic.

I was on my way to hell in a hand basket.

"Do you like the way Father died?" Clarissa asked, after mass.

Clarissa's brother made a gesture not unlike Mom's human hand peace sign puzzle, except he slid his right index finger back and forth within a tube that he had formed with his left hand.

"Father died of a massive heart attack," I said.

"Yeah, on top of a whore!" Clarissa said.

*Think of Easter…*

"But that can't be, Sister Mary Evangeline found him," I said.

"She did, dummy, and she covered up for him! Alcatraz, you don't know anything!" Clarissa said.

It seemed as if Clarissa was right. I knew nothing. How could Father have even been in a room alone with a woman, let alone having sexual relations with her? Priests weren't allowed to do that. It was mortal. Punishable by damnation. Mom-God hell for eternity.

On the way home from mass, I asked Lemonsucker and Dad if they were sad about Father.

Only Dad spoke, "The loss of life is always a shock."

*Is that Dad's "think of Easter"?*

"Clarissa said that Father was maybe with a woman when he died, in the biblical sense," I said.

I ducked, fearing the air's response.

But Lemonsucker and Dad answered like God—not at all.

I never did know for sure if Father died on top of a whore or not. I didn't care. It just seemed to me as if all of the adults made all of the rules but never had to follow any of them. And meanwhile, I was going to hell for breaking all of the commandments and all that Holy Spirit stuff. Even Jesus couldn't get it right—He only knew how to give hope through death. Nothing made sense.

My friend Dad was right—life was a shock.

## August 1978

Dad and I continued to go to the library, but he kind of ruined the fun by spending the whole summer reading one book: *War and Peace*. It was a gazillion pages long. It was fine that he wanted to, as he said, "tackle that book." But it wasn't as much fun running into the library to get new books by myself while Dad waited in the car for me.

Because of *War and Peace*, we didn't watch much TV that summer either. Lemonsucker took to knitting like a fiend, so the living room was all needles scraping and pages turning. Dad and Lemonsucker had found their own kind of solitaire.

And then it got paler than pale.

I was in my room playing my own game of solitaire.

Sin Baby barged in.

*Don't they teach you manners?*

She grabbed Aerosmith *Get Your Wings* and tried to remove the sleeve from the cover. I saved the album by default—it was on my turntable.

She mangled a paper crane that I had saved from Sister's Christmas wish tree. O flock of heavenly cranes, I shall refold thee.

Just as Sin Baby was clawing at Andy Gibb's thigh, hung as he was on my hard wall, Gina appeared at the door, distracting her.

"Maryanne, have you seen Aunt Kennedy's doll?" Gina said.

*What doll?*

Sin Baby lunged for Baby Crissy as fast as I did, and we played a ridiculous game of tug of war.

*Ridiculous.*

"What the hell is the matter with you?" Gina asked in perfect Dad form.

"You shouldn't say 'hell' in front of your kid," I said.

"Kennedy, let her play with the doll," Gina said.

"She's not a doll, she's Baby Crissy, and no one is allowed to touch her."

"How old are you?" she asked.

I was fourteen, Gina was twenty-three, and Sin Baby was terribly two.

"Gina, no. No one is allowed to touch her."

At that point, Sin Baby was crying.

When Lemonsucker appeared at the door sucking a gazillion lemons, I surrendered, at least temporarily.

*Sometimes you have to mess things up before you can put them back together again, right Schnapps?*

I borrowed Dad's logic.

"OK," I said, "she can play with her for a few minutes, but then she has to give her back."

Sin Baby dragged Baby Crissy by the hair down the hall and into the living room.

*Why are they letting her do this? Why doesn't anyone care about Baby Crissy? Or me?*

She threw her on the ground and punched her and laughed.

*Hail Mary full of grace…*

She picked up Baby Crissy by one arm and dragged her to the kitchen, where Lemonsucker and Gina sat drinking coffee.

*How can they just sit there and let this happen? Don't they know that I am one step away from having a massive heart attack just like Father? Why don't they care? What the hell is the matter with them?*

*Please don't hold Baby Crissy by the arm, please Sin Baby oh God, o flock of heavenly cranes can I please put her back in my room I don't want her to touch Baby Crissy I waited forever for my own baby Baby Crissy and my world is perfect when I am with her practice makes perfect people but does practice make perfect people I need her on my hip by my side so please don't touch my Baby Crissy she is all I have left of Rog.*

I took a calculated risk.

*One, two, how do you do?*

"May I hold Baby Crissy?"

And it worked. Alleluia. Aloha.

Sin Baby passed Baby Crissy to me and the world was right.

*Easy does it, Schnapps…*

And that's when it happened, just when I wasn't expecting it. Sin Baby howled like, well, I didn't even know, like a freakin' crazed baby wolf in toddler sheep's clothing. Lemonsucker and Gina were like "give her the doll" and I was like "no she's my baby" and then there was another ridiculous tug of war and when Baby Crissy's arm started to give way I let go because the one thing that I didn't want to do was hurt Baby Crissy and then it was over.

Screech! Boom!

*Do you need an ambulance, Boss?*

Gina got mad and Lemonsucker got mad and Gina announced that she was leaving and Sin Baby was crying and whining and dragging Baby Crissy toward our front screen door and I yelled at them *don't take my baby* and maybe they said stuff back to me but I could not hear them because the noise in my head and the heat in my ears were too loud and hot and all I knew was that I wanted to die because my heart felt like it was exploding like a massive heart attack on a whore or in a game of Baby Crissy tug of war or when your pilot got on an airplane and you didn't know when he'd be back again or when you got called Alcatraz for being Hawaii and were the only one unchosen for cheerleading and you didn't even know your so called best friend's father hurled off a bridge until your fat-assed frosted teacher covered a mayonnaise jar with construction paper so everyone could think that coins could help death or like when you had to do all kinds of shit penances from some priest who died on a Jezebel and all the while he and all the other adults and sin babies just ran around doing whatever the hell they wanted even if it hurt someone so bad they wanted to die of an exploded heart.

"Mom! Please don't let them take Baby Crissy!"

*No. Not my baby. Not my Baby Crissy. Not my everything. No. You can't let her take her away from me. I love her.*

I said it.

*I love Baby Crissy.*

*Use your greatest weapon, Kennedy, your gift from God, your love weapon against Satan.*

"I LOVE BABY CRISSY!" I said it out loud, Bea-screech loud.

*She loves me back. She loves me back.*

*No. God. Oh. God. No. Please. Oh. No. She's all I've got.*

My stomach surged and my fingers tingled *the loss of life is always a shock* and the world before me went to the whitest white that I had ever seen.

"Mom, no! Mommy, no! Don't let her take my Baby Crissy away!"

*Oh. No. I. No. Please. No. Don't!*

"You don't play with her anymore. You're too old anyway. The baby is crying. She wants the doll. Don't be mean to Maryanne."

*Mean? You mean ridiculous?*

"Mom! No!"

*Fuck you Lemonsucker fuck you Gina fuck you Sin Baby fuck the world fuck Jesus and Mary and Joseph and fuck the whole fucking Trinity and fuck you, aloha.*

I stood at the front screen door alongside Lemonsucker watching Baby Crissy's hair drag on the grass, her cheek bouncing up and down against the pavement, and I was purged pain.

I was numb and I was hoarse and I was screaming only inside huge unheard noes and wishes of damnation to everyone who ever lived.

*Fuck you, hope.*

Baby Crissy's head hit the side of their car, her cheek banged against the metal, her fixed smile looked just like the Joker from *Batman*.

*Boss, we've had an accident...*

And then she was in the car.

*Stand back, Boss, the creases are sharp...*

They stole my baby, my Baby Crissy.

*Thou shalt not steal.*

One hot tear, like Fab-faded pink paint running through the creases in sudsy streams, rushed down my cheek, reminded Lemonsucker of my existence.

"You're not *THAT* upset are you?" she asked in her French.

I answered her like God.

*Fuck you too, God.*

*Thou shalt not take the name of the Lord thy God in vain bless me dead Father on top of a whore for I have sinned...*

And that was it.

*Easy does it, Schnapps...*

Their car pulled away and they were gone. They kidnapped my baby. The only thing that I was allowed to—love?

Me. Gone.

Them. Thieves. Sinners. Pagans. Haters.

The trailing taillights of Baby Crissy's kidnappers were like streaks of blood on the road.

Lemonsucker closed the wooden door.

I was dead.

*I said no.*

**shatter** |ˈSHadər|
VERB
: break or cause to break suddenly and violently into pieces
: damage or destroy
: upset (someone) greatly
: how I was left alone, again

My bedroom was empty the second I entered it. I looked around as if I might find Baby Crissy somewhere in there by some miracle, but all that was left of her was a rosary and a lei.

I played Gilbert's 45.

I taped Andy Gibb's torn thigh and traced my finger along the bulge in his pink polyester pants.

*Why did Lemonsucker and Dad allow this poster? Were there really no rules and only I thought that there were? Who are the liars?*

I wanted to write a letter to Rog about the brutal kidnapping, but didn't want to upset him. One broken heart was enough. I felt as alone as I had that day that he was swallowed by the airplane.

After finishing the last of my three library books, I placed them on Dad's side table next to his recliner, covering his *War and Peace.*

Without permission, I grabbed a stack of Dad's newspapers.

*Thou shalt not steal.*

Back in my room, I found Sister's mangled crane, unhinged it fold by fold, and creased it back together deliberately, methodically, perfectly.

*Oh Rog, the creases are so so sharp...*

I cut perfect squares from used news, like the semi-frozen bread from *Dad's Production.*

Plastic Panasonic headphone foam wrapped around me, hugging me with words from the closest humans that I could find.

And then I began folding for Baby Crissy's return.

*O flock of heavenly cranes, cover my child with your wings.*

It took eighty-seven hours and eleven minutes to fold one-thousand cranes. I glued a scrap of yarn from leftover balls *this is so gauche, Kennedy* to each finished crane, and sang Sister's song each time I hung one from my ceiling.

Every time my bedroom door opened or closed they flew as if in a Hawaiian trade wind. Sin Baby couldn't reach them.

"MOM, why did you let KENNEDY plaster THESE THINGS all over her CEILING?" Bea never could help herself. Some things never changed.

No one bothered to ask me about the cranes, and that was all right with me. I would have lied to them anyway, the way that they do.

*Thou shalt not lie.*

My headphones hugged me.

Lyrics filled me and urged me to love somebody and drink whiskey. Stakes were high. People were sinning and dying and walking miles for tits and ass. There were games and players and lovers and prisoners and losers. People were missing people and I was alone.

*Is everyone alone again, naturally?*

Who needed Baby Crissy anyway?

I did. I almost threw up every time that I thought about her.

Sometimes, when we visited Sin Baby, I found Baby Crissy and held her. I thought of ways to steal her back, but I always got caught.

*Thou shalt not steal.*

Everybody yelled at me for wanting her back. For wanting anything.

*Thou shalt not covet thy neighbor's goods.*

If Sin Baby saw me holding Baby Crissy, she yelled, "Mine!" and it made me want to punch her.

*Thou shalt not kill.*

*Ugly kidnappers, able abettors: fuck you.*

I missed Sister Mary Evangeline and her Hawaiian voodoo and her aloha love. I missed watching the Lord move through her body like a trade wind. I missed Roger. I missed Baby Crissy.

The cranes helped.

## CHAPTER 13

# Midnight Blue

### October 1978

High school was very different than grade school.

The nuns were nice and wore wooden cross necklaces. They dressed in regular clothes instead of habits. They had hair.

There were brothers who were more like the new fangled nuns than priests.

There were teachers who called themselves doctors.

No one used pointers or yardsticks. Or if they did, no one swung them like a ruthless nun.

The girls in high school did not seem like fake Marcia Brady girls either. They seemed pretty nice and said hi to me in the halls. It was a relief.

Clarissa thought that it was gauche that I was friendly with all of the girls and told me that she was only friends with the "normal girls." This made me wonder if Clarissa was a fake Marcia Brady, and I did not miss having her in my high school with me at all. I enjoyed my new freedom.

*I am Hawaii...*

There were boys who looked almost like men.

There were machines from which you could buy amazing food like canned ravioli with mini meatballs, and a device called a microwave that heated it up in seconds.

*Like computers in Nebraska?*

You could buy pizza every day.

There were lockers wherein you could store all of your stuff and you were allowed to carry a pocketbook wherever you wanted.

They had their own library and a class called homeroom.

There was a man-boy in my homeroom named Jake who looked disturbed in the Jim Morrison way. He wore worn corduroys and flannel shirts half tucked in. He talked to me, unless he was reading some dog-eared paperback, which was most of the time. He asked me questions like what bus did I take and what books did I like to read and what kind of music did I like. He asked me about my schoolwork and my teachers, which I found peculiar because he was in most of my classes. I answered him anyway. He wrote poetry and all of the girls seemed to have a crush on him.

When Jake read in homeroom, I read too. Or I studied so that I could get one-hundreds in everything just in case I still wanted to make Dad proud.

It had been difficult to continue to try to be Dad's friend, because although he was not present for the kidnapping, he kept company with kidnappers, and was, therefore, guilty by association.

"Bad company ruins good morals," at least that was what it said in the *Good News Bible* that we had to buy for ninth grade religion class.

High school religion, at least in the ninth grade, was all about the *Good News*, which really didn't seem like good news at all, just like Miss Turtleneck and her Jesus-hope. Basically, you had to talk all about Jesus and how He spread the Gospel and how you would be a disciple and spread it too, and you got one-hundreds in religion class. It was pretty easy. There were no commandments in high school, or so it seemed to me.

The hardest part about religion class was that we were required to go to confession once a month in order to pass. It was uncomfortable because the new high school father had an office for a confessional instead of a dark velvet closet. His office was filled with comfy chairs, and plants, and books about Jesus and theology, and a full coffee pot and extra mugs in case you wanted some. To me, his office looked more like the near occasion of sin than absolution.

I felt bad lying to New Father, but I could not possibly tell him what I was really thinking. So I didn't.

But New Father was nice, and asked questions the way that Jake did. New Father acted like he cared, but I was afraid that he was a wolf in sheep's clothing.

"How are Dooley and Roger? And your sister? I forgot her name."

"Gina," I told him as he nodded. "You know Rog?"

"Everyone knows Rog, Kennedy."

We laughed.

So instead of listing sins, I told New Father about how Gina had a sin baby, except I kept out the sin part, and that she was expecting another non-sin one.

I told him how Roger worked on machines for the Air Force in Nebraska.

I told him that Dooley was a detective and that Bea was very tall and very blonde and very loud, and he laughed.

I wanted to tell New Father all about the kidnapping and the cranes, and how much I missed Baby Crissy and Sister Mary Evangeline, and how I missed being Hawaii, and how I missed Roger, and how lonely Gilbert O'Sullivan sounded on his 45. And me. I wanted to tell him that I was lonely. But I didn't.

New Father absolved me of the sins that I didn't confess with a blessing and a thumb-drawn cross on my forehead. And that was that. Confession done for another month.

*It can't hurt, Boss...*

I thought about my next confession and wondered if I should tell New Father about how something weird was going on with Dad and Lemonsucker.

Dad lay down a lot on Saturdays instead of mill shopping. *The Winds of War*, Dad's latest epic, remained untouched next to him on his side table. The TV was on, but he snored, even through *The Love Boat*. He coughed more than he talked, holding his chest like Roger did when he inhaled too much smoke from his cigarette. Sometimes Dad pounded his chest like Roger—like Tarzan—and choked out, "Wrong pipe."

Lemonsucker, well, maybe she wasn't quite sucking anymore. It was as if the lemons had been removed from her mouth, leaving a sunken corpse looking mouth, the way it looks right before they sew it shut. She looked as if she had just seen a ghost and gasped for air. Wrinkled-style. She looked too tired to suck.

I was silent and different, indifferently unnoticed.

## CHAPTER 14

# Tragedy

### December 1978

That year, I helped Mom wrap Christmas presents because Dad was too tired. Plus, I needed to wrap a gift for our homeroom's Secret Santa.

I was excited. I'd never engaged in a Secret Santa before. The rules were simple: pick a name out of the hat and buy a gift for that person. Label the gift with your recipient's name without telling anyone it was from you. So I did.

I bought the recipient of my gift, a very popular man-boy, a silver chain, the kind that men and man-boys wore. Sometimes they hung a cross from them, like Scott Baio, or a Miraculous Medal, like Dad.

I was real proud of my gift until it turned into a hot potato.

"Nice necklace. Turning into a girl?"

"Fag!"

The homeroom man-boys were teasing, and everyone was asking who bought the necklace, even the girls.

I opened my mouth but nothing came out.

*Think of Easter...*

Wasn't there safety in Scott Baio and Dad, in crosses and Miraculous Medals? In Jesus-hope? What about the *Good News*?

I stood and reached for the chain, but it was being tossed and I could not break into their tangled huddle.

*One, two, how do you do? The Angels!*

"WHO DID THIS?" our homeroom teacher asked in a Bea-screech.

*Alcatraz did.*

"There must have been a mix up," Jake said, reaching for the chain. "Here, let's trade."

Jake took the necklace and handed a book of Lifesavers and a giant Hershey bar to Very Popular Man Boy. The room quieted.

*Turn the other cheek...*

Jake clasped the chain around his neck, looking at me with eyes I recognized. Roger's eyes as he waved at the airport, Dad's eyes as he stood alongside Roger's crumpled car. The look of stolen babies.

*Jake gets it.*

I heard him; silent empathy.

He winked as the bell rang.

I ran to my locker and to the bus as fast as I could without looking like I was running away from pain, away from torment, away from everything sad and everything lonely. Away from kidnappers. The bus door closed me in, shielding me faintly.

*Easy does it, Schnapps...*

I opened my gift, my Secret Santa: Sweet Honesty perfumed soaps by Avon. *Perfect, Bea will love these.*

I thought about going home to the weirdness, where the sound of yelling and Dad questions and voices on the scanner were distant. Besides Dad's coughing, everything was just so quiet. The silence of the house was deafening.

I pressed my cheek against the cold bus window, cooling the flame of disappointment and shame. I wished the window a mute Merry Christmas.

The bus unleashed me into the cold. In my peripheral vision I saw its flashing red lights, like emergency Christmas lights.

*Like ambulance lights?*

Ahead, I saw Dad's car in the driveway.

I tried to remember if I had ever seen Dad's car in the driveway during the day, a school day, during the work week.

*No. Never.*

*Is Mom a possible cardiac?*

The neighborhood was still, as if maybe even it was trying to eavesdrop and decipher the unfamiliarity of Daytime Dad.

I walked up the driveway, past our huge six-trunked tree, *our history, our roots*, through the front screen door.

Dad sat in his seat at the head of the kitchen table looking straight ahead, with Mom alongside him, in her chair.

Dad's head was cradled in his open palms, like an open-faced prayer. He looked pale. *Paler than pale. Whiter than white.*

Mom looked like Mom usually looked, pursed and tight, corpse-like, her head turned toward me, emotionless.

We stared. A silent trinity.

Dad pronounced the problem, the reason why he was home in the middle of a work day, with one word, like it was my name or something. Like it was all encompassing, that new label.

I was fourteen and Dad was fifty-two, and even though Dad told me not to tell anyone, more secrets to have and to hold, I knew that the quiet neighborhood would soon be whispering that things for us would never be the same.

*Lord, will this day of secrets ever end?*

I shook my head up and down, letting them know that I heard.

I stood before them until I felt tears tugging at the backs of my eyes, and until Dad's eyes could not help but look away.

I walked to my room, numb, opened my door extra fast, watched the cranes fly in frenzy, and looked around for Baby Crissy, forgetting she wouldn't be there.

Immediately, I began to pray the rosary, attempting to hear their marital mumbling.

Dooley arrived with an urgent squeak of the front screen door.

Something was growing rapidly inside of Dad, certainly not a sin baby. Size of a tennis ball. Possibly matasti-something-ed. Operation. Something about next week, or maybe a few weeks. After the holidays.

I asked God if there would still be Christmas.

I wondered what it would be like if someone knocked on my door and told me, explained things to me like I mattered like Dooley, held me, the floundering bedroom crier that I was, the newly reassigned daughter of Daytime Dad.

"Cancer," was all Dad, or anyone, had said.

## December 1978

*Silent night. Holy shit. Now what?*

Christmas went on as usual, except for *Dad's Production: Christmas Edition*. This time Mom made the dressing with my help, employing my game-time cutting expertise.

Dooley put up an enormous live Christmas tree that took up most of the living room. We strung tinsel one by one on every branch.

Mom pressed out hundreds of butter cookies.

Mom and I neatly wrapped the remainder of the presents, including Bea's Sweet Honesty.

The perfect presentation. The quintessential facade.

It seemed as if everyone was trying to be super nice to everyone. Even Mom un-sewed her mouth to smile at the sin baby. It infuriated me.

## January 1979

Some time after cancer came and Christmas went, Dooley and Bea dropped off a dog for Dad—a stray someone at the police station found.

"Brilliant idea, Dool," I said.

"A pet can be cathartic in these situations."

I stared at him.

"Cathartic means…"

"I know what cathartic means, Super D," I said, cutting him off.

"Dad loves dogs."

"Dad is sick. Mom is…"

I didn't have a word for Mom.

*A possible cardiac?*

"She will help," Dooley said.

"How do you know? You don't live here," I said to Dooley, wondering if the "she" he was referring to was the dog or Mom.

*Turn the other cheek…*

"MOM. Why is Kennedy being so SELFISH and FRESH?" Bea couldn't help herself.

"Mind your own Bea-business," I said, shocked at my own voice.

Everyone yelled, "KENNEDY!" so loud it awakened Dad.

"Now look what you've done," Dooley and I said in unison.

Dad liked the dog; Dooley was right about that. He named her Cancer the Crab, or CeCe for short.

"Since when are you into the Zodiac signs?" Mom asked Dad.

*Astrology is the devil's science...*

"Since I got cancer and a dog born around July," Dad said.

Mom thought it was morbid, but I thought it was pretty funny.

I wondered if I should try to be Dad's friend after all, even if he continued to associate with kidnappers.

I spent more time out of my room, helping with CeCe and trying to eavesdrop.

"Getting my affairs in order, Schnapps," Dad said, as I watched them scurry from the sidelines.

Mom and Dad were busy gathering papers and going through strong boxes and passbooks.

I tried to forgive them for their sins.

*"Father, forgive them, for they know not what they do." I mean, that's what Jesus said when they were crucifying Him. Talk about turning the other cheek.*

I was no Jesus.

Once I was back in school it was easier to ignore the presence of Daytime Dad and cancer.

Jake never said a word about the silver chain, but he wore it every day, and we were best friends ever since.

That month at confession, I wanted to ask New Father how Jesus could forgive the people that hung Him on a cross, and if turning the other cheek was really what we were supposed to do.

Instead, I confessed fake sins and asked for forgiveness for lying about fake sins. I told truths through lies, like an adult. And then I asked New Father to pray for Dad, because as Dad said, it was showtime.

## February 1979

It was tragedy.

The Bee Gees said so through the transistor radio I had pressed to my ear on the way to the hospital in Dooley's unmarked car. They sounded void of soul and as desperate as I felt.

The gazillion below zero wind chill bullied me into wearing a scarf, and its frigidity forced tears from my eyes, which made me mad because I had been trying not to be a crybaby about the cancer thing. I pushed my scarf into my eyes to drain them.

"Does it have to be this Goddamn cold? I'm practically crying!" Dooley said.

It was *that* cold.

Since saying Goddamn was a sin, I answered Dooley like God—not at all. Only Dooley would cry practically. I didn't know superheroes cried.

By the time we reached the hospital's entrance, my forehead was aching. It was bone-chilling. Even CeCe was shocked by the bitterness outside, reluctantly stepping over her mini yellow ice rinks, doing her business, then sliding back into the house. The poor dog missed Dad, her new partner in cancer. Never mind the sub-zero temperature. I felt bad for her, having to go into the cold alone without Dad.

Dooley's navy-gloved finger pressed elevator buttons: arrow up, fifth floor. He told a stranger that his wife was afraid of elevators.

*Figures. Big blonde Bea afraid of elevators. Who even cares? At least it's warm.*

I was not afraid of the elevator. I was afraid of the tube. I did not want to see the tube. I was not going to look at it.

*I will look at Mom instead. No. I will try to look at Dad. Maybe Dad will like that. But I am not going to look at the tube.*

It was hard to look at Dad while he was sleeping or not wearing his glasses. I had never seen him without his glasses until then. I had never even seen him sleep so much until then. Plus, Dad had to wear an effeminate hospital gown and thick white stockings. Both were flat-out wrong. Dad would never have worn those.

*Gauche.*

Dad's surgery had gone well. I'd heard the lung surgeon tell that to Mom in the surgical patient's family waiting room after he was finished cutting Dad open and sewing him back up like a fish. He removed Dad's whole lung and even some lymph nodes. I had to figure out what lymph nodes were, but I guessed you didn't need all of them to live because Dad was still breathing.

*That clown machine is scary too. I Jesus-hope that they don't bring it in for Dad to blow.*

The lung surgeon made Dad blow into this machine that looked like a gumball machine. He was supposed to blow hard enough to make the little ball at the bottom inside the chute hit the clown's head that was at the top of the machine. It was like some sick circus game—the clown head like a monster waiting to be struck hard enough to ding with a happiness that hurt.

*Like the Joker from Batman?*

I felt awful for Dad. You could tell that it hurt.

I prayed Hail Marys ad nauseam. That's Latin for so fucking much.

Dad's eyes were open when Dooley and I walked into the room.

*Don't look at the tube.*

Dad liked the Bee Gees, so I told him that they had another new song on the radio.

*Tragedy.*

But Dad just closed his eyes, and although I tried not to look, I stared directly at the tube.

*Turn the other cheek...*

At the bottom of Dad's hospital bed, there was a plastic box filled with yellow and red fluid, tie-dyed but murky. It made me want to cry because the tube that went into the top of it also went into the top of Dad's chest.

The backs of my eyes ached with the involuntary insurgence of crybaby tears.

"What?" Dad asked, open-eyed.

Mom shot me a look like I was doing something wrong, and I was unsure which was the culprit—the Bee Gees or my visible tearing.

"Tragedy!" I said.

I thought that Dad almost smiled, but then he slept again, so I told Mom about how the cold made Dooley cry.

Practically.

She answered like God.

## February 1979

"Squamous cell carcinoma, that's the kind of cancer my dad has," I said to Jake.

"Squamous cell carcinoma sounds serious," he said, looking up from his paperback. "How do you know?"

"The surgeon told Mom in the waiting room. I listened."

I could not help but repeat it over and over, feeling guilty about loving the sound of the words as they twirled off my tongue and gouged terror in my gut.

*Squamous cell carcinoma. Squamous cell carcinoma. Squamous cell carcinoma.*

I attempted to use them in English class as examples of both alliteration and onomatopoeia, but the teacher-doctor scowled and said that we didn't need to use such words.

*No one asked her to.*

Admittedly, I could not have known the sound of such cells. However, if nothing else, they had alliteration and charming cadence. It was a lovely sounding cancer.

Jake agreed, but suggested that a haiku might be a more appropriate outlet for those beguiling words. Jake was always using big words. Maybe he was right.

So I wrote:

*Cigarette cancer*
*Squamous cell carcinoma*
*Incised, cut, and carved.*

In any event, haiku or not, I was pretty mad that God decided to give Dad squamous cell carcinoma, *squamous cell carcinoma*, because it is caused by cigarette smoking, and Dad quit smoking way back in 1969. He did it for Roger.

I was five and Roger was fifteen and Dad was a forty-three-year-old raving cold turkey.

"You're smoking," Dad said.

"No, sir."

Even I knew that Rog was lying. Rog always smelled like, well, *Rog.*

*Of summer and cigarettes.*

"Sit," Dad told Roger.

I crawled beneath our kitchen table, scared of what was coming next. I hated it when Dad yelled.

I don't remember what Dad said, but there was volume and there was banging and there was terror. I watched the tablecloth flutter when Dad pounded his fist on the table with every syllable.

But Roger was no cheek-turning Jesus, and he was no superhero like Dooley. He challenged Dad with words that I never forgot.

"Fine, old man, if it's so easy to quit, then let's see YOU quit."

Dad yelled, "Fine, then. I quit!"

Dad's crushed half pack of cigarettes flew from his rolled shirtsleeve and onto the floor, so close to me that I could smell their sweetness.

I watched Dad's feet walk to Roger, so close that their shoes touched.

"I quit. You quit. We quit. Together," Dad yelled.

Roger backed up the kitchen chair fast with a screech. His only response to Dad was a puff, a sound like he was losing a lot of air.

I wanted to scream at Dad, "Dad! Roger won't quit, you may as well smoke!"

I knew that Roger wouldn't quit.

And then it happened as it always happened. Roger left. Roger was leaving way back then, I just didn't know. From beneath the tablecloth, I watched his brown suede jacket fringe sway through our front screen door. Roger went to the fence.

I felt bad for Dad after that. He walked around a lot and stopped and looked at things, like he had lost something, like the way he looked when—years later—Dooley had stopped talking on the police scanner. Dad had the look of crumpled cars and kidnappers. The look of cancer. Dad looked afraid. Dad looked lonely.

So, yeah, it seemed pretty mean to me that God decided to give Dad cancer, specifically that cancer, after he did that for Rog. Dad was alone again, naturally.

Since Dad's eyes were closed a lot, and because Mom repeatedly said that there were too many people in Dad's hospital room, I hung out a lot in the regular waiting room with Aunt Aileen. She seemed to be in as much trouble for saying things like "tragedy" to Dad as I was.

I told Aunt Aileen all about the Bee Gees' new song and about my torn Andy Gibb poster, but I left out the parts about the kidnapping and the bulge in his pants. She smiled and said that she had a bit of a crush on Andy Gibb herself.

Aunt Aileen was cool. She brought cards and small puzzles with her to the hospital so that we could pass the time. That's what she called it, "passing the time."

Once, she even bought us Tabs from a vending machine with coins that she pulled out from her bag.

"Green grass and high tides!" she toasted.

"Ireland?" I asked.

"No," she laughed, "the Outlaws!"

We clinked cans and it felt right.

I wondered when it was OK to practically cry.

## CHAPTER 15

# Just What I Needed

**March 1979**

Aerosmith's *Bootleg* had two ringed coffee stains on the back cover. How could something so brand new be so defiled at the same time?

I felt bad, but sometimes I told Mom that I had too much homework to go to the hospital, or that CeCe needed someone to care for her. It worked. I got to stay home alone and listen to my music without headphones.

I traced the coffee stains with my fingers and thought about cancer and what my life might be like without Dad.

I Bea-screeched lyrics so loud the cranes shuddered.

I screamed.

Like a forest of falling trees, if no one heard me, did I still make a sound?

*Clarissa never hears me.*

*"Man falls to death…"*

*Does death have sound?*

I hadn't told Clarissa much about Dad because I was afraid that it would upset her. I only mentioned that he was sick and needed an operation.

"Well, it's under control then, it's not like he's dead," was all she said.

I played all of the Aerosmith albums I owned: *Draw the Line, Get Your Wings, by wind waves or wings*...and *Bootleg*, playing "Lord of the Thighs" over and over, ad nauseam, so fucking much.

I tried to decide which version of "Lord of the Thighs" I liked more: studio or live. The planned or the spontaneous.

I blared the *Bootleg* live version, staring at the delicious picture of Joe Perry on the *Get Your Wings* album, until my thighs had the answer: Live. Spontaneous. The *Bootleg* version.

I went louder and realized that silence was worse than death— invisibility worse than cancer.

I missed Baby Crissy.

I missed Rog.

I slid my hand down my pants and glanced over at the bulge in Andy Gibb's pants, feeling bad for him over there flat on the wall all alone while Joe Perry lingered beneath my fingertips.

I was fourteen and cancer was incalculable.

I closed my eyes and prayed Hail Marys for Dad. Then, I asked the Blessed Mother to intercede for me for forgiveness for what my fingers were about to do.

*Blessed is the fruit of thy womb.*

## April 1979

I got used to seeing Daytime Dad's car in the driveway, and eventually, he was released from the hospital. He spent most of his time in his recliner.

Mom reminded me in whispery words not to bother Dad, but I decided that that was bad advice. Look where it had gotten me with her when her own lady parts went missing.

I stood before Dad.

"Is cancer gone?"

He stared at me as if he couldn't remember that I lived there or something, as if wondering why I was there.

"So far, so good, Schnapps," Dad said.

"Does it hurt?"

When cancer moved out, it left an enormous scar that looked painful and gruesome, but Dad never seemed to notice it. It began kind of at his breast bone, like in the middle of his chest, and it arced around to the middle of his back, as if he had a pectoral fin that was sewn tidily to his body.

"Not too much, Schnapps."

Mom shushed me from the kitchen. She was standing in front of the window where the falling sun was illuminating her, translucently, as if she were radiated and levitating. I had never seen her look more alive.

I ignored her.

"Why do you keep this up?"

I pointed to a narrow, wooden, cigarette-dispensing box hanging behind him. On it was a painted camel, and underneath, inscribed in gold, it read, "Coffin Nails."

The box had been empty since 1969, after Dad quit smoking and after Roger stole what was left inside of it.

Dad smiled this time, only the look in his eyes was lonely.

"Hope. It reminds me of hope."

*Jesus-hope?*

"Like my president?" I asked Dad.

Dad half nodded.

I thought about hope, Miss Turtleneck's Jesus-hope through death, Dad's Coffin Nails hope, and President John Fitzgerald Kennedy's hope, which I recited for Dad, like a prayer:

"Now the trumpet summons us again; not as a call to bear arms, though arms we need; not as a call to battle, though embattled we are; but a call to bear the burden of a long twilight struggle, year in and year out, rejoicing in hope, patient in tribulation; a struggle against the common enemies of man: tyranny, poverty, disease and war itself."

I didn't know how anyone could rejoice in hope, even if the president of the United States and the Bible said so.

Dad stared.

"I failed gym."

Despite failing gym (Jake and I ditched it and hid in the library), I continued to attempt to get one-hundreds in everything. It was the least I could do for Dad, on account of his cancer and all. Plus, I was hoping to make Dad proud, and really had turned the other cheek about the kidnapping, Jesus-style, forgiving Dad, who was, after all, only guilty by association.

But Dad's eyes were closed again.

That whispering neighborhood of the newly reassigned daughter of Daytime Dad was right. Things were never the same.

## June 1979

Once it warmed up, Dad was meeting me at the bus stop in order to get his daily exercise. He was thin and out of breath. Sometimes he brought CeCe with him when it wasn't too much of a strain.

"Did Gina have the baby yet?"

Gina's baby's impending birth, and me asking, seemed to make Dad smile. So I asked.

It was a waiting time. Waiting for Gina's baby. Waiting for Dad to recover. Waiting for Dad to go back to work. Waiting for whatever normal was going to be.

To help Dad pass the time, I became the waiting room Aunt Aileen. I set up a TV table in front of Dad's recliner and we played Yatzee or Got a Minute, our two favorite games. I talked to Dad, telling him about my day, or Jake, or the way that religion in my new high school seemed to disappear, or how good I was at math, or how I thought that hope was hogwash. Sometimes, we played silently, with just the rattle of the die between us. To lighten the mood, when Dad won a game I would tell him that it was because I let him, and that seemed to make Dad smile. I liked making Dad smile. It seemed as if the harder I tried, the more Dad smiled, and the more sewn shut Mom's mouth became.

Time did pass, with and without TV tables and games, and Daytime Dad was back in the swing of things, as he liked to say.

Ninth grade ended with a perfect report card from me, all one-hundreds. I even got a 100 percent in gym class because, much to the dismay of my gym teacher, New Father said that it was more cathartic for me to take solace in reading at this difficult time than to engage in exercise.

In simpler terms:

*Score:* Gym teacher: 0

Cancer: 1

"Atta girl," Dad said, after reviewing my grades.

Maybe I was making Dad a little bit proud.

# CHAPTER 16

# Adam's Apple

**July 1979**

The summer began with a bang, literally, a loud pop of the champagne bottle that Dad opened in the hospital room where Gina was staying after giving birth to her newest Mary—Maryjo.

"Have you lost your mind?" asked Mom.

"Nah, just a lung and some lymph nodes!" Dad said.

Dad cracked me up. He was big on cancer jokes, but they seemed to make Mom pretty mad. Everything about Dad seemed to make Mom pretty mad.

"Are you going to name all of your babies Mary?" I asked Gina.

I knew that it was mean, but she deserved it, and my anger toward her was justifiable. It said so in the Bible of good news:

"God is a righteous judge and always condemns the wicked."

In this case, I was the righteous judge and Gina was the wicked. There. Justified.

I was sure that New Father would have agreed with me if I had bothered to tell him during confession about my justifiable anger towards kidnappers.

I was convinced that Gina used the name Mary again (along with Dad's middle name, which also happened to be the name of Jesus's chaste father, Joseph) to gain favor with Mom and Dad, God, and maybe even the Blessed Mother, since she fucked up so badly with the sin baby. But maybe that was just my interpretation.

Clarissa thought that it was gauche to have two babies named Mary, and I agreed with her.

Clarissa had gained favor with a lot of public school boys on account of having to ride the bus with them on the way to—according to her—the better, all girls, Catholic high school.

"Nonna says I will get a better education without the distraction of boys," Clarissa told me.

Maybe Clarissa's nonna was right, but at least I didn't have to ride the bus to see boys. Besides, if I hadn't had boys in my school then I never would have met Jake, and he was a far better best friend than Clarissa—unbeknownst to her.

"So what's with the bike?" she asked, circling me.

"Dad got us both some new wheels!" I attempted to tell her, but she was already talking over me about some boy with a boombox.

**boombox** |ˈbo͞om ˌbäks|
NOUN *informal*
: a portable sound system, typically including radio and cassette, capable of powerful sound

I had been admiring the his and her 10 speeds from the living room window. Both were yellow, with drop handlebars covered with black tape.

"I didn't know Mom could ride a bike!" I said to Dad.

"She can't," Dad said, "the bikes are for us!"

If I knew how, I would have hugged Dad the way that Sister Mary Evangeline had hugged me. I was almost as excited about the bikes as I was when Roger gave me Baby Crissy, but…well, not quite. No, not at all. But my very own 10 speed wheels! I couldn't wait to write to Roger to tell him.

Not only did Dad come home with a bike that Mom couldn't ride, but to make matters even worse, he came home with a brand-new car that she couldn't drive.

"Where's the old one? What do we need that for?" Mom squeezed out.

"I traded it in. And to drive," said Dad.

"But it's a standard," said Mom.

"Nothing to worry about. You have no license and no business driving anyway!" Dad said.

*Turn the other cheek…*

Dad even added an FM converter to his new car so that we could listen to my music.

*My music!*

On some Saturdays, Dad and I rode our bikes around the neighborhood, or sometimes to Gina's to visit the babies, both sinful and pure. That was fun, but I was obsessed with how to abduct Baby Crissy while straddling a 10 speed.

On other Saturdays, we went to Aunt Aileen's house, something that infuriated Mom even more than the bikes and the stick shift.

I loved going to Aunt Aileen's house, but even I had to admit, she was a bit pretentious. And even though the *Good News Bible* said that bad company ruined good morals, I liked that about her, and I could tell that Dad did too.

They acted like rich people, Dad and Aunt Aileen. I wondered if maybe Aunt Aileen was actually rich, on account of her piano and powder rooms, and her rosemary lamb.

It was cool that Aunt Aileen had nice rich people things and toasted with her pinky out. However, she was sinning against a gazillion commandments, not to mention the offenses to the Holy Spirit. Sister Mary Ruthless, Miss Kinstler, and Dead Father would have had a field day at Aunt Aileen's. What would that nice bishop have said?

But surely, New Father could have found good news to support such ideals.

But not Mom. Mom continued hating everything about Aunt Aileen, the wine seeming to bother her the most.

"Good to the last drop! Right, Double A?" Dad said.

Mom refused to drink their wine. Their Jesus blood.

But Dad? He swallowed. Dad looked, well, happy, when he was with Aunt Aileen. They talked and laughed and drank and it made me miss Roger. And Baby Crissy.

"We have experience with toasts, don't we Kennedy?" Aunt Aileen said as she poured wine for everyone, including me. But out of respect for Mom's tight lips, originally, I had refrained.

But while Mom and Uncle Bob (Aunt Aileen's better half, as she called him) talked about the Mets, I chugged that wine because I really wanted to forget about hospital waiting rooms and tragedy and missing Roger and Baby Crissy. So I swallowed, just like Dad.

I wrote to Roger about everything: baby Maryjo and her stupid name, our bikes, Dad's car, the FM converter, my perfect grades, Jake, New Father, Aunt Aileen, everything. Life felt almost like the good old days, when Dad and I used to read and watch TV, and when Sister Mary Evangeline made it almost OK to feel OK.

## August 1979

Dad continued with his summer escapades, as Mom called them, and instead of mill shopping, we went to Sears and Dad bought Levi's and Jockey briefs.

Mom was like Bea, she couldn't help herself.

"Since when do you wear dungarees?"

"Since now!" said Dad, very pleased with his new non-mill wardrobe.

"What was so wrong with your boxers?" asked Mom.

"Look your best while you wear your least!" Dad, a slogan machine, said, as he showed Mom the Jockey briefs we bought.

I laughed.

I wasn't sure which disgusted Mom more: the Jockey ad's slogan or Dad.

"Besides, boxers are old-fashioned. The girls at work say men wear briefs now," Dad added.

Well, that went over like a lead balloon.

Throughout the rest of that summer, Dad took Mom and me to all of his old stomping grounds, which were more like taverns than restaurants. Dad said that they weren't much for atmosphere, but rather good food and free alcohol. Turned out Dad knew a lot of bartenders.

It was fun meeting all of Dad's tavern friends. They pinched my cheeks and told me that I was the apple of Dad's eye, being born on his birthday and all.

"Hey Mom, I'm the apple of Dad's eye!" I tried.

Mom answered me like God, then turned her attention to Dad.

"You're going to ruin your liver with the drink," she said.

"I already ruined my lung with the smoke! And that was a lot less fun!" Dad said.

He raised his glass to toast.

"Erin Go Bragh!" I said, even though it was not St. Patrick's Day, just to make Dad laugh.

We toasted, pinkies out, and I clinked my root beer mug against Mom's coffee mug, even though it stood alone on the tavern table, unraised.

I was fifteen and Dad was fifty-three, and I thought that maybe, just maybe, we were kind of like Irish twins.

*Slainte!*

## CHAPTER 17

# O Holy Night

**September 1979**

"All you need is love!" proclaimed the poster on the door of Mr. Meany's homeroom.

*Love?*

I wondered what kind of love this Mr. Meany meant. The bishop's weapon? Sister Mary Evangeline's Jesus commandments of loving the Lord your God with all your heart, and with all your soul, and with all your mind? Or loving your neighbor as yourself? Or loving God by letting Him flow through you like a trade wind? I didn't know. Really, it was just a poster for a Beatles song, up for anyone's interpretation, I supposed.

I scanned the room until I found Jake. *Whew.* Thank goodness for alphabetically sectioned homerooms.

"All you need is love," Jake said to me as I sat down.

"Apparently, yeah. You know this guy?" I thumbed at Meany.

"Yeah, he's cool."

Jake was a breath of fresh air, as Dad would say, compared to Clarissa and her Boombox Boy turned Boombox Boyfriend. No surprise there.

I was envious, I'll admit. I wondered what it was like to have someone that close. I wondered what it was like to make out like they did, all the time, so fucking much.

Anyway, the new-all-you-need-is-love Mr. Meany stared at me too long as he called out my name during attendance.

"Roger?" he questioned.

"No. Mary Kennedy," I answered, "but, yes."

He laughed, "How's that crazy brother of yours?"

*Roger is famous here.*

Mr. Meany told me three or four stories about Rog, and then asked me if I, too, excelled at math.

"Infinitely," I added, and he laughed again.

*All you need is love.*

I glanced at Jake and gave him a thumbs up.

Mr. Meany seemed safe so far, *like a blanket on cold Nebraskan nights* despite the collection of untouched rulers of varying lengths standing in a corner.

I was happy to be back in school even though the summer with Dad was fun.

"Back to business now, Schnapps," Dad said as I left that morning.

*Back to business.*

## October 1979

It turned out that I was even better at math than Roger on account of the fact that I actually handed in my homework. It continued to be easy to get perfect scores in math because everything could be proven. Everything added up. Nothing was up for interpretation. It was absolute.

*Math is abounding! God is abounding!*

Religion, on the other hand, was not so infallible that year. It had returned with a vengeance. New Father, who had been all about acceptance and scriptures and the bright side of things the previous year, appeared like a wolf with all the rules. It was like the blue confirmation booklet all over again.

But New Father was sneaky about it. He taught to us the same rules that we had learned in grade school, but he left them up to us to interpret. He used phrases like "examine your conscience" and "listen to your inner voices."

*Huh? Aren't inner voices hushed with pointers and yardsticks?*

The commandments were back, the Trinity was back, and even hell in a hand basket was back at our evil teenaged finger-tips, ours for the taking. It was up to us to resist, to make the right choices, to listen.

According to New Father, all we had to do was be exactly like Jesus.

*Oh, you mean perfect or more perfect.*

To me, it seemed as if New Father had set us up to be comfortable with the no-religion thing so that he could sneak up on us and eat us like a big bad wolf.

*What do I always tell you, Schnapps?*

Yup, the invisibility of religion was too good to be true, for sure.

New Father had the scripture from the *Good News Bible* to back up all of these new ideas, had it proven through words out of the mouth of Jesus Himself—unless you counted the part where the other four dudes wrote it down for Him.

I was good at telling New Father what I thought he wanted to hear, and I was good at knowing how to answer the test questions, subjectively objective as they were.

But Jake, like Bea, couldn't help himself. He questioned everything. Jake and New Father cited scripture back and forth until finally New Father told Jake that he needed to simply accept the teachings of Christ, or come to confession to speak with him privately. Jake, the consummate Doubting Thomas, never stopped questioning, in any forum.

I was afraid to question anyone or anything the way that Jake did, and I was afraid of God and I was afraid of hell. But my voices, the inner and the outer, didn't always agree on much of anything.

Confession changed from being a talk over coffee to an outward examination of my inner conscience, with New Father acting more like a questioning attorney than a caring listener. It was typical. Never trust a New Father in sheep's clothing.

Jake and I had each other, though, and we talked on the phone every evening, and wrote notes to each other on ripped notebook pages hidden beneath sheets illuminated by flashlights in middles of nights. Eventually, I shared my cancer haiku with Jake, and he confirmed that the words were better in that context. Jake shared his poems with me, which were much more sophisticated than my haiku, some of which I wasn't even sure I understood. Sometimes we shared lyrics.

I wrote to Jake all about the loft warehouses in Troy that I found while mill shopping with Dad. Jake said that we could convert one into an apartment exactly as I had imagined, except Jake added a handful of Persian cats and loose teas to the mix. I said that we would sip wine from pretty glasses, pinkies out, and stare out the vast windows at the people below on sidewalks or the stars above us in the sky. We would paint and write and read and watch movies and play albums and listen to each other and ponder abstract realities, as Jake called them, ad nauseam.

Jake said that we were like-minded.

I let our friendship flow through me like a trade wind, just like Sister taught me, and I hung on Jake's words like a crane scotch-taped to a ceiling by a string of hand-me-down yarn.

All fall I listened to Clarissa tell me all about Boombox Boyfriend, so I took a risk and told her all about Jake and our letters and our plans and ideas. I wanted to share with her something about my life too.

"It's gauche to write letters and dumb to imagine things that can never happen, Alcatraz," she said.

*Turn the other cheek...*

I answered her like God, not at all.

Mr. Meany, though? He laughed at Jake and me and said that we were going to make a fine, old, married couple someday.

I wondered.

## December 1979

"Midnight mass is better high. Suck in a little," Rog instructed.

I knew it wasn't a mortal sin to get high, but I did worry about the implications of attending mass while high. It was next level venial for sure. I fumbled with the pipe, holding the lighter to the bowl part. I sucked.

Thou shalt not, well, I didn't know. I'd need confession for sure.

Roger surprised us just like he did the last time that he came home, except he flew on an airplane and called a cab.

Mom, and even Dad, seemed happy to see him.

I thought that maybe Roger was Mom's favorite the way that Dooley was Dad's favorite. I understood, because Roger was my favorite too.

"I can't tell you anything about my job or I'd have to kill you," Rog said to Mom and Dad.

Mom looked like, well, Mom, but almost unsewn as well as unsucked.

Dad almost smiled.

Dad and Roger actually spoke to each other. They talked about Dad's new car and FM converter. Dad listened to Roger when he told him all about computers and military weapons (not the bishop's love weapon). They joked about how an actor could be our next president, and how President Jimmy Carter had committed adultery in his heart. Dad didn't yell, and Roger didn't argue or bite his lip as if he wanted to lie or cry.

*Maybe even the president of the United States can go to hell in a hand basket.*

Roger's midnight-mass-while-high gospel was right—the poinsettias on the altar were more brilliantly red, the gold on the priests' stoles glistened and danced off of the candlelight as if alive, and the ringing bells were sharp and crisp, each note lingering in the air until the next one pinged.

Even carols took on new meanings.

"Joy to the world, the Lord is come..." the church choir sang.

When Roger turned to me in our pew and announced out loud, "The Lord is cum," we had two choices—leave or die laughing.

So we left.

We drove to Denny's on the slippery roads through the newly falling snow in silence, listening to the snowflakes hitting the windshield. I stared at them, trying to decipher their differing shapes, thinking that we, God's children, should be treated like snowflakes—each different but equal and loved for our individual beauty—rather than being shoveled into piles of unworthy sinners who God loves unconditionally, yet only if we are perfect, or even more perfect, exponentially, and showing us that love by running us over and crushing us beneath tire treads and yardsticks.

"Mr. Meany would love these snowflake shapes," I said to Rog.

Rog answered like God, not at all, but I knew that he didn't mean not to answer. He was just being introspective from the weed we smoked.

Once out of the car, we spent a gazillion hours or maybe thirty seconds with our faces tilted toward the sky, feeling the snowflakes drop and melt like tears. We watched our feet rise and fall on the sidewalk as we set the first footprints into the virgin snow, looking over our shoulders at our powdered paths in history.

I spotted Mr. Meany while scanning the restaurant for Valerie.

"Mr. Meany! Boss was just talking about you!" Rog said as they shook hands.

"Kennedy," Mr. Meany said as he shook my hand, as if I counted, as if I were seen like a snowflake.

Rog and Mr. Meany talked about computers and the military, and Rog told him how he used math every day.

"Thank you, sir," Roger said.

"All you need is love, right Kennedy?" Mr. Meany said, smiling.

*Love?*

Mr. Meany sat down, and Rog and I walked to what had become our regular table.

"Is it, Rog?"

"What?"

"Is love all you need?"

Rog stared at me for about a gazillion hours or maybe eleven seconds until he answered with a question.

"How do we want our bacon tonight, Boss? Next to our eggs or on our burgers?" That was all Rog said about love.

It didn't bother me that Rog didn't answer because I was much more concerned about Mr. Meany and the man he was with, so I asked Rog about that instead.

"Everyone knows Mr. Meany is a fruitcake, Boss."

Roger didn't mince words.

I hadn't known that Mr. Meany was a "fruitcake," and I wondered how Roger knew. I mean, just because he was with a man? Or maybe, I supposed, it was because they were laughing and touching like *The Love Boat* actors, or maybe I could tell by the way that they were holding hands.

*Turn the other cheek...*

Maybe it was obvious.

But being a homosexual was not allowed—*thou shalt not commit adultery*—a sin worse than Gina's premarital sex, a sin worse than Clarissa's dad's suicide. Even New Father said that some dude in the Bible named Leviticus warned: "No man is to have sexual relations with another man; God hates that." Besides, what kind of a human hand puzzle could Mom have configured for that?

"How come Mr. Meany is allowed to teach in a Catholic school if he is a perpetual and intentional mortal sinner?" I asked Rog.

"Cuz he's fucking great at math."

I couldn't figure out if Roger stopped telling me the truth like every other supposed adult, or if he was as doubtful as Jake, or as sinful as Mr. Meany, or if maybe, like me, he just didn't know.

"You have to stop worrying so much, Boss. You're a good person. The weed made you paranoid," Roger laughed.

But I *was* paranoid. I was worried about Rog and his soul and the souls of Mr. Meany and his man friend. I was afraid of all the lies. I was afraid that all you needed was love and I wasn't sure where I was going to find it.

"What's with the birds?" Rog asked.

"My cranes? Oh, I got high with Clarissa and we made a gazillion of them and watched them flutter all night long," I said.

*Thou shalt not lie.*

I was afraid to tell Rog the truth about Baby Crissy. I was afraid that it would break his heart too, knowing that she had been kidnapped.

It was my first lie to Roger, ever. It felt awful. Since when was my truth not good enough for us?

Roger accepted my lie as truth, which made me feel even worse, and we ate bacon alongside our eggs in silence together, over hard and scrambled.

By the time Roger and I got home, fake Santa Claus had already left presents beneath the tree. Despite the deception, it felt magical. There were so many presents—more that year than ever before. A tiny box, a cube, for Mom, whose tag was written in Dad's script, his near-perfect non-chicken scratch. A few albums, 12 3/8 × 12 3/8 squares with perfect corners. A couple of unusually large ones, perhaps albums incognito.

*Like wolves in sheep's clothing? No, like sheep in sheep's clothing. Loved like snowflakes.*

All of the geometric shapes of the wrapped packages overwhelmed our senses—cubes and squares and rectangles and irregular quadrilaterals.

The colored illuminating light from the Christmas tree bulbs twinkled off of the tinsel and the shiny wrapping papers.

We determined that the tinsel strands were curves, not lines.

Rog tried to remember the technical term for Christmas bulbs, until we decided together to call them truncated cones.

"But what about the tree?" I asked. "It's nowhere near a triangle."

Rog stared until we laughed, until he suggested that we take a break and think about the tree while devouring Mom's pressed butter cookies.

"Mom will kill us if we eat all the cookies, Rog!"

"Nah, she won't, she'll think it's funny."

*Mom? Old Lemonsucker? Will laugh?*

I wasn't so sure. I would not have even thought about eating Mom's cookies until tomorrow, until it had officially become Christmas. Until Mom said so. But Rog, he marched to the beat of his own drum, as Dad would say. So, we sat, we stared, we devoured.

"Pretty much it's a reuleaux triangle, Boss," Rog said about the questionably triangular tree.

"Is it?" I asked. "Or is it a summation of mini lines and curves pretending to be a reuleaux triangle?"

*Stand back, Boss, the creases are sharp...*

"Yes," Rog said, but I was not sure that he meant affirmative to my question, or affirmative to the way he abruptly moved the presents into better, more pleasing positions.

"What are we gonna tell Mom about the cookies?" I asked.

"The truth, except leave out the part about the hash pipe."

"And the Mr. Meany part?"

"Affirmative, Boss. Leave it out."

I had no idea which truths were the right ones and which truths were the wrong ones. But for that night, that middle-of-the-night Christmas Eve, I was OK with that, because I was fifteen and Roger was twenty-five and I could not have loved him more than when he said, "Nah!" because the arrangement of the presents was once again, all wrong.

Yup. That was exactly what I was feeling for him as I watched him rearrange.

It was love.

Together, we moved presents long into the night, until we decided that we had to lie down because soon it would be Christmas morning and soon it might be OK to feel OK.

It was all I needed.

Dad's perfectly wrapped and inscribed cube to Mom was something called a mother's ring, which made Mom cry a lot. Each gemstone stood for each of us, kind of like our huge six-trunked tree, only without the mom and dad trunks.

I'd never seen a face on Mom like the one that she wore that Christmas morn, that crumbled crushed crying face.

*Like the Joker from Batman?*

It was kind of like the Joker from *Batman*, only happy-smiling-crying-style.

"I hope you like it," Dad said, staring at Mom, diametrically unemotionally.

Maybe Dad was afraid that Mom would hate it. Maybe he was afraid of what it stood for. I didn't know. It was just a weird stoic look that Dad had, especially for someone giving someone a ring with such meaning.

One of the sheep in sheep's clothing—that is, one of the unusually large packages that Roger and I had rearranged so fucking much—was an album for me from Rog, Pink Floyd's *The Wall*.

"It's epic," said Rog.

I had given Rog an engraved pen. "Wish you were here," it read.

"Yo, Boss, we simultaneously Floyd-ed!" Rog said.

Mom and Dad looked at us as if we were high.

We probably were.

When Mom asked what happened to the cookies, Rog told her the truth, and I swear, Mom almost smiled. Maybe Roger was in charge of making Mom happy.

*What do I always tell you, Schnapps?*

The day after Christmas, Roger left with Valerie in something called a rent-a-car, despite my efforts to make him stay by replaying "Please Don't Go" by KC & The Sunshine Band ad nauseam, so fucking much. At least Rog had someone with him, someone to love, and someone to love him back.

Valerie returned on an airplane alone. She handed me a keychain, a souvenir, in the shape of Nevada—a trapezoid—that read, "Battle Born."

"Because you're getting your permit this year, Kennedy! Then you'll be a pilot instead of a copilot!" she said.

Battle born.

*Born during a war? Born to fight? Or maybe President Kennedy's call to bear the burden of a long twilight struggle? Battle born, b-a-t-t-l-e-b-o-r-n, battle born.*

"Thanks!" I said to Valerie, but she was already gone.

## CHAPTER 18

# Dirty Deeds Done Dirt Cheap

**January 1980**

After Christmas break, I unleashed onto Jake and told him every-thing about Baby Crissy—the kidnapping, the emptiness, the lie that I told Roger about the cranes.

He held my hand *Boss, we've had an accident...do you need an ambulance?* and scribbled a haiku onto my palm:

*Heart robbed. Breath stolen.*
*Her face a driveway's skateboard.*
*Baby Crissy gone.*

No one ever held my hand except for Roger and only when it decided to crash into the dashboard. It felt weird having someone hold my hand, even if it was only to write a haiku inside of it.

Jake's hands were hard—unlike Roger's, there was nothing soft about them. He closed his haiku in my palm and hand hugged the fist he made, holding us shut.

Instinctively, we both made a steeple out of our index fingers and recited the childhood poem, the one about the church and the steeple and the people.

Although it worked much better when one person executed this, our fingers danced like moving people inside our intertwined hands, tapping against the haiku.

*One, two, how do you do? The Angels!*

"You two have made progress over break, I see," Mr. Meany said, as he sat in an empty desk across from us.

Embarrassed, I sat my retracted hands into my lap. Jake folded his arms tightly against his flannel.

"We were just haiku-ing," Jake said.

"Perfect!" said Mr. Meany. "That's exactly what the doctor ordered!"

Mr. Meany explained that he was in a "rather sticky predicament." He had volunteered to help with the literary magazine and knew nothing literary, although he did admit that in addition to math, he was a whiz at copying and stapling.

At Mr. Meany's suggestion, Jake and I attended the literary magazine meetings, and soon after, officially joined as staff members, as well as contributors.

I was excited about the prospect of the literary magazine, about maybe being able to express thoughts and feelings with words. It sounded like the opposite of math, and it seemed to be up for interpretation, which scared me, considering my track record. We both submitted poetry, and Jake submitted book reviews, some of which got rejected, like the ones he wrote for *Go Ask Alice* and *Giovanni's Room.*

"Too controversial. You're way before your time," Mr. Meany explained, when Jake asked why.

Some of my poetry was rejected also.

"Too raw, Kennedy. Father will have the men in white coats at our door if we print these!"

Mr. Meany suggested that I write about something other than kidnapping and cancer. So Jake and I settled into writing what we were asked to write, and continued sharing the raw and controversial pieces with each other, by flashlight, always on time.

## February 1980

Bon Scott, the lead singer for AC/DC, was found dead in his car in a place called London. He hadn't jumped off a tower or bridge like Gilbert O'Sullivan's song dude or Clarissa's dad had. The blurb that I found in Dad's newspaper said that he had asphyxiated on his own vomit, poisoned by alcohol. I tore out the article and made a crane.

"Do you think he knew he was dying? Do you think he coughed, like choked, before he suffocated? Do you think he was asleep when he threw up? Do you think he cried for help? How much do you think he drank?"

Jake's questions were relentless. He was obsessed. He wrote a tribute for the literary magazine, and Mr. Meany found a nice picture of the band to put beneath it. Researching this death, and the death of other musicians and artists, became like a hobby to Jake. It made him question God even more.

To make matters darker, Jake had developed a habit of drawing bricks on his forearm when he was bored, which, while in school, was pretty much all of the time.

"You're going to poison yourself with that ink!" Mr. Meany warned.

"We're all already poisoned, Mr. Meany. Or dead like Bon Scott," Jake said.

"Why bricks?" Mr. Meany asked.

"Why not bricks?" Jake said. "Maybe they're for protection. Maybe they represent oppression."

I knew that Jake's bricks were from Pink Floyd's *The Wall*, and totally due to boredom. I was sure that they didn't mean as much as Mr. Meany thought that they did. But Jake was wayward when under attack.

## April 1980

As soon as the weather permitted, almost lilac season, I had my 10 speed up and running. I filled the tires, oiled the chain, checked the brake pads, and *gave her a tune up*, as Dad would say. And while I was at it, I tuned up Dad's 10 speed for him too.

I rode and rode some more. I thought of ideas for the literary magazine and of ways to stop Jake from challenging New Father so much about God and religion. It was not as if the rules were going to change anytime soon. But Jake was like Bea, he couldn't help himself.

I thought about Jake's bricked forearms, and his response to Mr. Meany about protection and oppression. Too many rules felt like prison, and too much protection was oppression.

*The Wall?*

A moving van was backed up into Marcus's driveway and I wondered who was breaking this joint this time.

"Rents are moving south!" Marcus yelled out to me, as he lifted a box onto the U-Haul.

"Are you staying here?" the funny feeling against my bike seat asked.

Marcus had been moving in and out of his parents' house for years now, back and forth between women and jobs.

"Affirmative, Boss," he said.

*Whew.*

I hated it when people left.

When I wasn't riding, I was studying or playing albums or writing for the literary magazine. I wrote a few different kinds of poems about people leaving, and one about death. I was grateful for a place to put my words.

*Like Karen Carpenter and Gilbert O'Sullivan…*

Dad was on some sort of a mission, bringing home supplies from the lumber store every weekend for what he called his summer projects. Little by little, the cellar became a mini warehouse of Dad's imagination waiting to come to fruition. I couldn't wait to see what would become of it all.

One evening, a Sunday before *60 Minutes*, he handed me a multicolored cube, obviously six sided, each side divided into nine smaller colored cubes.

"Can you solve it?" he asked.

"Solve it?"

I fingered the perfect squares, reminded of Christmas cubes and dancing colors.

"Yeah, put it back together—make each side its own solid color. Twist it!" Dad said.

*Will this make Dad proud?*

I twisted and turned the movable cube, rotating each of its three sections one at a time, wondering how to make even one side of the cube solid colored.

"This is a 3-D puzzle," I said.

*A human hand puzzle?*

"It's called the Rubik's Cube. I saw it at Western Auto, thought we would like it," Dad said.

He was right, this was right up our alley.

"You want to try?" I asked, handing him the cube.

"I got three," Dad said, "one for each of us."

He handed Mom a cube, her second cube that year, and she just held it.

"But mine is already solved!" she said.

Dad and I laughed.

Mom was right. Hers was untouched, unscrambled, unadulterated.

*Immaculately conceived...*

"Sometimes you have to mess things up before you can put them back together again, right Schnapps?" Dad said.

"Right, Dad."

I twisted.

After about three weeks of wrestling with the Rubik's cube, I handed it to Mr. Meany, who had it solved before homeroom was over. He knew shapes.

But Mr. Meany was right—he really didn't know a lot about anything literary, but he sure knew a lot about how to arrange things on a page and how to include photographs and graphics alongside the submissions. He was a whiz at the copy machine, and we copied and stapled right through lilac season, and by the end of it all, our magazine, our words, our thoughts and feelings, were ready for distribution.

## CHAPTER 19

# Shadow of a Doubt (A Complex Kid)

**June 1980**

By final exam time, not only had we solved the Rubik's cube, but Jake and I were in a groove studying together, well prepared and ready to ace them. We had to rely on our busses for transportation on account of the fact that both of Jake's parents worked and Mom didn't have a license. But it was OK—we studied even more in between tests, and when there were no tests, we did a variety of things.

On Monday, after exams, we walked to the Mohawk Mall and pointed out all of the things that we would buy for our loft apartment. We found bookshelves on which to store our books, mugs for our tea. We found pretty glasses out of which we could drink wine, pinkies out. We sniffed candles and found scents on which we could agree. We passed by the bedding department, quickly, silently; somehow it felt to me as if Jake and I would have separate beds.

At the pet store, we chose cats and named them after literary characters: Holden Caulfield, Ponyboy, Alice. We named a dog Mr. Meany.

We shared a malt from Friendly's, and even drank from the same straw, which was even more forbidden in our house than saying "belly button." It was beyond crass.

We played a few games of pinball at the arcade with what was left of our pooled money, and at times Jake's arm brushed back and forth against mine. It gave me that Marcus feeling nowhere near my navel, but somewhere dark where the body part didn't even have a name. It was crass with a vengeance. It was the same feeling that my fingers gave me when they found the folds. Jake's flannel sleeve unrolled and fell just like my poise and pinball game.

On Tuesday, the following day of finals-boredom (replete with inked bricks on both of Jake's forearms), we walked to the convenience store and bought lunch: two boxes of Cracker Jacks and a pack of coffin nails called Marlboros, the kind that Angel from *Little Darlings* smoked.

We sat on a curb and smoked as many cigarettes as we could until we got dizzy, and ate our Cracker Jacks until we found our toy surprises. Jake got a horseshoe charm, which immediately he strung through the chain that he hadn't removed since that awful Secret Santa day. I found a toy figurine, an army man with a rifle.

*The bishop's love weapon?*

"I would trade, but this is perfect for my chain," Jake said as he refastened his necklace. "I need all the luck I can get!"

*Luck o' the Irish?*

"We'll write a story about this little man."

Jake fingered the weapon.

On Wednesday, we rifled through the baby name book that I stole from Gina. (It was only fair. Baby Crissy was still their hostage, plus she named all her babies Mary, anyway. I'd return it in good time.) We looked up people's names, matching personalities with their names' meanings.

Jake, or rather, Jacob, was, in fact, a "supplanter." He replaced a brother who was a stillbirth a year or two before Jake was born, alive and well.

"Imagine being dead before you were ever born," he said.

*I can.*

Jake always felt as if he could never live up to that legacy, and I got it. I told him all about Dooley and Dad, and how I wanted to please Dad and befriend him and make him proud. I knew that it wasn't the same, but the empathy seemed to make Jake feel better about not being good enough.

Kennedy was, of course, not in the baby name book, but Mary was. Jake and I marveled at the fact that Mary meant bitter and rebellious. Odd for someone who said yes when the Angel Gabriel asked Her if it was OK if the Holy Spirit put a baby inside of Her without the human hand peace sign puzzle or a penis, or that She was going to be the Mother of God, for that matter.

Why was everything seemingly so opposite?

"When we get our loft apartment, we're not having kids, are we?" I asked.

I was like Bea, I couldn't help myself.

Jake answered like God—not at all.

On Thursday, Jake brought in his boombox, and we played AC⚡DC's *Highway to Hell* so fucking much, in honor of Bon Scott. Jake was still wallowing in sorrow and morbid curiosity. We mulled over Jake's new copy of *No One Here Gets Out Alive* (the

Jim Morrison biography), and I mentioned to Jake how much he
and Jim Morrison looked alike.

"The lizard king?" Jake said, swirling the air with his tongue
like a serpent.

*Like the Joker from Batman?*

Jake was undeniably good looking. All the girls thought so. I
thought so.

"All you two need is a coupla rockers and a front porch!" Mr.
Meany said, and then asked who was raging from the boombox.
When we told him, he said, "AC⚡DC. Interesting name for a band."

Then he said, "Next year, since you two are obsessed with
music, let's start a music club. We will listen to songs and artists
and discuss what they mean to you. We can interpret lyrics and
maybe you two can even write your own songs. And you—maybe
you'll stop drawing all over yourself!"

We laughed. Poor Mr. Meany sure did want to be creative.

"Mr. Meany, you're living vicariously through us!" Jake said.

"Where'd you hear a phrase like that?" Mr. Meany asked, smiling.

"I dunno. 'Vicariously' was a vocabulary word."

I loved the way that Jake was so smart and creative. I loved
lizard kings.

On Friday, we sat backs to lockers trying to decide what to
do with our afternoon. Jake took my hand, opened my palm, and
haiku-ed in it for the second time:

*Jake. The lizard king.*
*Backs splat against steel lockers.*
*He wants to kiss her.*

I read. I stared. I listened to what my palm was telling me but
I couldn't hear it.

*You two are going to make a fine, old, married couple someday.*

*Jake wants to kiss me?*

I was afraid to look up from my human hand haiku.

A gazillion years, or maybe about seven seconds, passed. Jake dropped his pen onto the hard floor. And then he kissed me. Or maybe I kissed him. It mattered not who started. I could have calculated with the distance formula whose lips met whose first, but it was more a function of magnetism than math.

Kissing was so much softer than I had imagined. It was confused, like peanut butter and jelly ice cream. It was dizzying, but not in the smoke-too-many-cigarettes type of way, but in the full body swirling type of way, like being on the Scrambler from the neck up. What was most fascinating to me was the smell of his upper lip, and the closeness; God it was so close, he was so close.

*Stand back, Boss, the creases are sharp...*

Eventually, his hands moved in jerky apprehensions, like he was going to grab something that he was dropping, but decided not to.

His flavor made me forget everything else in the universe. There was only Jake, his mouth, his jerky hands, and the steel against my back.

I wanted more.

*Thou shalt not commit adultery.*

We kissed for what must have been a gazillion years or seven seconds, but more likely about two hours, and then Jake walked me to my bus.

At the bottom of the bus stairs, he kissed me as if he was sealing me up, his non-jerky hand solidly around my neck. His rolled-up flannel hugged my ear.

"Mary—bitter and rebellious," Jake said with his index finger on my lips, and walked away.

*Mary—reeks of sin, smells like lust.*

I pressed my deflowered mouth against the bus window until fog formed, and wrote "Jake" inside my drawn heart.

I had kissed the Lizard King.

Mom and Dad didn't seem to notice anything different about me or my mouth that night at supper, but I sure felt different.

When Jake called, we talked about the music club that Mr. Meany suggested to us. We spoke about my Driver's Ed course, which was beginning right after the Fourth of July. But we spoke nothing about peanut butter and jelly ice cream.

I did not hear from Jake the day after or the day after that. I was alarmed, but figured that maybe since it was summer we weren't going to talk every single day like we had during the school year.

By the fifth day, I tried to call him, an offense punishable by Mom-God hell, according to Mom. Calling boys was beyond crass. But I was like Bea, I couldn't help myself. I was driven by the power of the Holy Spirit's tongues of fire.

There was no answer at Jake's house. I was not sure if that made me feel better or worse, and I wondered if my sinful offense was absolved via silence.

*How can Jake kiss and not call?*

"Don't be so desperate, Kennedy," Clarissa said when I told her that Jake hadn't called.

But I was desperate. Clarissa didn't understand. My real best friend who had kissed me didn't call me—it was a big deal.

"It was just a stupid kiss, Kennedy. He just wants to get in your pants," she said, eye-rolling me.

*He does?*

I didn't think so, but what did I know? I was no Jezebel.

"A music club sounds almost as gauche as standing in front of the classroom doing the hula next to a nun, Alcatraz!" Clarissa said when I told her about Mr. Meany's idea.

*Turn the other cheek...*

"Driver's Ed should be fun," I tried again.

It was challenging firing things at Clarissa and then waiting for her recoil. Like ping pong.

"What could be fun about having to go to school over the summer? My uncle already taught me to drive, and as soon as I get my license, he's buying me a car!" she said.

Clarissa had failed her road test so many times that she had to wait a while before they allowed her to take it again.

"Well, I'm excited," I said, because I was.

"Sometimes you worry me, Kennedy."

She sure didn't seem to care very much for someone so worried.

I tore out all of the used pages from my school notebooks, and on the blank leftover pages, I began to write everything...everything...to Roger.

And thus, another summer began.

## CHAPTER 20

# Burnin' for You

**July 1980**

I had never been inside of a public high school. It was darker, vaster, more foreboding than my welcoming, smaller, more inviting, cloistered, parochial high school.

There were no smiling teacher-doctors, no welcome banners, no near-naked dead men in loin cloths on crosses, no Blessed Mothers, or any other mothers, for that matter, and no posters telling you that all you needed was love.

Just boys. Tall boys, medium boys, dangerous looking boys, friendly freckled boys—boys of all flavors—standing backs against lockers as if in a police lineup.

I was one of two girls, and her femininity was questionable at best.

"Hey, you here for Driver's Ed?" she asked.

"Yeah."

"Oh, thank God. Hot damn! I thought I was going to be the only girl amongst these hooligans." She gestured to the lineup.

*Fence hooligans? Hot damn? Like hell? Like fiery tongues?*

"Kennedy," I said, following her to the end of the lineup, already deciding which contestant that I would pick from the Whitman's Sampler of man-boys.

*I'll take the strawberry blonde with the Andy Gibb package in his pants behind door number two, please.*

But all I could think about was Jake and how he tasted and how I still hadn't heard from him.

It made me miss Roger, and Baby Crissy, for that matter.

The Driver's Ed teacher was a regular mister like Mr. Meany, not a doctor. (Although, in reality, Mr. Meany was a Dr. Meany, but he thought that it made him sound too evil, like Dr. Frankenstein, so he called himself regular Mr. Meany.) The Driver's Ed regular teacher didn't make me feel strange because I was not from their school, but introduced me to everyone else who already knew each other, including the not-so-girly girl. He was as good at teaching about driving as Dad was, and laughed at me when I raised my hand every time he asked a question.

"Is Miss Kennedy the only one who actually read the driver's manual?"

Everyone laughed along with him, and it didn't feel mean, it just felt like laughing. And he let them. Like fun.

*Is this what public school is always like? Is school without God and commandments more fun than my school? Not damnable?*

After a couple of days of class instruction, groups were chosen for Road, the driving portion of Driver's Ed. Four were in my group: the not-so-girly girl, the strawberry blonde Andy Gibb look-alike who walked off of my bedroom wall and from behind door number two (my chosen chocolate from the sampler), one of the friendly freckled, and me.

Regular Teacher explained all of the functions of the car, and the benefits of having Driver's Ed in general, even if you already had a license.

The strawberry blonde was the first to drive since he already had his license. I guess his father, like Dad, knew the benefits of having Driver's Ed under your belt.

*I wonder what's under his belt...this is how you accelerate through a curve, Boss...*

"Since I have my license, I can drive Kitty around. Right, Kitty?" Strawberry Boy asked the rearview mirror.

"Kennedy. Her name is Kennedy," the not-so-girly girl corrected him.

"I'll call her whatever I want. Right, Kitty?"

"Eyes on the road, son," Regular Teacher said.

*Is he talking to me? Is he calling me Kitty? What is going on here?*

Only two of us got to drive that day, Strawberry Boy and one of the friendly freckled. Thank you sweet Jesus and the Blessed Mother, because I probably would have plowed us right into something, what with the feeling below my belly button—yes, I said it, BELLY BUTTON—the feeling in the part of my body that Mom and I would never talk about, the crassest of the crass.

After Road, I stood against the public school building in the shade, waiting for the other students to disperse. I was kind of embarrassed about having to walk home on account of Dad working and Mom not having her license, but I didn't mind the walking part. It was only about a mile or two, and the sun felt safe and warm.

But the shade felt good. I was hot from being squished in the non-air-conditioned Road car with four others, not to mention the heat from my crass and Strawberry Boy's mirrored stare.

And there he was *oh my God oh my God oh my God* walking toward me with that package in his pants, his eyes pinned against me as my back pressed against the cool brick.

"Want a ride home?" he asked.

"Me?"

*Is he talking to me? Does he want me to get in his car?*

"No, the Kitty behind you."

"Oh, no thank you," I answered.

*Fuck fuck fuck fuck fuck how stupid am I the Andy Gibb packaged Levi's strawberry blonde is wanting me in his car alongside him and I am saying no to him what is wrong with me?*

He approached, closer and closer, until he was almost against me, his arms up above me, palms flat against the brick, nearly pinning me to the building. I could smell his nicotine, and I saw in his eye, a look that sometimes Jake had.

*Like crass with a vengeance?*

Like a cartoon, easily, I could have melted and slithered away between his faded Converse. But I didn't.

I tried to breathe.

"I don't need a ride, thanks."

He backed up.

"Kitty, Kitty, Kitty. I didn't ask you if you *needed* a ride home. I asked you if you *wanted* a ride home."

He kicked some stones and reached into his pocket.

*Oh my God his pocket why is he talking to me why is he calling me Kitty what would Sister Mary Ruthless say I was committing a gazillion acts of lust and adultery just like President Carter to hell in a hand basket for me...*

He knelt before me, asked for my hand, and put his car keys into my open palm.

"Dear Kitty, will you ride with me?"

He closed my palm, stood up, turned, and walked away.

*Why does everyone give me their car keys?*

I thought about Jake—how he tasted and how he hadn't called.

*Mary, Mary, quite contrary...*

I wondered if Andy Gibb looked like Strawberry Boy when he walked away, if the strawberry in his blonde hair danced in noon suns, *shadow dancing* and decided that I was tired of watching people leave.

I followed behind him until he turned.

"Are you afraid of me?" he asked.

*Fear not said Jesus oh sweet Jesus I cannot be thinking about Jesus oh I am so afraid of you and your Andy Gibb package and your strawberry blonde hair and your nicotine sweat...*

I was so afraid that I was going to throw up. My face was hot and my crass was out of control. I'd never been in a car with a boy before where sex could happen. *Oh my god I wish sex would happen but then hell and thou shalt not and all that shit but yes please drive me plow me home.*

"C'mon," he said.

I felt like a dog on an invisible leash, following him, watching his Levi's as he walked toward the passenger door. His fingers wrapped as if in slow motion around the metal handle.

"Get in."

I looked over my shoulder to make sure that he was actually going to walk around the back of his car and get in, wondering if there was a car bomb or something, *Boss we've had an accident* hoping that all of this was not some cruel setup, some joke of Clarissa's.

*I am Hawaii. You are Alcatraz. So gauche.*

Not-so-girly girl gave me a thumbs up from the sidelines.

It was hazy, hot, and humid. Life was foggy.

He got in.

*Oh my God Strawberry Boy is next to me and his door slammed shut.*

We were locked in.

I couldn't breathe.

*Don't take candy (or rides, for that matter) from strangers.*

Jesus Christ.

*Thou shalt not take the name of the Lord thy God in vain.*

There was a cigarette.

"Here...kitty kitty..." he said as he pushed the cigarette lighter further into his dash, his unlit cigarette dancing between his lips.

I watched his finger push and I wanted to grab his hand and hold it, but I just stared at its slow motion pumps.

"What do you want to listen to?" he asked, and then guessed, "Journey? *Infinity*? Side B? That's right, Kitty."

I watched his liquid fingers pump a cassette into the slot and felt the volume ripple and slide into my jeans when "Wheel in the Sky" began to blast from speakers behind me.

The lighter popped and I watched him bring it to his mouth, lighting the cigarette. His cheeks hollowed as he inhaled, his lips wrapped around the filter.

That sexy smoky smell of cigarettes from Roger's car of summers past filled the air and my nose, and all I wanted to do was drown or suffocate in it. *Like Bon Scott?* I was cigarette dizzy. I was Strawberry Boy dizzy. I was disbelieving on the sidelines of *Strawberry Boy's Production.*

He cranked his window open and we sat in the car, sharing his cigarette. Moms and dads drove by us, staring. I worried about the cigarette on school premises, but it wasn't my cigarette and it wasn't my car. Or my school, for that matter.

"So you're one of those smarty pants Catholic school girls, huh, Kitty?"

"Am I?" I asked.

He sucked.

We drove to a gas station where he handed me a dime and told me to call my mother to tell her that I wasn't coming home because I was in love with a boy from public school. Seemed reasonable, so I did, except I told Mom that I was walking to the mall with the group from Road.

*Thou shalt not lie…*

I couldn't believe that I was back inside of his car, my back against his red interior, air smoky and summery, music loud. Me. Kennedy. And a primordial public school pagan.

He ran the back of his bent index finger along the outside seam of my jeans. *Oh my God touching he is touching me why is he touching me this cannot be happening how am I going to explain the smoky smell to Mom fuck Mom how am I going to explain the bad boy in the bad car and why I am in it?*

I watched his finger, wondering where I might let it go next if he tried to digress from the sideline seam. I wondered what gave him the right to touch me, and I thanked Jesus and Mary and Joseph for whatever it was.

But I just listened to the songs and smelled his smell, and let him play me, his ever-changing instrument, drumming and strumming my leg to the sounds of his favorite band.

We drove, and finally, he spoke.

"Do you like Journey? It doesn't matter, it's the only band my cassette player knows how to play since they're the best and only band in existence."

*I suppose Andy Gibb and Aerosmith are out of the question…*

I got nervous and asked him if he knew Clarissa.

"What? No. I only know Kitty. Kitty cat."

*Can this be real?*

*What do I always tell you, Schnapps?*

I didn't care if it was too good to be true.

We drove until both sides of the cassette were spent. We parked by a river and he asked and he talked.

I mean, it wasn't that I didn't care about his alcoholic father or Jezebel sister or his mother named Connie, but I was much more interested in his mouth than what was coming out of it, and I wondered what it was like to be his cigarette.

His drags were slow and creamy and I was in love.

I had no one to tell—no Jake, no Baby Crissy—about Strawberry Boy. I was afraid to tell Clarissa.

Finally, Dad asked, "What's with the car and the coffin nails?"

"Just a guy from Driver's Ed. Gives me a lift so I don't have to walk in the heat," I said.

*Do you mean gives you sweat and makes it hot and hard to walk?*

"I hope you're not smoking, Schnapps."

"Nah, Dad, it's just a ride."

"It's never just a ride."

*Why is Dad trying to ruin my life?*

Some of my cranes had fallen from the humidity. Sometimes I rehung them, *"O flock of heavenly cranes, cover my child with your wings,"* wishing for Baby Crissy's return or Jake's phone call. Sometimes I threw them away, my Jesus-hope ever teetering.

In worn notebook letters, I told Rog all about Jake not calling and he told me that I probably scared him away because I was prettier than Gina and Valerie put together. I didn't know how Jake could be afraid of me. After all, the kiss was his haiku idea.

I told Roger about Strawberry Boy and Roger said that he was going to kill him for touching me.

"Unless you're cool with that, Boss," he wrote.

Roger got it.

I was so cool with Strawberry Boy playing my pants like an instrument and fingering my seams. But I was worried about all of the sins that I was committing in my conscience just thinking about Strawberry Boy. I was as worried about hell as I was excited about his fingers. Exponentially.

## August 1980

I convinced my friend Dad to buy Journey cassettes for the boombox we had gotten ourselves for our birthday so that we could listen while we worked on Dad's newest projects—his *Summer Productions*.

Dad's first project was constructing a game room in the cellar by hanging paneling and pegboard on the studded walls.

"Gotta start somewhere, Schnapps," Dad said.

Soon after the walls were completed, a pool table with a removable ping pong table topper arrived on a Sears truck.

We played ad nauseam, so fucking much.

"Aren't you two tired of playing?" Mom yelled down at us.

Dad and I just laughed. It was a challenge—both losing to Dad as I learned to play, and then, eventually beating him.

With the extra pegboard, and to help Mom organize her kitchen, which she insisted needed no organizational assistance, Dad hung pegboard on both sides of the cellar stairs so that she could hang anything she wanted from metal hooks.

"*More pegboard?*" Mom asked in her italicized French.

"The better to hang you with, my dear."

Dad and I laughed.

Mom's anger and Dad's pegboard were exponentially married.

As for me? I felt safe surrounded by pegboard. Each of the four equidistant holes made squares, and the squares made rectangles or larger squares, until they filled one large square or rectangle. I could stare at it for hours. Plus, if you drew diagonal straight lines from one hole to another, gazillions of perfect hypotenuses formed one side of gazillions of perfect right triangles. It was simple math.

"Hey Dad! The pegboard has a gazillion hypotenuses!"

He smiled. He heard me.

*He hears me.*

Dad spoke more, joked more. Sometimes we had actual conversations while Dad hung, banged, built, me on his sidelines, holding, handing, helping, being.

That summer, we even found two new dramas on TV that we liked—*Dallas* and *Knots Landing*.

We read.

We played Got a Minute.

"Don't you two get tired of that game?" Mom asked.

We rode our 10 speeds.

"You two are going to fall or get hit by a car out there!" Mom warned.

We lay in the sun on our newly laid patio, Dad's pectoral fin fading as he tanned.

"You're going to get a sunburn!" Mom insisted.

We listened to our boombox so fucking much.

"You're disturbing the peace!" Mom cited.

We drank way too much lemonade.

Mom sucked her lemons silently.

"We're on a highway to hell, Schnapps! Cheers!" Dad said as we clinked lemonade glasses, basking in the hot sun after long bike rides, or marathon Got a Minute or ping pong sessions, boombox beside us, blaring Journey.

I was sixteen and Dad was fifty-four and it seemed as if all of Dad's inhibitions were gone, and mine were begging to follow.

*What do I always tell you, Schnapps?*

## August and Everything After 1980

It had not taken long to find out what it was like to be Strawberry Boy's cigarette.

His mouth was soft but his lips were hard and tasted like sweet cigarettes, the way they smell before they are lit. His kiss pressed against me much harder than Jake's, and he used his tongue in a way that pushed right through me in a stabbing-renting-out-space type of way that didn't seem to want to leave.

By the third make-out session, one of his hands found the back of my bra, tugging at it as if it were a boomerang, then unclasping it, while his other hand tugged at the bottom of my shirt. His hands moved as if trying to hold on to something, nothing like Jake's at all, and he held my hipbones for dear life, his thumbs pressed so hard they left bruises. He wasn't rough. He was unyielding.

"You're gonna do it eventually, Kitty. It may as well be with me," he said.

Although that may have been true, I wasn't about to have sex with him no matter what. That was a mortal sin, and look where it got Gina. With God watching us, and hell at our fingertips, how could I have done it?

"I can't," I'd say, squirming away, feeling his thumbs press even harder, and then shrivel away as desperately.

It never deterred him—he was persistent, and so fucking sexy and good at anything he did with his mouth or his hands that it left me feeling melted and wanting.

By August, the temperatures lowered and my shirts rose. Sometimes, Strawberry Boy stopped making out and pounded his fist into his dashboard *Do you need an ambulance, Boss?* Other times, he left the car and smoked a cigarette, staring me down with a look I didn't recognize. It wasn't quite angry, but it wasn't quite friendly either.

I felt bad, but I had my soul to worry about. It wasn't like I didn't want to be with him. All I could think about was what it would be like to have sex with him. With Strawberry Boy on my brain, it was easy to imagine that Andy Gibb walked out of that poster off of my wall to right on top of me to do everything I imagined Strawberry Boy may have done, had I let him.

We were sixteen and it felt so good to be seen.

## CHAPTER 21

# Back in Black

**August 1980**

Dad had a big day at the horse races planned, especially for Mom, who enjoyed the track. But then Dad ruined it on account of inviting me, and worse, Aunt Aileen.

Aunt Aileen came wearing a self-embellished picture hat which Mom thought was ridiculous. Even I had to agree with Mom—it was ridiculous. But Dad and Aunt Aileen thought that it was appropriate for Saratoga. It was.

Poor Mom, happily hatless and helplessly angry, was beyond lemon sucking.

Dad and Aunt Aileen drank a lot of wine from clear plastic cups, pinkies out, from the concession stand beneath the grandstand. Dad drunk-promised that if he won, he would buy us all something special with his winnings.

"Yeah, sure, you won't even remember saying that." Mom eye-rolled at Dad, adding that she wanted nothing with his winnings.

Dad was a man of few promises, so I believed that he would do what he said he would do.

Aunt Aileen, also believing Dad's drunk-promise, squealed and clapped a bit like a circus seal, and said that she had been wanting some new paints. Aunt Aileen was finding herself through her art, through her paintings, or so she said.

"What would you want if Daddy wins, Kennedy?" Aunt Aileen asked.

*"Freedom at Point Zero!"* I said.

*New freedom?*

"You want *freedom?*" Mom asked in her italicized French.

*Very badly, Mom. So bad you can not even imagine. I want to break this joint. I want to get into Strawberry Boy's car and never come back. I want to smoke cigarettes like Roger and ride on airplanes and name my babies and have sex all night long with Joe Perry or Andy Gibb, if it is even possible to have sex all night long.*

"Yes. At zero point," I said.

Dad won.

"Luck o' the Irish!" Aunt Aileen said, thanking Dad as we dropped her off, waving the twenty dollar bill that he gave her for paints.

"Paint me a shamrock!" he said to her.

"Good luck with your freedom album, Kennedy!" she said as she closed the car door.

On the way home, we stopped at Record Town to buy my album, and that was when I saw it. It was a perfect 12 3/8" square, naturally, but surprising and sinister. It seemed to speak.

"Dad! Look!"

Immediately, I held it, and slid my finger over the nearly invisible embossed letters.

**BACK IN BLACK.**

I traced the ϟ between **AC** and **DC**.

"Dad! They're back!"

"In black!" Dad said, reading beneath the line on his glasses.

Miraculously, AC⚡DC had released *Back in Black* with a new singer, just months after the death of Bon Scott.

"Can I get this instead of Jefferson Starship?" I asked.

But Dad was a man with winnings, so we got both. Me and Dad really were like friends! I couldn't believe my own luck o' the Irish.

After Record Town, we stopped at K-Mart to get Mom some new Cozy Cups and a non-human hand puzzle for her, a regular jigsaw puzzle. That was what Dad decided she wanted with his winnings.

And then Dad really ruined race day by showing up later that week with what *he* wanted with his winnings: a motorcycle.

I wrapped plastic Panasonic headphone foam around me and entombed myself in *Back in Black*, so that I could not hear what ensued between them.

## AUGUST 1980

Dad thought that *Back in Black* was a little loud for the patio, but appreciated their tenacity as a band, their forging on after the death of Bon Scott, and their ability to *bear the burden of a long twilight struggle, year in and year out, rejoicing in hope, patient in tribulation* carry on. Dad was giving his own inaugural speech.

Strawberry Boy, well, he didn't think anything of *Back in Black*, because all he played was Journey. I was as sick of hearing "Wheel in the Sky" as he was of hearing me say no to fucking him.

As for me? I was spellbound, as with Sister Mary Evangeline's Hawaiian voodoo. I listened to *Back in Black* over and over, so fucking much, and blew my cranes. I thought about death and hell and bells and being shaken all night long by a Strawberry

Boy. It was all so contradictory. Like Jesus-hope. Through death we had salvation. *Like being Back in Black?* I wondered how Bon Scott's family felt about Jesus-hope.

**AC/DC** was back in black and Jake was back in flannel. He called me, finally, at the end of August, all apologetic and repentant. His parents had sent him to Jesus camp where there were no phones or stationery or stamps. He worried all summer that I would be mad at him for not calling or writing.

"Kissing and ditching is not very Christian-like. Besides, I found someone else to kiss while you were away," I said, punishing him with the venom of Dead Father's penances. And then I told Jake all about Strawberry Boy and his thumb bruises and his sweet cigarette mouth. Jake was mostly silent on the other end of the phone, adding polite interjections here and there.

Finally, Jake spoke.

"Kitty, huh? Bittersweet and rebellious, Mary Kennedy, alas."

And then he did the worse thing possible. He pulled a Jake. He haiku-ed:

*"He calls her Kitty.*
*Bittersweet, rebellious.*
*Mary is her name."*

*Jesus Mary and Joseph. Jake is going to haiku me when HE is the one who kissed and ditched? When he is the one who pulled a Roger and left?*

"Jake! You're the one who kissed and ditched," I said.

"They sent me to camp, Mary Kennedy. Fucking Jesus camp. Fucking brainwashing Christian camp. No phones. No stationery. No stamps. What the fuck, Mary Kennedy?"

"Stop calling me that."

"OK, Kitty."

*Turn the other cheek...*
Jake made me feel dirty and sad.
*Is this his Jesus camp speaking?*
So I haiku-ed back:

*"Jake, my best friend, left.*
*Strawberry Boy tastes so sweet.*
*Don't call me Mary."*

*There. I'll fix him for leaving.*
Jake hung up on me.
*Whatever.*

I had Strawberry Boy and I had my friend Dad and we were all back in black in the saddle again.

## September 1980

When Driver's Ed ended, almost daily, I dragged Clarissa to the hamburger joint where Strawberry Boy worked, an outdoor drive-in type of joint. After all, she owed me.

He handed out free food through the pick up window, and if we timed it right, he took his break and we made out against the side of the building while Clarissa and Boombox Boyfriend got high in the nearby woods.

"Must be gross to have to kiss an ashtray," Clarissa said.

"Kinda like swapping spit on a joint?"

Clarissa hated it when I was right—it shut her right up.

At least we both had boyfriends, I thought, even though Strawberry Boy and I never really talked about it.

But once the drive-in hamburger joint closed, so did Strawberry Boy. He never asked for my number, but I gave it to him anyway, a move that Mom would have called loose, and a move that was clearly Mom-God punishable.

*Dear Jezebel,*

*Why wouldn't Strawberry Boy want your number? Because he never intended to call you, that's why.*

*Yours truly,*
*That Little Voice Inside New Father Told You To Listen To*

"Why'd the smoker stop sniffing around?" Dad asked, almost too happily, as if it were a riddle.

*Like the Joker from Batman?*

"I dunno."

But I knew.

*Cuz he's sniffing somewhere else, Dad…*

"Boys and girls, there is no such thing as Santa Claus. Go home and admonish your parents for being pagans. Believing in Santa Claus is a sin against the first, God's ultimate, commandment," Sister Mary Ruthless had said.

Yet somehow, I continued to believe in the unbelievable.

To cheer me up, or so they said, Clarissa and Boombox Boyfriend invited me to the movies, a double date without the double, and this was where I became a believer in the believable.

I saw her before I saw him, the awkwardly skinny, bird-looking girl with the Aigner pocketbook, her arm locked around Strawberry Boy's, and folded.

*That fuck! What is going on here?*

Strawberry Boy saw me, untwined his arm, and ushered her by the elbow *like a prom queen* to a seat below us.

"Clarissa?" I asked.

"Well, I thought you should know why he hasn't called," she said.

*She knew?*

181

"It was obvious that he had a girlfriend, Kennedy."

*It was?*

"How did you know? Why didn't you tell me? And how did you know he'd be here today?"

Clarissa thumbed at Boombox Boyfriend.

*Oh.*

"He's had the same girlfriend for two years, Kennedy," Boyfriend boomed at me.

"And you never told me? Why?" I thundered back.

*Clarissa knew? How could she not have told me? Man plunges to death... How could she bring me here knowing how much this would hurt me? I am Hawaii, you know! You are Alcatraz...*

Strawberry Boy walked toward me and summoned me with an eyebrow and a head nod toward the back door of the theater.

I followed him into the light.

*This cannot be happening I need to taste him again sweet nicotine who is she why is she here with him he is my Strawberry Boy why is he with her?*

"Who is she?"

We sat.

He kissed my neck, his breath in my left ear.

*Like Marcus and Valerie?*

He whispered, "Kitty, don't do this here. Who is who?"

He slid his hand up my left thigh until his fingertips hit the seam along my crotch crass. Electricity shot between my legs and I started to ooze because slow motion's fingers were pumping the insides of my thighs *lord of the thighs* and I was liquid and we both knew it.

All of his stupid songs from his stupid cassettes that his fingers pumped into his dashboard's slot ran like a ticker tape across both my forehead and the movie board.

*"Journey? Infinity? Side B? That's right, Kitty."*

*Who is she? O flock of heavenly cranes please save me because…*

He was breathing on me and his lips brushed against mine until I tasted his tongue and his lingering cigarette.

"She's my girlfriend. I'm really sorry, Kitty."

*Smoky mouth.*

Fire rose in me and wetness seeped from me. I needed to cry. I wanted to hurt him. I wanted to fuck him.

He kissed me hard like he was sealing me up.

I was gaping and he was gone, into the black theater, cancer incised and carved out.

"Hey!" I yelled to no one. "I fucking hate Journey. And my name is Mary Kennedy, you dumb fuck."

I waited for Clarissa and Boombox Boyfriend in the light because the dark theater was full of monsters like strawberry cancers and skinny birds.

*You mean like long skinny red taillights that looked more like eyes surrounding a big monster-mouth tailgate like a hearse like back in black like the Joker from Batman?*

*Think of Easter…*

We got high on our walk home. Boombox Boyfriend was good for something, at least, and I almost didn't mind his third hand spliff spit.

I was nothing but silent.

Once at home, the high made both listening to Mom yell at Dad about that Goddamn motorcycle more palatable and my courage more tangible.

"Don't you remember we're on a highway to hell?" I asked Mom, my question actually hushing her for the first time since Dad came home with it.

Mom looked hurt and I didn't care, even though I tried to care. I mean, her complaining about the motorcycle was more words than I'd heard Mom speak in the previous six years combined. I should have been grateful for her voice. But I was angry, hurt, and hungry, and I needed to be filled.

I phoned Jake, who, *thank you silent God and the Holy Spirit and the cranes and everyone else*, accepted my call. We sat, phones to ears, mutes, answering each other's wordlessness like God.

Jake spoke first.

"Gotta go. Dinner."

Click.

I blew the cranes and watched them flutter and sway like Sister's Hawaiian fingers and her hips reigned in by her black *in black* habit.

*Hail Mary full of grace...*

I said a rosary because I felt guilty for wanting Strawberry Boy and for hurting Jake and Mom, and then begged the mute Trinity for deliverance.

I was ready for junior year. I missed Mr. Meany and his love poster. I missed Jake. I missed Roger and I missed Baby Crissy. Still.

Does everyone leave? Does everything end?

*What do I always tell you, Schnapps?*

## CHAPTER 22

# Behind Blue Eyes

### September 1980

Back in the school saddle again, in homeroom, I handed Jake our
Cracker Jack army man as a peace offering, wrapped in haiku-ed
loose leaf.

*Cracker Jack surprise*
*Gun, the bishop's love weapon.*
*Best friends, battle born.*

"What the fuck is the bishop's love weapon?" Jake asked, hard,
and smelling of a new kind of musk.

"I'm not sure yet."

Jake was still mad, I could tell. I tried to be mad back, but I just
didn't have it in me. It wasn't his fault that his parents sent him to
Jesus camp, of all places. It wasn't his fault that I got creamy with
a Strawberry Boy turned malignant.

"Are you two married yet?"

Thank the mute Trinity that Mr. Meany was our homeroom teacher once again. Perhaps there was safety in some things, like the alphabet and pegboard.

"Nah, we're chaste," Jake said.

**chaste |CHāst|**
ADJECTIVE
: abstaining from extramarital, or from all, sexual intercourse
: not having any sexual nature or intention
: what me and Jake were with each other

*Ouch.*

Jesus camp coached Jake well.

Quietude was contagious.

Mom stopped nagging Dad about the bike, not because she chose to, but because he put it away for the fall.

Dad seemed quiet too, seemingly sad about retiring his bike early to please Mom. Or at least that's what he called it. It was as if she nagged the ride right out of him.

In general, it was quieter at the house without our patio boombox booming and Dad's *vroom vroom.* Sure, we still watched our shows and read our books and played our games, but there was something missing again, and I Jesus-hoped it was just Dad's zero point non-freedom. Mom's needles scraped and our die clanked against the plastic Got a Minute cube.

Finally, Jake broke his silence over the placement of one of his literary magazine Jesus pieces, insisting it not get printed on the same page as one of my "sappy love poems."

*Sometimes you have to mess things up before you can put them back together again, right, Schnapps?*

Tit for tat, I spat back.

"Jake, you never called."

"Mary Kennedy, I was at Jesus camp. I was in hell."

"Your irony is not lost on me, challenged as I am," said Mr. Meany, between us. "Now shake and make up."

We didn't shake, we held, and I wanted to cry, because holding hands with Jake was so much closer than kissing him or Strawberry Boy. It didn't feel like lust. It didn't feel crass. It felt safe, like pegboard. It felt contained, like die in plastic. It felt OK to be OK, our hands locked.

Jake called me every night on the phone thereafter. We mapped out the literary magazine and made plans for our new music club, as Mr. Meany had suggested.

But something about Jake had changed. Something about everything was changed.

## November 1980

For Mom's birthday, Dad bought her a car—his Cracker Jack toy surprise peace offering for buying a motorcycle, which should have made Mom happy, and it did, but for two things: it was Aunt Aileen's hand-me-down, and Mom didn't have a license.

I made her a cake, her favorite, a pineapple upside down cake. Dad decided that, as a joke, he would write on it, upside down.

HAPPY

BIRTHDAY

MOM

It was written as if in Hebrew gibberish, wishing someone named "Wow" a cockeyed and capsized "happy birthday," which it kind of was.

Poor Dad was like Bea, he just couldn't help himself.

The cake went over as well as the car—like a lead balloon.

Although I thought that Dad and I had become friends again, when I announced that I had been invited into the National Honor Society, Dad barely looked up from his newspaper.

*Are we really back to this?*

I mean, they showed up to the ceremony and all, went through the motions, but it was more like old times than new times—times when I paled in comparison to Dooley, when Dad barely curled his newspaper down to answer me like God. Not at all.

I didn't know what else to do to continue to make Dad proud, so I did what I knew how to do: my best.

*Dad's Production* went on as usual with a little more beer and a lot more soliloquy from me. That's an SAT and Shakespearean word for talking out loud never-minding if anyone hears. Sideline soliloquy or not, I would have walked a highway to hell to have summer Dad back by my side. But autumn had fallen.

*Like a pineapple upside down cake?*

When Mom turned her back, I added more salt and Dad chugged the remainder of his beer and we were finished with the production for another Thanksgiving.

Part of my production soliloquy to Dad was about the literary magazine and how Jake and I were senior staff members, even though we were just juniors. I told Dad that I wrote about unrequited love and that I composed haikus and poems. I told him how I arranged others' works on pages, ad nauseam. I even told Dad that ad nauseam was Latin for "so fucking much," and Dad didn't even flinch.

I continued, saying that Jake wrote about the struggles of keeping Jesus present amongst our teen challenges. I explained to Dad that it was Jake's Jesus camp shit, and that Jake didn't believe in any of it, but that it flowed out of him like lava.

I did everything that I could to break Dad's silence. I solved the Rubik's cube over and over in different ways, all sides, some sides, just corners—and showed them to him, Jesus-hoping for a response.

I let him win Got a Minute and he asked me why I was cheating.

He said no to playing pool and ping pong.

We watched *Dallas* and *Knots Landing* in silence, which I supposed was simply the normal way that people watch TV, but it was solemn, like Sunday mass.

I was missing Baby Crissy and Roger more and more, so I folded and hung fallen cranes Jesus-hoping for their return.

I confessed to New Father fake sins and performed my penances without protest.

As I said, I tried my best.

## December 1980

Mr. Meany did not believe in Secret Santa, thank you Silent God and Mute Trinity. For Christmas, he gave to each of us a piece of paper folded in half forming a card, a Christmas card. Mr. Meany sure was a pro at copying, and apparently, folding.

*Like origami cranes?*

On the front was a Christmas tree comprised of names, the names of my homeroom classmates, handwritten by Mr. Meany.

"I concrete-poemed," Mr. Meany said, beaming with pride at his creation, "and then made you all into an irregular isosceles triangle."

That he had.

On the inside it read,

"Blessings to you at Christmastime.

Love, Mr. Meany"

*All you need is love?*

Third line from the bottom, one in, was Kennedy, my label, like a branch in between and among everyone, like our looming, steadfast, tried-and-true tree trunks at home. Together we formed something. An irregular isosceles triangle. A tree.

I slid my finger over my name.

*Back in black?*

It moved me so, like a Hawaiian breeze, this gesture, so painstaking and heartfelt. Uncreative Mr. Meany had taken the time to make me into a greeting tree, to make me into something special, to make me into something alive on a piece of paper, of a tree, formed into a tree. It felt more like a circle than a triangle. Safe.

I looked around, confused, the only one remaining in the classroom with him, the only one who continued to hold their card as if it were a twenty-four-inch, cuddly, life-sized, nine-month-old Baby Crissy doll.

He stood, studying me, his eyes framed in thin worry lines running in parallels between and above them.

I tried to thank him, but nothing came out.

"Kennedy, you're crying."

Tears teemed like raindrops out of me as if someone had just let them loose, like someone had turned them on. I hadn't even noticed.

"It means..."

I fingered my evergreen name, making sure that I was still a part of it all.

Mr. Meany reached out, took my hand.

*Boss, we've had an accident...*

I wanted to tell him everything. I wanted to ask him everything. I wondered what this was, this circle feeling of bittersweet OK. I wondered if this was Jesus-hope or the bishop's love weapon.

But all his hand hug pulled from me was, "Aloha."

Embarrassed, and not embarrassed at all, I ran for the bus.
*Stand back, Boss, the creases are sharp...*

## December 1980

Silent night, holy fuck.
*Now what?*

We were a trinity for Christmas—Mom, Dad, me—which substantially reduced the number of arrange-able wrapped shapes beneath the tree. Mom made a quarter of the cookies she normally made, and *Dad's Production: Christmas Edition* was cut in half. We ate Christmas dinner while playing Perquackey, the new game that Fake Santa left for us, a rectangle wrapped in red.

New Year's Eve was a rockin' eve, with Mom sleeping by ten o'clock and Dad complaining about the absence of some dude he liked named Guy Lombardo. The highlight was when at midnight, Dad poured us champagne and took his to bed, leaving me with a sleeping Mom, a glassful, and the rest of the gigantic bottle.

## January 1981

I rationed the champagne and spent the break in my room mildly buzzed on bubbly, listening to albums and reading a stack of paperbacks Jake lent to me. I didn't mind the solace.

In homeroom, after Christmas break, with worry lines intact, Mr. Meany asked, "Kennedy, are you OK?"

"Yes! I am OK."

And I was.

"Is your father OK? He's not sick again, is he?"

*What? No, Dad isn't sick. Cancer is gone. Dad is just mad at Mom about the motorcycle. Dad is just back to being Dad before it all began. Dad is fine.*

"He's good," I said.

"You had me worried there with your 'aloha' and all," he said, whisking away his angst with flapping hands, without the gracefulness of Sister Mary Evangeline.

"Oh. No, Mr. Meany. 'Aloha' is just something we say."

*Who says it, Kennedy? Nobody says it. Only you and your phantom nun. Kennedy, sometimes you worry me. Think of Easter.*

## March 1981

School was harder than it had ever been, especially with the addition of studying for the SATs and thinking about college.

Religion class was rough, all church history and crusaders, but the confession part was particularly tricky. I had so many feelings and voices that I wasn't sure which ones were good and which ones were bad, except that I knew for sure that I couldn't say any of them aloud to New Father.

Jake offered no consolation. He was a true apostate since Jesus camp.

"Fuck the rules, they're all fake anyway," he said.

But I remained worried about my lust and my feelings of anger about Dad being quieter again and how I drank that whole bottle of champagne by myself and how Clarissa and Boombox Boyfriend and I got high not just once and how I let my fingers do the walking.

Also, I was confused by this new feeling that I had. Sometimes it felt OK to be Kennedy, OK to be OK. Surely that was a sin against every commandment, every deadly sin, and all of the sins against the Holy Spirit. I was doomed.

And Music Club? Well, it may as well have been called Hells Bells.

It began with just music, listening to it and interpreting the sounds or the lyrics.

I led the discussions when Jake, who was either excessively verbal or utterly despondent, didn't.

We discussed the music's relevance to history or literature, we dissected lyrics, and eventually, we included our own poetry and personal essays that were too controversial for the literary magazine. These topics boggled Mr. Meany's mind, which was the fun part of it all—he seemed to be exploring and learning too. It was as if in Music Club, we were equals.

Mr. Meany allowed us to dislike things without a reason, he allowed us to question things without dissent. Mr. Meany allowed us to express ourselves, that was what he called it, in any way we needed.

*Inner and outer voices?*

Other times, we were still—and simply listened—lyrics and music conduits of expression and relaxation. Mr. Meany believed that meaning could come from silence.

*It can't hurt, Boss...*

Mr. Meany reminded me of Sister Mary Evangeline, her aloha spirit, her voodoo attitude. It was all wrong but it felt all right, and I liked it too much not to participate.

*But that's how the devil works, isn't it, Mary Kennedy?*

I presented my new *Point of Entry* album by Judas Priest, maybe simply to listen to, maybe to explore the album cover artwork, maybe to understand the raw sexuality, *the crass* I felt when it thundered through my headphones.

On the cover was a flat spongy or stony landscape with a narrowing rolled computer paper highway that extended off the top center of the album to an unknown blue dusky horizon; to a place that might be promising, maybe to freedom, maybe to ecstasy, maybe to a destination, or maybe even to nowhere.

After having listened to the album so fucking much, I thought that perhaps the computer paper tunneled highway was a metaphor for a lady part, a vagina.

*Bless me Father, for I have sinned, am I allowed to say vagina in Music Club? Is Mr. Meany allowed? I mean, if he is indeed a homosexual, surely that sin is worse than saying "vagina." Crass.*

"That album cover is compelling, Jake. Photograph that for our literary magazine. Maybe we can use it somewhere," said Mr. Meany.

*He sees it. Mr. Meany gets it.*

We listened to a few of the songs from the album, my selections, and everyone in Music Club agreed that they were provocative. At least I wasn't alone in my opinion, again, naturally.

Mr. Meany did not seem to notice that there were a multitude of sins occurring.

"What does it mean to you, Kennedy?" Mr. Meany asked.

"To me?"

Jake sat forward on his elbows like a private dick and everyone else just stared at me.

*It means belonging. It means smoky nicotine tongue. It means my palm haiku-ed inside of Jake's fist. It means that people like Sister Mary Evangeline and Mr. Meany may be on to something with their voodoo and that my interpretation of Catholicism is fail worthy. It means feeling OK to be OK. It means freedom at point zero.*

I was afraid...*fear not, Jesus says. Well, who the hell is HE to talk? He's got God for a fucking Father*...but not really afraid. I was terrified of not being terrified, for once. I was scared of what it might feel like to let go, to feel what it might be like to listen or to be heard, afraid to feel me, afraid to be me. Kennedy. Mary Kennedy. To tell the truth like Roger, to tell my truth.

The album was about yearning and love and need and hope. *Jesus-hope?* It was about loneliness and vibrations and desire. *And towers and bridges?*

"I'm not sure," I said.

*Oh fuck oh fuck oh fuck. I flinched. I hate me. I want Baby Crissy. I want to be seen, be heard, I want to be sure and provocative, secure and confident. Understood and accepted. I want it to be OK to be sexy. I want to be told that it is OK to be so confused about morality and mouths. But I flinched.*

I could not bear to look Mr. Meany in the eye, as if he had any clue how terribly I had failed myself, my chance to feel OK to be OK. My chance to take a chance.

It was Jake who saved me, *a superhero?* fingering the Cracker Jack horseshoe around his neck. I could almost see my thoughts ticker-taped across his Doubting Thomas forehead.

"I get it," he said to me, giving my arm a hand hug.

I knew he did.

"Mr. Meany, is that a vagina?" Jake asked.

Jake was never afraid to speak my words. Only his own. Just like me.

We were sixteen.

## April 1981

I presented a perfect quarterly report card to Dad.

I never forgot what Dad was wearing that day: the peach dress shirt that I loved, a tie of a paler than pale shade of peach, traversed by green and taupe stripes. He wore brown slacks, cordovan belt and shoes, brown socks that blended perfectly. He always matched. He always looked nice, crisp. He smelled like an office and looked worried.

He tilted his head back and moved his eyes down to the bottom of his lenses like he had so many times before. He had never gotten used to his bifocals. They made him feel old and he hated that. He scanned.

"It's good," he said, "very good," and tossed my perfection onto the kitchen table.

*Hold on, buster, I waited all quarter to show this milestone, this perfect report card, to you. Do you know how hard it is to get one-hundreds in everything in junior year? Isn't this what you have wanted all along? I even went to gym class for you. What do I have to do to make this guy proud?*

I used my words. I didn't flinch.

"Yeah? Really? It's good? Very good?" I asked.

Dad answered like God, not at all.

But my sarcasm, my tone, my anger, my volume, was enough to swivel Mom from the stove, spoon still in her sauce.

*Fuck the fourth, honor thy father and thy mother. What the fucking fuck?*

Dad shuffled through the rest of the mail, tossed it as well, readjusted his fucking old-man glasses.

"What's for supper?" he asked the stove.

My words followed him down the hall.

"I have all kinds of letters from colleges about scholarships, you know, and invitations for tours," I begged.

*I bet Dooley, Gina, and Roger never got those. Aren't I proud-worthy yet?*

I stormed out of the front screen door, and went to the fence like a hoodlum. Alone. Again.

The neighborhood was quiet, but the sound inside my head was screechy and achy, like the boom of Roger's car exploding, like the click swirl tick-tock of Dooley's cop car lights, like all of the car doors slamming, stealing—the ambulance, the kidnapper's escape vehicle, the cabin door of the metal bird—the pain from which was paramount to the numb throb of my fingertips holding onto the fence rail for dear life.

I was finished flinching.

Everything was wrong with Dad, *"Is your father OK? He's not sick again, is he?"* and I did not know what.

*I will fix Dad. I will play the dicey word game with him, Got a Minute, whose die are enclosed safely in a plastic cube, its egg timer adhered to an inner corner always counting down the time. We will feel safe because the letters are inside the plastic and they can never be loose. They can never be free. They can never be defiled. They can never change. We will make tons of noise shaking them up, then watch them tumble and fall into place, watch them become separate and then together, mold them into silent words, so many unspoken words. I will say Hail Marys, full rosaries, so fucking much, I will light candles in the chapel at school, go to confession. I will fix Dad.*

Something was wrong. Something was bigger than I. Something was stealing from me and from him. Something was on his mind or in his head and nothing to him was ever just "good" or "very good."

I was panicked.

*Everything was good, very good. Dad and I were friends forever, right?*

I reentered the house, glancing at the wall to make sure that Coffin Nails was still hanging on.

## May 1981

We had lasagna and lemon cake for our birthday—not because Dad and I discussed it, but because that was what Mom made.

I got a card signed in only Mom's delicate cursive with a twenty-dollar bill in it, which was weird, and by most standards, a lot of money.

"For your albums," Mom said, "or whatever it is you listen to in there."

It was like a surprise birthday party, except backwards. It was as if it were the guests who knew nothing about it, a secret to everyone, unobserved and overlooked. Unattended and non-existent—invisible.

I bought Dad some new ping pong balls and a cassette by REO Speedwagon with "Keep on Loving You," on it. He looked at both as if they were foreign, as if I were foreign.

## June 1981

Our second literary magazine was published and distributed for a "nominal fee," that's what Mr. Meany called it. Felt amazing to be marginalized, once again. That's an SAT word for insignificant and peripheral, infused with sarcasm.

Our last meeting was a goodbye party, a celebration for all of our hard work. Mr. Meany thanked Jake and me for our contributions. At least someone noticed something.

Jake and I sat stacked on the cement stairs in the front of school, waiting for our fathers to pick us up.

Since Jesus camp, Jake's father decided that Jake should be more proactive around their house, to keep up the tenants of camp, and assigned a lot of manual labor to Jake. The blisters inside of his palms were evidence of yard work, of spring clean up, but Jake had aches that could not be seen.

"Can you rub my back?" he asked, his back already between my legs, hair at my chin.

"Lower," he directed.

I rubbed him with the insides of my thumbs in the tiny soft part of his lower back where his corduroys fell parallel to the ground, the elastic waistband of his graying underwear like gossamer between my thumbs and his skin.

I touched above the underwear too, because the soft spot that ached was higher than the elastic, sliding my thumbs, making sure to do a good job.

*Perfect. One-hundred percent.*

I thought about the smell of his hair or the words that he was saying and I was lost inside until my fingers felt the connective thread reminders between us.

Jake was hard and lean and...

"MK?"

"Yes?"

"I love you."

...puzzling.

*Like Mom's human hand peace sign?*

*No, like the bishop's love weapon.*

"Fuck. Daddy Dearest is here," he said, leaping up like a Mexican jumping bean before I'd even had time to react to his words.

*I. Love. You.*

I had never heard those words before. Not ever. Not from the lips of another living soul. Not from God. Not from Mom. Not from Dad. Or Rog. Or anyone. I repeated them over and over in my head and wondered what he meant.

**love** |ləv|

NOUN

: an intense feeling of deep affection

: a deep romantic or sexual attachment to someone

: (Love) a personified figure of love, often represented as Cupid

: a great interest and pleasure in something

: affectionate greetings conveyed to someone on one's behalf

: a formula for ending an affectionate letter

: a person or thing that one loves

: (in tennis, squash, and some other sports) a score of zero; nil

VERB

: feel a deep romantic or sexual attachment to someone

: like very much; find pleasure in

: what Jake felt for me

By definition, love was big.

I swallowed it whole.

"Buckle up!" Dad said as I entered the car, changed forever.

I click-clicked the steel into my slot, and once safe within Dad's restraints, I thought about love.

## June 1981

"No one loves anyone in high school, Alcatraz," Clarissa said. "They are just stupid words."

*Are they?*

I sat with those words until the last day of school. Nothing about them seemed to change anything about Jake and it made me angry. He wasn't allowed to say them if he didn't mean them.

*What does he mean?*

I didn't know what he meant. Was it the feeling that I had for Baby Crissy? For Roger? Except, if you were a boy and you loved a girl, shouldn't there have been romance or a kiss here and there? Like on *The Love Boat*?

I didn't know how to be loved. Jake loving me made me feel lonelier than being unloved altogether.

*Alcatraz.*

So I un-flinched and confronted him in homeroom.

"What do you mean you love me?"

Jake stared. He was four-Mississippi silent.

"What do you mean what do I mean? What don't you understand?" he said.

It didn't seem as if the love word mattered to Jake at all. He had no clue why I was confused with his words.

*Is Clarissa right?*

I stared back.

*One, two, how do you do? The Angels!*

"I love you, MK, is that so hard to believe? What is your fucking problem?"

"Children children children, stop your squabbling," Mr. Meany said, hands fluttering, after Jake yelled loud enough for the whole Goddamn school to hear.

I didn't know what my problem was. I didn't know what love was.

I did know that the dismissal bell and the end of another school year could not have come soon enough. I was tired of Jake, Mr. High and Dry. I was tired of getting one-hundreds in everything. I was tired of being unnoticed. I was tired of trying.

I was tired.

## CHAPTER 23

# Suddenly Last Summer

### June 1981

I awoke to so much fucking noise.

I knew from the sounds of pitter-patter and plastic hitting hard wood that Sin Baby and the kidnapped and abused Baby Crissy were in the house.

*When will this imp be done with her assault?*

The cranes were flying on their own from a vibration I could not identify.

I was unable to look at my beautiful Baby Crissy and had stopped attempting to kidnap her back. I used my words instead, albeit, to no avail.

"When your sin baby is finished assaulting my Baby Crissy, will you please return her to her rightful place? That is, to me, in case you don't know. And by the way, thou shalt not steal or covet thy neighbors goods," I recited to Gina, too often.

Gina always just stared at me. Everyone always just stared at me, answering always like God.

*What the hell is wrong with these people?*

As soon as I stood, I saw trucks and men outside of my bedroom window. There were ropes tied around the trunks of our six-trunked tree. There were saws laid like offerings, like jagged Christmas presents, beneath it.

I ran.

"Mom! What are they doing to the tree? Are they taking down the tree? What is going on here? Mom!"

My face was hot and I wanted to throw up.

"But that's our tree! Our family monument! Dad said each trunk stands for each of us! It's symbolism! It's alive! It's who we are! Dad promised he would never take it down!"

And he had.

"It's just a tree. It's clogging the new sewer pipes," Gina offered with a flick of her wrist and a wave of her hand.

*Think of Easter…*

I did the math, the absolute: effectively transporting shit was greater than roots and symbols and foundations and promises.

*Got it.*

I ran through the front screen door, but Dad stopped me midflight with the look on his face and the halt of his hand.

*Stand back Boss, the creases are sharp…*

So Dad approved this, this ruthless uprooting.

"Dad! It's our tree!" I yelled, inaudibly.

But the ropes strangulated. The saws severed the surrendering trunks. They plummeted to the ground like tired cranes. Pieces everywhere of things past flew. Memories. Chopped up and taken away on a flatbed.

I rubbernecked the wall behind Dad's chair, checking for Coffin Nails, Dad's mini monument of hope. The empty coffin remained.

After the tree murder, I hugged my head with headphones and allowed the music to flow through me like a trade wind and transform me the way that Sister Mary Evangeline and Mr. Meany had taught me.

I stayed in my room for a gazillion days, or however long it took for Mom to career into my room like a crazed cartoon roadrunner.

The cranes flew.

"What are you doing? Are you on psychedelic drugs?" she asked.

The excavation of her lady parts really had kidnapped her.

"I'm listening to music," I said.

"I don't understand them," Mom said, alluding to the fluttering origami.

"I know," I said to her, elucidating nothing. I felt bad for Mom, standing there alone, in her own personal lurch. I watched her watch the cranes, trying to read their old news as their freedom wings fluttered. I was tired of leaving her alone. "Want to learn to drive?"

Mom was not a natural at all, but it was the closest that we had ever been—pilot and copilot—and that was worth something.

Dooley, in his unmarked car, pulled us over and asked me if I were credentialed to teach someone to drive, as if he didn't already know the answer.

When I told Roger about that scene, he laughed and said that I was a good sport and a great copilot, teaching Mom to drive.

I didn't bother to listen to what Gina-the-kidnapper said about Mom's driving lessons.

And Dad?

*Did Dad even know?*

If he knew, he answered like God, not at all.

## July 1981

"You should get a job for the summer, save money for college," Dad said.

So I did.

On my first day on the job at our local grocery store, a bunch of us sat in a room not unlike a classroom, with cardboard boxes of unpacked goods lining the walls like wallpaper. Whole peeled tomatoes, Minute Rice, A.1. steak sauce, maraschino cherries, Bosco, and *oh,* a serious-looking boy in a stiff white shirt. I caught a glimmer of his tattoo falling from beneath his shirt cuff. It was enough to raise my eyebrow, which he saw. In turn, he stared me down, and answered me by pushing his own eyebrow up with the eraser of his pencil. We were training to be cashiers. I was training to keep my eyes to myself.

"Having a mainstream job is gauche, Kennedy," Clarissa said. "It must be so embarrassing to cash out people's groceries. Especially people we know. Aren't you embarrassed?"

I wasn't. Nor was I sure about what I should be embarrassed.

Clarissa would never do something so mundane as be a cashier where everyone we knew shopped; she would never have to. She'd melt like the Wicked Witch of the West under the scourge of water if she had to be so ordinary. So she wasn't. She worked at a used bookstore in Troy, not far from our lofted mills.

"I got your friend a job at the bookstore yesterday," she said to me, arms crossed, watching me bag her mother's groceries. (For the record, I *was* slightly embarrassed while bagging Clarissa's mother's groceries; it seemed as if I was unsuspectingly privy to something personal or intimate about them.)

"What friend?" I asked.

*Jake?*

"Don't you only have one other friend besides me, Alcatraz?"
*Ouch.*

I waved her away with an extra long cucumber.

Jake hadn't told me anything about his job. He was silent for the second summer in a row. I guess he was still mad at me for wondering about love.

"Who's the mean girl?" someone asked after Clarissa and her mother left the store.

I froze behind my register, trying to keep my eyes to myself, knowing it was HIM, Tattoo Boy, questioning me.

"My best friend," I laughed.

"I bet all the guys want to do her," he said, "but not me."
*How does he know this? Why doesn't he want her?*

"She's not even pretty," he said as he scanned groceries, one in each hand, like a swimmer, brown ink peeking from beneath his crisp white cuff.

I bagged for him.

I wondered how long it would take for Clarissa and Jake to hook up—Jake in his angst, Clarissa with her claws. I knew before they did that they would lie to me about their relationship, and that it was only a matter of time before Clarissa infiltrated Jake and me, our friendship. Our love.

"Your car's a classic," Tattoo Boy said as we left work.

"I hadn't thought of it that way," I said.

And I hadn't. I had been worried that I would be made fun of. Although in great shape, Aunt Aileen's hand-me-down was a battle-born veteran.

"It's got nice lines," he said, looking into the window, "you could lie down back there, that seat is so big!"

His tone was marveling, not sexual. Like a little kid who found a toy that he liked.

As for me, I felt sexually marveled.

"See ya," he said, and ran to a car awaiting him.

*That's it? Huh.*

I thought about the ink beneath his cuff all the way home.

## July 1981

And then it came. The kiss of death friendship letter in the mail. All about love, and nothing about love at all.

> MK,
> I love you, but don't get caught up on those words. Let them stand for what they are, they are truth and they are memory. I love you. You are a special part of my life as my friend, and I will always be thankful for having you in my life. Let our love always be our memory.
> Jake

*Well, what the fuck? Memories are a thing of the past, Jesus boy.*

I didn't understand Jake and I didn't understand love. But I understood that Jake and Clarissa were on a their private highway to hell.

And I knew what this was; I had seen this before. This was my best friend stealing my best friend. This was kidnapping.

## August 1981

Without the tree, the house looked naked and gaping.

I hated passing the empty hole that it used to fill. All that was left of the tree were some graduation photographs in which it starred and the 8mm film, *Roger's Production, Goodbye to Innocence.*

I took on all of the hours at the store that I could, earning and saving as much money as possible, as Dad had suggested. It was fun. Plus, I got to drive the classic and see Tattoo Boy. I had stopped trying to stop looking, and he knew it.

Mom and Dad were back to their motorcycle wrangling. Two things were different: Dad didn't care or hear anything that she said, and Mom threw in some new low blows about running him over since she could drive, which Dad either ignored or didn't hear.

I was no longer bothered by their bickering until the day that Dad wiped out turning our corner.

"Is that Dad?" I asked Mom.

"I hope so. He's going to get killed on that thing."

*She hopes so? Jesus-hopes?*

I became Dooley. I grabbed the keys as if in slow motion and rushed to the car like a superhero, music from *The Six Million Dollar Man* playing in the background.

*Come in, Adam-12.*

I drove to the corner and helped Dad off of the ground and into the car. He looked pretty banged up, but was coherent and able to walk.

*Do you need an ambulance, Boss?*

"Your mother is going to kill me," he said. "It would have been an easier death on the bike."

"Well, before you walk through the valley of the shadow of death, let me get you home," I said, disgusted with both of them.

Dad was pretty banged up. Clearly he needed urgent care, an emergency room, but I wasn't going to be the one to say that—or worse yet, call an ambulance.

But like a drill sergeant, as soon as we drove into the driveway, Dad directed from the copilot window.

To Mom: "You. Call Dooley and have him send someone to bring the bike home."

To me: "You. Drive me to the Goddamn hospital."

*Thou shalt not take the name of the Lord thy God in vain, but OK, sir, yes sir.*

Mom was relieved.

Turned out that Dad had quite a few scrapes and bruises, a sizable burn on his right calf, and a serious case of road rash along the entirety of his left side.

"Are you always so short of breath?" the ER doctor asked, seemingly more concerned with Dad's breathing than Dad's accident-related injuries.

"Comes with having only one lung, champ," Dad answered, annoyed, rolling his eyes at me.

"And this hoarseness? How long have you had that?" the doctor asked, flipping through Dad's chart more earnestly.

*How long HAS Dad had that hoarseness?*

There hadn't been much yell left in him, but that doctor was right, there was a distinctly fresh rasp to Dad's voice.

Dad became furious, knowing that the newbie doctor was being super thorough, overcautious, and annoyingly exuberant while ordering off of his new-doctor menu.

By the time Dooley arrived, Dad was somewhere awaiting—amongst other tests—a chest X-ray.

"Why are you here?" I asked Dooley. "I can handle this."

"I thought Dad might want someone with him."

"You're probably right, Dool."

*Someone more hero-like, someone more proud-worthy, someone who didn't have to get one-hundreds and still got all of the credit as if they had. A superhero. A Super Dooley.*

"I'm leaving, then."

And I did.

I drove home to steal beer. Raspy Dad wouldn't miss it.

"Gotta run into work," I told Mom as I left through the front screen door.

She hadn't even asked about Dad's condition.

I went through Tattoo Boy's grocery line with some Cracker Jacks. They had worked well in the past. I raised my eyebrow.

"I get off in fifteen," he said, ink peeking through his white cuff.

"I know."

I wondered what lay beneath his crisp white shirt cuff...and the rest of it, for that matter. Tattoo Boy's appearance was impeccable. He was clean cut, well ironed, well polished.

"Delectable" was the SAT word that I would use to describe him, and to say that something about him was "provocative," that is, deliberately arousing sexual desire, was an understatement.

I watched him trot like a race horse over to Aunt Aileen's hand-me-down, and, without asking, took the copilot seat. I wasn't at all nervous about him the way that I was with Strawberry Boy. I was the pilot this time.

"What's the deal?" he asked.

"My mom hates my dad because he fell off a motorcycle and my dad likes my brother better than he likes me," I said.

He took a piece of red licorice from the pen holder inside his crisp white shirt pocket and silently looked straight ahead for way too long.

"There's a lot of information there, Kennedy. But what I was really asking you was—here, us, the car and the Cracker Jacks—what's the deal?"

*Oh.*

"I'm bad at interpretation," I blundered again.

*Some pilot I am.*

"Licorice?" he asked.

"Sure."

He leaned over and dangled his remainder toward my mouth, again, not really sexually, but playfully, like a kid.

I bit.

*Who is this creature?*

"Beer?" I asked.

"Yeah…sure…" he answered, his eyes wide, irises like green stained church glass, like rosary beads, his sandy bangs and his glasses shading them. He was almost studious. His features were delicate. Almost pretty.

"I know you want me, but why are we here right now?"

"I don't…"

I didn't finish.

*Don't flinch, Kennedy.*

He held up his hand.

"Of course you do. It's in your eyebrow. Don't be embarrassed."

"I'm not…"

"You are, but I don't mind you not admitting it. I already know you want me."

He chugged his beer faster than I'd ever seen anyone chug. I'd barely sipped mine.

"Mom's here. Can't keep her waiting!" he said as he left the car and trotted to hers.

"Thanks!" he waved, his mother's car swallowing him.

*Didn't he know we were supposed to get buzzed and make out? Didn't he know I was taking charge here? Why does his mother drive him around? Why is he so self-assured?*

I still hadn't seen what was below his cuff or any other part of him, but I was hellbent on trying.

Mom didn't notice when I entered the house holding a near full can of beer. I went to my room and thought about crisp white shirts and stained glass eyes and slept for the rest of the summer, or days, or maybe just minutes, the screech of the front screen door awakening me.

*Rog?*

*What do I always tell you, Schnapps?*

I heard three kitchen chairs screech against the hardwood. I knew that Dad and Dooley had returned from the hospital and were filling Mom in on the details. A family meeting. The three of them. Typical.

I descended the hallway, buzzed from the beer, peeked around the corner to prove myself right, and sat in Dad's recliner, beneath Coffin Nails, eavesdropping outwardly.

"She'll need her license," Dad said.

"I have my license," said Mom.

"Since when?" asked Dad.

"Since I got it. I've told you a thousand times."

*She had.*

"Who taught you to drive?"

"Kennedy," Mom said.

"She's been taking Mom driving for quite some time, Dad. I thought you knew," said Dooley.

"Certainly not. You have your license to drive a car?" Dad asked again.

"I do," was all Mom said.

I could tell that Dad felt duped, and I felt a little bad.

"Well, I guess that solves that problem," Dad said.

"So, we'll need another operation," said Dad.

*An operation? Again? We who?*

Then Dad coughed, the old cough, that familiar breaking silence cough.

*Here we go.*

And then he gave more details to Dooley and Mom as I listened, huddled on the sidelines.

## CHAPTER 24

# On This Day,
# O Beautiful Mother

### August 1981

"Recurrence" was what they called it when cancer moved back in to eat the rest of your dad.

I never thought that squamous cell carcinoma was going to kill Dad.

I was right. Adenocarcinoma was.

I was seventeen and Dad was fifty-five and recurrence was ageless and enduring and we were part of some sad trinity that had come with a vengeance to make us holy again.

*Bring it on, bad boy.*

**surrender** |səˈrendər|
VERB
: capitulate, give in, give (oneself) up, give way, yield, concede, submit, climb down, back down, cave in, relent, crumble; lay down one's arms, raise the white flag, throw in the towel

: give up, relinquish, renounce, forgo, forswear; cede, abdicate, waive, forfeit, sacrifice; hand over, turn over, yield, resign, transfer, grant
: abandon, give up, cast aside
: when I became thoroughly convinced that hope was death

It was hard to be mad at Dad about the tree with recurrence shadowing us, so I stood before Dad and recited what he had taught me long ago:

"Now the trumpet summons us again; not as a call to bear arms, though arms we need; not as a call to battle, though embattled we are; but a call to bear the burden of a long twilight struggle, year in and year out, rejoicing in hope, patient in tribulation; a struggle against the common enemies of man: tyranny, poverty, disease and war itself.

"We can beat it, Dad. With Coffin Nails hope and Miss Turtleneck's Jesus-hope and the bishop's love weapon and flocks of heavenly cranes and the Blessed Mother and maybe even God and all of His alter egos, we can beat it. You and me Dad, we're battle born like Nevada. We got this."

Dad just stared.

"We're going to rejoice in hope, be patient in tribulation about recurrence itself," I paraphrased and prophesized.

*It can't hurt, Boss...*

"What the hell are you talking about, Schnapps?" Dad asked right through me.

"I'm talking about President John Fitzgerald Kennedy, like you always told me, Dad. Remember, you couldn't help but name me that? Remember our birthday, Dad?"

All I meant was Dad, where is your fight? All I meant was Dad, I'll be your friend through this. All I meant was Dad, I'll make you proud. All I meant was Dad, please don't die.

"Let's take a ride. You drive."

Dad threw me his keys.

"But Dad, I can't drive stick," I said.

Dad stared at me, thinking.

"If not us, who? If not now, when?" Dad quoted President John Fitzgerald Kennedy.

So we drove stick.

I stalled a few times, I bucked a bunch of times, and I slid backwards on every hill.

Dad didn't yell. Dad didn't get mad. Dad barely said anything as we lurched our way toward the Family Rosary Society.

The Family Rosary Society was a creepy Catholic office, bigger than a closet confessional and nowhere near comfy, with a judgmental lady behind a desk who looked like a nun in street clothes. A wolf in sheep's clothing.

Dad bought a bunch of rosaries, one for each of us. *Oh, like the tree trunks, here we go again, what do I always tell you, Schnapps?* Maybe they were Dad's peace offering for ripping out our tree, I didn't know, it didn't matter. Dad believed that these rosaries in particular held special powers because they had been created for and blessed by some guy called Father Patrick Peyton.

"He was sent to Albany, to my high school, to teach, to spread his word. He had great devotion to our Blessed Mother, Our Lady of Hope," Dad said.

*Jesus-hope?*

"Father Peyton began a crusade. He made it his life's work to honor the Blessed Mother through prayer, through the rosary," Dad paused, swallowed, "and now we have his rosaries. I've always wanted to get these for all of us."

No wonder Dad had such devotion to the Blessed Mother and the rosary. No wonder Roger told me to say Hail Marys when I was scared. Roger got it from Dad.

I'd never seen Dad so close and so faraway, he was so soft and humble, his shoulders lax against his seat belt.

"Eyes on the road, Schnapps," he warned me back into reality.

Father Patrick Peyton's family was from Ireland, like President John Fitzgerald Kennedy's, like Dad's.

"Dooley's name comes from my mother, it's her surname. And of course, Patrick is from St. Patrick and Father Peyton. Patrick Dooley," Dad continued.

A destined superhero.

I guess I wasn't the only one with a special name.

"What about Rog and Gina?" I asked.

"Mom named Roger after her father. And then when Gina was born, well, since they were like twins, your mother wanted their names to be similar. Regina, Queen of the Angels. Our Blessed Mother strikes again, Schnapps."

And so she had.

*Roger and Regina. Irish twins.*

The rosaries had taken on a symbolism stronger than a six-trunked tree, and I was going to pray on mine ad nauseam, so fucking much.

"Thank you, Dad," was all that I could manage.

I bucked and Hail Mary-ed all the way home.

## August 1981

I fingered Father Patrick Peyton's rosary relentlessly for the five hours it took to carve out and incise recurrence.

The same lung surgeon told Mom that everything went well, but that recovery could be more challenging for Dad, since he only had two-thirds of one lung left to do all of the breathing that he needed to do.

"Margins were clean," he added, staring at the glass beads I was holding between us—in the air—like a priest holds a crucifix to a demon.

The post-op (that's a cool hospital term meaning after the operation) was déjà vu. Aunt Aileen brought cards. We played. She bought us Tabs. We drank. I told her about Music Club and National Honor Society and my job. She smiled. I showed her Got a Minute, our cubed word game that I carried with me, just in case Dad wanted to play, even though he mostly slept.

"It's too noisy," Mom said when I showed Aunt Aileen the cube, letters clinking safely inside the plastic.

*Who thinks of noise when cancer is eating Dad?*

But the whole hospital part was not as bad as it was the first time. I could drive, both Aunt Aileen's hand-me-down and Dad's stick, which meant that I could come and go alone. Naturally. I had the excuse of my job anytime I didn't want to be there, and took responsibility for lonely CeCe, Dad's Cancer dog. Recurrence was fun that way—I could do almost anything, sans permission.

I didn't tell Jake or Clarissa about recurrence or its ensued operation. They were too busy in their fake relationship anyway, pretending not to be real, the opposite of Santa Claus and the Easter Bunny. I didn't tell anyone until I told Tattoo Boy.

In between work shifts and the hospital, I spent time at the library trying to figure out what the hell adenocarcinoma was.

**adenocarcinoma** |ˌad(ə)nōˌkärsəˈnōmə|
NOUN (pl. adenocarcinomas or adenocarcinomata |-ˈnōmətə| )
*Medicine*
: a malignant tumor formed from glandular structures in epithelial tissue

By definition, it was simple.

But I needed to know more.

How was adenocarcinoma different than squamous cell carcinoma? Why was it called recurrence if it was a different cancer? What were margins and wasn't it good that they were clean?

*No one wants dirty margins.*

What I really needed to know, more than definitions and textbook explanations—they were clear cut, *carved, incised*—were all of the variables, all of the unknowns. Squamous cell carcinoma and recurrence were wolves in sheep's clothing whose variables were degreed exponentially with duplicity; seen and unseen like the Holy Trinity, wherein Dad was the visible one, the one made of flesh, Jesus Christ.

I remembered:

*And like every other day, Miss Turtleneck ended the last day of sixth grade by saying, "Remember class, this is why we all suffer each and every day, but Jesus brings us hope."*

*I raised my hand. I had to know.*

*"How does Jesus bring us hope?" I asked.*

*"Through His DEATH, Kennedy!"*

*Miss Turtleneck screeched "death" in a Bea-voice, laughing as if the joke was on me once again. In fact, everyone in class laughed, including Clarissa.*

*I didn't think it was funny, nor did I understand how something like death could bring hope to anybody.*

*I remained silent.*

*I didn't even turn my other cheek.*

I could read and study all I wanted, but really, all I could do was Jesus-hope that Dad's surgeon knew what the hell he was doing. And hang on to my Father Patrick Peyton rosary beads for dear life.

## CHAPTER 25

# Desert Plains

**September 1981**

Even though I suspected that Clarissa and Jake were committing mortal sin on the sidelines, she kept Boombox Boyfriend around, which was a good thing—he scored us front-row seats to Judas Priest, my *Point of Entry* band.

From behind the scenes, I felt the vibration of sound first, and then came a deeper, more guttural shudder.

Rob Halford, the lead singer, appeared from backstage, dressed in leather, mounted on a motorcycle.

*Stand back, Boss, the creases are sharp...*

He was sweaty, and the vibration of the engine revving between his legs rumbled between my thighs.

It was my album, it was my song, my flinch-in-Music-Club song come to life.

*Mr. Meany, is that a vagina?*

The music began, like the galloping of horses—the bass, the drums—and the motorcycle's engine drove through me like the paper road on the album cover, split, carved, plowed up, and through. Incised. It was the rumble of speakers held by wires and Journey from the bottoms of my feet and up my legs and inside my jeans, all seams.

One of Boombox Boyfriend's buddies was stiffened against me from behind like a human wall, holding a beer that I was allowed to share, in exchange, I assumed, for this free feel from behind. His hardness was all I needed to help me stand as I watched as if I had never seen before.

Mom's human hand peace sign began to make so much more sense, and I understood how Wayne had no problem figuring out the angle, the sum of the measures, the trajectory of it all. It was as if mathematics met magnetism again, where there was indeed a certain formula, yet a variable, a minute variable, of degree.

*God is abounding! Math is abounding!*

I studied the 45-degree angle of Rob Halford making love to his motorcycle.

*"You need a special license for that,"* Mom told Dad.

He was atop me, ten feet away, maybe fifteen,

*"You need a helmet for that, you know. Protection,"* Mom said.

straddling, moving back and forth, pushing, forcing almost,

*"You need to follow the rules of the road,"* she said.

insisting, persevering, all the SAT words in a

*oh!*

nearly parallel thing.

As I did the math, pondering what the exact angle was...*39 degrees...27 degrees*...a mouth nestled my neck.

"More beer?" he whispered, his kisses climbing forward toward my collarbone.

*Dad bought a motorcycle, weird, no wonder Mom was so mad, it's so crass...*

I swallowed his beer, the cold racing through my body, landing atop the hottest spot.

I sipped, turned to lock lips, cold beer mouths, thirsty, yearning, and I wondered what it would be like to spread my legs for the tempestuous, tenacious, and tireless Rob Halford.

Boombox Buddy's kiss was weak, hesitant and worried, lukewarm. He kissed openmouthed and soft, limp. His tongue wiggled like a snake trying to make sense of its surroundings instead of finding the lust we craved. It was insulting to the band, really.

But I liked the way that his hands held my hips, sturdy, reminding me of Strawberry Boy's thumb bruises. The more beer I drank the more tolerable was his kissing, until he tried to go beneath my shirt, until my hands stopped him with superhero speed.

"What the fuck?" he said, waveringly.

"Pass the beer," I said, eye-rolling.

Who knew that kissing could be so exponentially dichotomous.

I swallowed more beer from the clear plastic cup and took a hit from the joint that was passed from I don't know where. I broke all the rules. I took drinks and hits from strangers, I allowed strangers to touch me inside and outside, I forgot the drinking age and the illegality of weed. I forgot the commandments, *keep your nose clean, Mom warned*, and the seven deadly sins, all of them vroom vrooming into tidy oblivion, into angles and shadows and mouths and tailgate monsters and smoky spit, so languid and tasty. *So fucking tasty.* My legs were closed but my nose was dirty...*so dirty...sorry Mom...*

I wondered what it was like to be someone's motorcycle.

*Deliver us from evil, amen.*

I used enough mouthwash that night for a third world country, antisepticising the bad-kisser-from-behind.

*What if Andy Gibb and Joe Perry were bad kissers?*

Shag carpet hugged my neck beneath my headphones. I couldn't remember that boy's name, Boombox Buddy, and I couldn't remember if I ever even knew it to begin with. But I couldn't get the motorcycle off of my mind, or the man straddling it, or the way that he moved on it. What would I tell New Father in confession? And poor Andy Gibb, his torn thigh, still on the wall with his mysterious junk. He looked so wholesome when I was high.

I tried to form SAT words with the letters that I found in the hanging cranes' old news until I was dizzy—a variation of a word game. I ate all of the Cracker Jacks that I could find. I finger-drove straight along Rob Halford's album cover computer paper road *a vagina?* and thought about fleshy angles. I thought about Tattoo Boy on the motorcycle and rocked myself senseless.

I awoke the next morning to the screech of the front screen door—some things never changed—and Dad coming home from the hospital.

This time he came with a crew—a nurse, I assumed, and a guy with a portable *clown machine* spirometer that Dad had to blow into several times a day. The man nurse kept track of Dad's clown performance in a marble notebook, and then gave him some sort of steamy treatment from a different machine and a mask.

*Like the Joker from Batman?*

No, not like the Joker from *Batman*, more like a ghost, a shadow, a glimpse of the guy that used to look like Dad, a waif version beneath a mask too big for him, all the *vroom vroom* cut out of him.

*Had his hair always been that color?*

Dad seemed to be in more pain that second time around, or maybe I was older and more aware, or maybe he just acted that way more so that time.

"How about a milkshake?" he said to me as I thumbed through the marble notebook marked "private," looking for cancer clues, as soon as the man nurse took a break.

After fumbling through the freezer to find ice cream, *whew*, I made Dad a milkshake, hoping, Jesus-hoping, to please him. It seemed as if nothing else had.

"I'll bring home more supplies from work," I said to him, handing him the shake.

Dad answered like God.

"We need to keep this area clear," the man nurse said, scooting me away with his widespread arm gestures.

"I am Hawaii," I answered him back, making my own solo hula movements, forming the state with my arms, as Sister Mary Evangeline had taught me.

He stared at me as if I were the one who looked like an odd, dangerous, rare bird.

He made me laugh.

I went to work.

"Who says I don't want you?" Tattoo Boy said.

He prodded my back with, and then bagged, an enormous eggplant.

"Pardon my crudeness, ma'am," he said to the customer who was glaring at him and her fleshy fruit with reproach.

"Do you want to see my tattoo?" he asked.

"I thought you'd never ask," I laughed. "What time do you get off?"

"Generally, at my leisure," he said as he raised his eyebrow.

*Oh goodness gracious, Mary, Mother of God, Our Lady of Hope, Child of Grace, Father Patrick Peyton, what am I going to do with this? I've been waiting a gazillion years to see what's beneath his crispness.*

Leaned up against Aunt Aileen's classic, I finally saw it. He unbuttoned his white cuff, and the brown ink that I had seen peeking out from it was the bottom of the Crucifix, the cross upon which Jesus hung. As he rolled, the funny feeling below my belly button, my crass, wasn't funny at all, but rather like a jolt of electric lightning. My crass was on fire.

*Your Point of Entry?*

I saw the nailed feet first, then the detailed wood, *he smells so good*, the boney knees, the worn loin cloth, *always so crisp and starched*, the sunken ribcage, the fallen shoulders, *rock star skinny*, the nailed wrists, the bloody hair, *the mystery of it all*, the tormented face, and the crown of thorns.

"Watch," he said, and began contorting his forearm, moving in such a way that made Jesus writhe, from the bottom up.

I could not have been further into hell in a hand basket if I'd tried. The thoughts of dead Jesus turning me on to such a degree were lascivious, contemptible, sinful, and immediately damnable.

*What is the matter with me?*

"Do it again," I pled.

*O flock of heavenly angels this boy's Jesus tattoo is flowing through me like a trade wind of liquid sex. As if I know what that is.*

I could do nothing but watch the body of Our Savior, Our Lord Jesus Christ, mesmerized, and the more Jesus flailed, the more I hungered.

*Give us this day our daily bread.*

We were equally roused, Jesus and I.

Tattoo Boy had me ringing hell's bells.

## CHAPTER 26

# Shine On You
# Crazy Diamond

**September 1981**

After recurrence was moved in and carved out, and shortly after
the nursing crew left, Roger came home for a visit. He brought with
him a model of an F-16 Fighting Falcon for Dad and a diamond
ring for Valerie.

"This is what you've done with your life?" Dad asked.

"You betcha," said Rog. "I worked on something called the soft-
ware. It tells the computer on board the aircraft what to do."

Dad's face.

I had seen this face before. It was the face of Dooley's police
hero plaque. It was the proud face.

This Fighting Falcon model was another milestone monument
for Dad.

"Atta boy," Dad said, pounding Roger's back, holding his chest with his left hand in backwards I pledge allegiance pose, clutching the side where the lung surgeon had given him a smaller, second pectoral fin.

I wondered if it was possible for Dad to live long enough for me to make him proud like Dooley and Roger.

"I guess you figured it out," I said to Rog.

"What's that, Boss?"

"The big dad question of what the hell you were going to do with the rest of your life," I said.

Roger laughed.

"Boss, go get Valerie—and the rents over there too."

So I did.

"Is he home?" Valerie asked as she opened her front screen door, her eyes sparkling like diamonds.

I knew what Roger was going to do, right in our living room, right beneath Coffin Nails, in front of Dad, Mom, and Valerie's parents too. Roger was making good on an old promise.

As soon as Roger reached into his shirt pocket, Valerie jumped up and down like a cheerleader with invisible pom-poms and a bad cheer squeal.

He held her left hand and kissed it.

He said, "Valerie? Will you be Boss's sister for the rest of our lives?"

Valerie looked slightly confused.

My heart filled like the Grinch's, almost to bursting. I started to cry.

Valerie cried, Dad hunched a huddled cough, and Mom and the Nelson parents stood unwaveringly, perhaps all confused by Roger's unconventional question.

"Yes! Yes! Yes!" Valerie yelled, jumping on Roger and most inappropriately wrapping her legs around his waist like a human pretzel.

They twirled and kissed right in front of both sets of moms and dads. Rents.

"Let's do it as soon as we can!" Valerie said, staring at the ring, the size of which seemed to swallow half of her ring finger.

"We'll figure it out," Roger said, hugging her, sneaking a peak at Valerie's dad who was red in the face.

I was so happy for Valerie and Rog, but also, I knew that this meant that Valerie would be moving away too, to be with Rog once and for all. It made me sad, thinking about her leaving. But I was excited for Roger, who now had someone to love him and someone to love back, like Dooley and Bea, like Gina and Wayne. I was happy about the way that he got to be all wrapped up in a human pretzel girl, just like a present beneath a Christmas tree.

Roger and Valerie spent some time talking with the rents, all four of them.

I spent some time checking my school supplies.

It was the eve of the first day of my last year, my last first, or maybe it was the other way around. My senior year. I was looking forward to it, eager to study and maintain a perfect average, excited to see the teacher-doctors, especially Mr. Meany, longing for routine, and ecstatic to be out of the recurrence recovery room. No offense to Dad.

I heard the rents leave, soon followed by the sound of Valerie and Roger going to the fence.

*Hmmmm.*

I followed them. After all, I was old enough, if not older than Rog was when he first started going to the fence. Perhaps, I was even of an age where I no longer had to get lost.

Except no one was on the fence, and there were no cigarettes, no alcohol, no weed, no kissing.

I watched Rog and Valerie disappear into Marcus's house, the door closing behind them.

So I mustered the Marcia Brady in me and took a calculated risk.

*One, two, how do you do? The Angels!*

*Three, four, guess who's gonna score?*

*Kennedy is.*

*Five, six...*

I knocked, silently chanting my impromptu tryout cheer:

*"'Twas the night before school, after the rents,*
*Not a creature was stirring upon the old fence.*
*Marcus's door was closed up with care.*
*I Jesus-hoped his six pack was safely in there.*
*And what to my wandering eyes should appear—*
*Marcus half naked, holding a beer."*

*Hail Mary full of grace...*

"Many is the man who's been missin' you..."

Marcus fucked up or made up a lyric and sang as he opened the door. Some things never changed.

*One two three four five six. Yup. All the abdominal muscles are accounted for.*

I stood.

"Holy motherfucking God. Do enter my holy house," he said.

*Thou shalt not take the name of the Lord thy God in vain, but OK.*

Marcus was a walking lyric, a sinful soliloquy. But he sucked at it.

He handed me his beer. I mean, I was almost legal.

*Keep your nose clean...*

There were other people there, stoned, hazy people.

The homey appearance and familial décor had definitely changed into something much more smoky and groovy since the last time that I had been there, many years ago, trick or treating.

Valerie was showing all of the other girls—*women? how old are these people?*—her ring, and Marcus was showing me to the bong.

He led me by the wrist, both like a little kid and a determined adult, and we sat on the tie-dyed covered couch, so fucking close.

I'd never seen a bong before, it was big and glassy, misty, and very sexy. Smoke was swirling in it, lingering, as if it was half-used and half-wanting to be used. It smelled sweet and felt hard.

"This is Boss."

Marcus introduced me to the house with the flick of his wrist.

Someone lit the bong in Marcus's lap and he told me to move in.

"Closer."

I thought that we were as close as we could get; I leaned.

"Relax, sugar. You haven't seen nothin' yet..." he sang.

Marcus took a hit from the bong, and then hand hugged my jaw, hard, and covered my mouth with his.

*Oh my God oh my God oh my God one two three four five six muscles his mouth is over mine plunging the dipstick back into its hole wiping it clean...*

It was like...I don't know what it was like. Marcus was beautiful. Marcus was sexy as hell. Marcus was a dream come true. Marcus was a poster walking off of my wall. Marcus was old. Marcus was good at this, whatever this was that he was doing.

I stood up and walked to Valerie's side. I was terrified of his mouth, of his singing soliloquys, of his raw and charitable free-spirited sexuality, and his hard smoky bong.

*Marcus kissed me, right? Kind of? It didn't seem like a kiss kiss, but unequivocally, his mouth was on mine.*

I told Clarissa that I had been kissed, or at least shot-gunned, by a rock star, or at least by a rock star look-alike. A mature man of twenty-six.

"That's disgusting. Who wants some dirty old man's old dry lips anywhere near them? Plus, smoke is gross," she said.

*I thought she was in love with Robert Plant.*

"Well, you get high all the time," I said.

"Not from the mouth of a pedophile. Kennedy, sometimes you worry me. You're so gauche."

And sometimes *she* worried *me.*

## October 1981

Clarissa and Jake continued to lie about their thing, but I just knew that they were in deep.

Jake was my friend, my love memory person, as he stated in his love note, but his dishonesty poisoned our water. Also, his grades slid somewhere between Jesus camp and his own personal point of entry into the lying Clarissa.

I started hanging out with some of the nice girls who were in all of my honors classes. It was a breath of fresh air, as Dad would say.

"What happened with you two?" Mr. Meany asked.

"He's fucking my best friend, lying about it, and forgot that he loved me," I answered.

"Kennedy, language, please..."

But Mr. Meany's expression did not match his words, even I could interpret that. He looked as hurt as I felt.

"I do love you. Plus, I thought *I* was your best friend," answered Jake.

"That was clever," I replied, because it was. He had me there. He was my best friend. Until he lied.

"Besides," he added, "you have all of your boy toys."

"I have my virtue."

I had won. I knew it. But it didn't matter. If it weren't for the lying, I really would have been OK with them being together. It was them playing real-life Santa Claus and Easter Bunny that I couldn't deal with.

*Turn the other cheek...*

I missed him and I missed us. I missed Clarissa too, although I was beginning to see her true colors, and she was Crayola Ugly.

Her claws were in him as soon as she had gotten him the job at the bookstore. She began her attack with quotes and short poems. She added some Lene Lovich and The Clash and The Pretenders, and he was a goner.

Even Jake tried to ease me into their whole clandestine summer fling by being a pretender himself, as if their relationship, by fall, was just at its beginning stages.

Jake: "Your friend Clarissa is nice."

Me: "She'll break your heart."

Jake: "You know she lost her father."

Me: Silent stare.

*Oh, really, smarty pants? I may have noticed her dead father. Has she told you how she never bothered to tell me and how she calls me Alcatraz?*

Jake: "Her bangs are like Chrissie Hynde's."

Me: Eye-roll.

*Has she mentioned a boy with a boombox?*

Ugly kidnappers, able abettors: fuck you.

Despite Jake and his lies, our literary magazine was up and running, and with Mr. Meany's help, I recruited some of the honors girls to dilute Jake's poison.

Music Club, however, became an impossibility. Every song that Jake brought in to share was a Clarissa song and I knew it, and he knew that I knew, and although I tried my best to be mature about the whole thing, it always turned sour.

It was reciprocal. Everything I shared became an accusation about me with some boy toy, his label for any male I mentioned, even if it was Roger. Jake became a walking hyperbole.

Meanwhile, I watched Dad like a hawk, and tried to engage him in any way I could. I recited the fall lineup on TV, and bought him a copy of *War and Remembrance*, the sequel to *The Winds of War*. Always alongside him on his side table, beneath his rosary in its pouch, was *All For Her*, Father Patrick Peyton's autobiography.

"Whatcha reading, Schnapps?" Dad asked one Saturday while we were parallel reading like old times, sans the screened-in porch.

"*I Am the Cheese*," I answered, shocked by his initiation.

Dad had been pretty silent since recurrence moved in and got carved out.

"Is it gone?" I asked.

"So far, so good, Schnapps," Dad said, much less convincingly than he had the first time that I asked him if cancer disappeared.

"What's it about?" Dad asked.

"A kid who feels all alone, like Gilbert O'Sullivan's 45 guy," I said.

"Is it for school?"

"No, but this is, " I said, holding up the one-two punch, *The Iliad* and *The Odyssey*.

"I would be dead before I could get through those," Dad laughed, still loving those fucking cancer jokes.

CeCe the Cancer dog sniffed the air at his side.

## CHAPTER 27

# More Than a Feeling

**November 1981**

Tattoo Boy was making me insane with his detached provocation; he was the consummate C-word tease. He stared at me relentlessly while we worked—cashiering, bagging, cleaning, counting— fucking the air with phallic foods and constantly making sure that his perfectly pressed shirt was perfectly tucked into his perfectly creased pants beneath his perfectly shined belt buckle.

The curious kitty in me could not help but wonder of the perfection beneath it all. If I caught his eye he would never break the stare, always sending me back into my corner, cowering, peeking, and starved. He reduced me to puddles; his hard-to-get game was burgeoning.

"I'm getting a new one for Christmas," he said. "You'll like it."

"Skipping right over Thanksgiving, huh?" I asked, intrigued by what he meant, but trying to act cool and disinterested, working on my own hard-to-get gig.

"I already have a Thanksgiving tattoo," he said, and right there on the front end, all belts and registers and people we knew buying groceries, he rolled up his stiff white cuff and killed the writhing Jesus all over again.

"Hallelujah," I prayed.

"Thanks be to God," he answered.

*I mean, I didn't really mean "Hallelujah." I meant your Jesus tattoo and your arm are enough to make me come right here standing in front of everyone we know how gauche buying all of their Thanksgiving groceries. I meant sheer blasphemy. The only praise I am giving is for every inch of your crazy sexy existence, including the Lord Jesus dying over and over with the rippling of your forearm.*

Thanks be to God?

"What are you?" I asked, my interpretive light bulb pulsing.

"That's a broad question. Could you be more specific?" he asked, scanning can by can, box by box, the bleep bleep of the holiday approaching.

Jesus twisted and contorted as Tattoo Boy's arms swam.

"Religion. What religion?"

"Oh. Episcopalian. We go to Saint Michael's, don't you?" he said.

"Everyone goes to Saint Michael's," I answered, which was a generalization, and a near true one, nonetheless. Everyone who wasn't Catholic *did* go to Saint Michael's. Episcopalians. Pagans.

I didn't tell him that I didn't go there because it was plain to see. We would have known each other already.

A pagan, though, was not the type of boy that I could bring home to Dad. Having pagans as neighbors, like Marcus, was bad enough. Having them as suitors was out of the question.

My disappointment showed.

"You're saving yourself for marriage too, I assume?" he asked, squirting my register's belt with all purpose cleaner.

Thou shalt not commit adultery included premarital sex. I didn't think that was in the Episcopal rule book like it was for Catholics, but locally, there was a trend amongst Christian teens to be doing so.

*My perfectly put together Tattoo Boy was chaste?*

*Like fake Jake?*

"What kind of tattoo?" I managed, finally.

"It's a surprise," he answered.

Of course it was.

## November 1981

*Dad's Production* was up and running.

I could smell Mom's job, the bacon and the onions and the celery already simmering on the gas fire. I heard Dad's knife swoosh-tap against his cutting board.

"Where's the beer?" I asked, tongue in cheek, entering the kitchen.

"You keep that nose clean," Mom warned from the stove, not budging.

She was pretty paranoid for someone who never got high.

Dad head-nodded me toward the refrigerator. I wasn't sure if that meant that he was ready for more perfectly frozen bread to cube, or to grab a beer, so I did both.

I poured.

"How were the SATs?" Dad asked.

*See? Dad is OK. Recurrence is gone. So far so good, Schnapps…*

Dad remembered that I took the exam. We were back to normal. Me and Dad were friends again. Everything was going to be OK. I was in the game, drinking with Dad.

"So far, so good, Dad," I said.

Awkwardly, Jake, Clarissa and I all took the test together, along with Boombox Boyfriend, Strawberry Boy, and his bird-like girlfriend. I hadn't seen that one coming, but I guess that I should have, knowing that the SATs were held at the pagan high school. We were alphabetical by room, so I was spared everyone except Jake and the vulture. I turned the other cheek, thought of Easter, and did my best. I was sure that I did well, and Jesus-hoped that it would make Dad proud.

Three quarters of the way through my beer and *Dad's Production*, I decided what I was going to do after they went to bed. Mom and Dad's bedtime got earlier and earlier as I got older and older, and after this production, they'd be wiped out. Plus, since recurrence moved in, their rules boiled down to Mom's singular one about clean noses.

I put on my tightest jeans and my Gunne Sax blouse with lace splayed like a V between my bosom. I sprayed perfume behind my neck—I don't know why, it was just what I did. I pulled my Frye boots over my navy Catholic school girl knee socks, and headed to the new fence.

*One, two, how do you do?*

I knocked.

Marcus didn't say anything when he opened the door, but never took his eyes off of the bottom of my blouse's V as I slid past him into his house of the holy. The front room was permanently hazed, but the house smelled of safety—turkey, dressing, weed.

I followed him into his kitchen.

"I'm preparing my feast tonight. 'Going away in the morning with my hurting heart,'" Marcus half sang his botched explanation.

My interpretation was that he wasn't spending Thanksgiving at home, but I wasn't sure. He stirred something on his stove, turned, traced the lace V with the back of his index finger, and then lit a joint.

"You gonna put me in jail?" he asked, taking a hit, and turning off whatever was on the stove.

I looked at him funny, I know I did, like the little kid that I was trying not to look like, and shook my head. I inhaled and stared.

He took my hand and led me to his couch where we sat, finishing the joint. His finger traced the V again, down and up, then back the other way.

"You eighteen yet?" he tried again.

"Yes," I lied.

"You sure about that? If you don't put me in jail, Rog'll put me in the hospital," he said, lighting a cigarette.

I watched his mouth suck and marveled at his ability to blow smoke circles in the air.

I stared him down the way that Tattoo Boy stared me down, but Marcus seemed more concerned about his Thanksgiving meal than he did about me.

"You know how to bake a pie, pretty Boss?" he asked.

"No."

*Jesus Christ—thou shalt not take the name of the Lord thy God in vain. Of course I know how to make a pie, you dumb fuck, but can we do it first and then bake? Why is Marcus ruining everything? Why won't he hit on me the way he did the last time I came here? Doesn't he know that I may be ready to be deflowered and that I choose him, an older, more experienced man? A rock star look-alike? Roger's best friend? I wore my nicest blouse for this!*

"I'll teach you," he said, and led me by the hand like a little girl *like a baby like a child* to his kitchen.

"I gotta go," I said, and ran home crying, just like, well, a little girl.

Thanksgiving was hard to swallow, especially after Marcus's rejection.

Dooley and Bea, Gina, Wayne, and their Mary-babies were all there. Roger couldn't make it, but was going to be back for Christmas and New Year's, as Rog and Valerie were being married the day after Christmas.

Gina and I held a modest bridal shower for Valerie in our pegboarded basement the weekend after Thanksgiving. Since Gina was busy with her Mary-babies, I did most of the decorating by myself. To Gina's credit, she made gazillions of finger sandwiches and bought a whole bunch of chips and dips and fancy fruit kabobs. She ordered a huge cake and I made punch and it felt like happiness. I was impressed, and almost wanted to be Gina's friend again, even though she was a kidnapper.

"Sorry you can't be my best boss," Rog wrote in a letter.

But it was OK, because Valerie had asked me to be a bridesmaid since I couldn't be the best man. I was a copilot of sorts.

Gina was matron of honor; Marcus was the best man.

Rog asked Dooley to be an usher.

"It's the right thing to do, Boss. He's our brother," Rog wrote.

Roger always had all the answers.

## December 1981

Christmas was sandwiched between the wedding rehearsal and dinner, where Dad welcomed Valerie into our family, and the actual wedding.

Rog and I did not go to midnight mass because he went to church with Valerie and her rents. Another "right thing to do," I supposed.

I went to regular Christmas eve mass with Mom and Dad, and saw Clarissa, just like grade school times. I saw Miss

Turtleneck, who was now a Mrs. Turtleneck, in a Christmas turtleneck. She asked me all about mathematics and I told her about Mr. Meany and his irregular isosceles name triangle Christmas tree, his concrete poem, but she did not seem to appreciate what I was saying. I wanted to ask her about Jesus-hope, but thought better of it.

I knew that Sister Mary Evangeline would not be there. She had asked to be transferred back to Hawaii, but had been sent to a school in the Philippines instead. I Jesus-hoped that she was happy.

Mom didn't make cookies and there was no *Dad's Production: Christmas Edition*. The presents were put beneath the tree days before Christmas, and I rearranged them alone, ad nauseam, so fucking much.

"We don't have time for tinsel," Mom said, after I had adorned nearly a third of the tree.

I put it on anyway, and no one seemed to notice, and if they did, I guess they didn't care.

It was like *The Year Without a Santa Claus*. I was the only straggling believer.

*I am the cheese.*

Roger and Valerie's wedding was small, with just close family and friends, at Valerie's family's church. The reception was held at the restaurant where Rog worked before he left for the Air Force.

Valerie made lace dresses for all three of us, and we wore velvet gloves that went all the way up our arms, almost meeting our capped lace sleeves.

Valerie's rents were angry with her for not wearing white.

"It's winter!" she exclaimed, but everyone knew that it meant that she wasn't a virgin.

I understood. Rog and Valerie had been getting married since the beginning of the universe. Valerie's lace was seasoned, warmed, genuine. White seemed stale and certainly not illustrative of the time they'd spent together. It was white that was indecorous.

But what I could not understand was why everyone got all hung up on things like the color of Valerie's dress, but couldn't manage to find or share the bishop's love weapon; or why they lied about things all the time; or why some people could sin and others couldn't; and why kidnapping was OK, and hugging or saying "I love you" wasn't.

*Why didn't Mrs. Turtleneck understand Mr. Meany's irregular isosceles name triangle and how in God's name is hope garnered through death?*

What I did understand was that I was going to hell just thinking these things, and for all of the other bad things that I had been doing, like lusting after Marcus. Valerie's tinged white innuendo lace paled in comparison to the sin that was happening all around that best man tux.

*Stand back, Boss...*

I tried to be pious and all since it was a wedding, a supposed sacrament, and tried not to stare at Marcus and think about his abdomen beneath his tux.

*Sit tight, Boss...*

I focused on Valerie and Rog, how they looked at each other, Valerie all glassy eyed and eager, Roger a seesaw of tender allegiance and hunger. They made me cry tears of delight. It was a childhood dream come true before my eyes. A real-life fairytale.

Mom shot me a look, and I wasn't sure if it was because of Marcus or my tears, but either way, I had done something wrong.

*Keep your nose clean.*

I straightened up and dried out, and kept my gaze and attention on the priest for the rest of the ceremony, which lasted about four more seconds.

Much to Mom and Dad's surprise and horror, the simple sacramental ceremony did not include a Catholic mass. I thought about how brave Valerie and Roger had been by not informing Mom and Dad beforehand. I mean, there was a priest, a Catholic priest, and I heard Dad grilling him afterwards about the validity of the sacrament without a mass. It was valid. I felt bad for Dad. He was a man of such faith, but it was Valerie and Roger's marriage.

Valerie's family was rich enough to afford a limousine in which the bridal party rode to the church, and then, from the church to the restaurant.

I'd never been in a limousine before, but it was equipped with a driver—a pilot, who opened and closed the doors for you, and it had comfortable benches instead of seats to sit on.

*You could lie down back there...*

After the ceremony, when we entered the limousine, there was a platter of Aunt Aileen's long-stemmed glasses filled with champagne—one for each of us. Dooley balked about me being underage, but Roger handed me one anyway, giving Dooley a flaccid middle finger. Dooley declined the champagne, and Marcus chugged his and then sipped Dooley's.

Marcus was looking at me with a look of, well, not quite tender allegiance or hunger, but maybe of contemplation. I tried to hold his stare but the feeling in my crass sabotaged me.

Dooley watched back and forth between us like a tennis match, and when we got out of the limousine he told me to back off of Marcus.

"Back off?" I laughed, and huffed as if puffing imaginary smoke in his face like Roger used to.

I hadn't known that I was backing in, or onto, or up to, or whatever it is you did in reverse of backing off. I wasn't sure what I had done wrong, and surely Dooley could not have known about the day at Marcus's when he shotgunned me with his mouth and his shameless smoke. Or his Thanksgiving rejection, for that matter.

At the restaurant, Dooley and I were introduced first, followed by Gina and Marcus. Marcus and I held each other's stares—*finally*—as he and Gina made their way to the head table. I contemplated the hell right out of him.

"What's with you two?" Gina asked. "It's creepy. He's old enough to be your father."

*Well, no Gina, actually, he's not, but nice try.*

Maybe Gina just couldn't count, which was how she got pregnant to begin with.

I answered her like God—not at all.

Typical wedding regimen followed: a first dance, a toast, dinner, cake, and dancing.

Marcus held his hand out before me, and we danced. He held me close like he held Valerie at Gina's wedding, and I could not believe that I was the girl whose ear he was breathing into. His fingers pressed into my back, sometimes running along the seams, searching for the bra strap that wasn't there, or so I imagined. His hand held mine, his thumb caressing the inside of my haiku-less palm.

*So fucking grown up*
*Robert Plant is holding me*
*I think I'm in love.*

I swear that I felt his muscles as we danced, as he pulled me closer as the music got slower.

"Boss, when did you grow up?"

His rhetorical question was music to my ears. Maybe he didn't see me as a little girl anymore.

The bummer of it all was when Dooley cut in, as if he were my father or something.

"Cut it the fuck out before you kill Dad," he dictated, pinning my arm to my back like a criminal, pushing me back to my place at the head table.

"I'm not what's going to kill Dad, you jerk," I cried.

"You're not even eighteen. I'll have him arrested," he said.

I had already researched that at the library, and Dooley was lying. The age of consent was seventeen.

"I'll be watching you," Dooley said.

Just what I needed. Someone else watching over me, like God.

I huffed and puffed and accepted Marcus's extended hand, over and over, despite Dooley.

*Bring it on, bad boy.*

Mom cornered me a few days later and told me to stay away from Marcus, reminding me to keep my nose clean.

I went to work.

The walkway to the break room was more of a warehouse aisle than a hallway, cases of soda bottles and cans of food and boxes of cereal and paper goods were stacked to the warehouse-type ceiling.

Halfway to the break room, Tattoo Boy pushed me deep into one of the tunnels, pinning me against a stack of something hard.

*Finally.*

"You want to fuck me, don't you?" he asked.

*Didn't we already establish this, Tease Boy?*

"I do," was all I said.

"Well, isn't that a mortal sin for you, Little Miss Catholic Kennedy," he asked and then questioned. "You are Catholic, right?"

"Yes, but..."

"But what? I'm worth going to hell over? Really? I choose no. What happened to your conviction, Kennedy?"

*Um. I left it in the smoke between the bong and Marcus's mouth, I guess. Um, it's drowning in your smell and your crispy white shirt and your stained glass eyes?*

I felt ashamed. He was right. What was I doing?

I leaned in to kiss him, more of a thank you than a sexual kiss, and he grabbed both of my arms, wrists up, elbows bent, as if I had dog paws, and shook his head slowly no.

His detached, hard-to-get game seeped into my underpants.

He backed up and leaned against the stack across the tunnel of groceries.

"Do you know who the most important person in the world to me is, Kennedy?"

I had only one guess. The right guess. The guess I had been taught since the beginning of time.

"God," I announced, proudly.

I mean, he had dancing Jesus on his forearm for God's sake.

He stared at me as if I had three heads, like Dad's man nurse, and shook his head no as if he was still deciding whether or not to continue with his line of questioning.

"No, Kennedy. I'll show you," he said like an exasperated father, "follow me."

We walked to the break room.

"It's still a little bloody," he said, taking his crisp shirt off altogether.

The gauze bandage was not quite covered by his underlying t-shirt. The muscles of his arms reminded me of Marcus's six pack, and the funny feeling below my navel stood at attention. Marcus had trained me well.

Tattoo Boy lifted the cloth tape and revealed his Christmas present: a tattoo of a swollen heart with an arrow through it, a banner flying over it inscribed "Mother" in pretty script.

"My mother. She is the best person in the world. It's about respect. My mother is my hero," he said.

*Like Super Dooley?*

I felt a little confused, exponentially turned off and on.

*Hail Mary full of grace...*

He re-covered his bloody mother and we shared a coke.

Tattoo Boy and I were friends.

*Sometimes you have to mess things up before you can put them back together again, right, Schnapps?*

Life was a shock.

## January 1982

Roger and Valerie did not take a honeymoon, but rather saved their money to help defray the cost of Valerie's move. Plus, Roger said that he wanted to spend time with Dad.

I was thrilled to have Roger home.

Mom and Dad went to bed around nine o'clock that year, well before the new Guy Lombardo—some dude named Dick Clark—dropped his ball on TV.

Rog, Valerie, and I were invited to Marcus's house for a New Year's Eve party. Mom, Dad, and recurrence approved this and seemed unfazed—recurrence, my real parent.

Marcus was sitting on his couch amongst several other smoky creatures, also rock star look-alike types. They all stared.

"Down, boys," Rog said, "she's my little sister."

*Ouch.*

The creatures didn't seem to regard what Roger had said at all.

There was punch—not the wedding shower kind, but a yellow spiked kind. Two bongs were bubbling.

Roger and Valerie disappeared into one of at least two other den-type rooms, where groups of people were gathered, talking, drinking, smoking.

I sat down between Marcus and some other liquidy creature.

The bong was bubbling and I leaned in for a hit.

Marcus sucked, covered my mouth with his, just like the last time. Smoke filled my mouth as his hand curled around my neck like a snake. When his tongue entered me, it filled my cavity and sealed me so completely that I think smoke came out of my nose. It was a sweet suffocation and I was under water and I was holding my breath *one oh two oh three oh four oh five oh six and I was breathing for the first time.* I felt numb I felt alive I felt embarrassed I felt wanted.

He looked at me, the way I think that I had been trying not to look at him since, well, like birth, and we kissed again, hard, crazy hard, and I wanted to fuck so bad. That was what the feeling was, so unequivocally. I forgot that we were in a house full of strangers, a house with Roger and Valerie, Marcus's holy house.

"I'm going to jail," he joked, his hand sliding up my back, beneath my shirt, searching, his thumb resting in the hollow of my spine.

I leaned in for more bubbly water smoke. I breathed and swallowed. The room tightened and his tongue was in my mouth and smoke was everywhere and I was getting higher by the second, on weed, and on Marcus.

*Is this happening?*

Mom would kill me. Dooley would kill me. Dad, well....

Roger came over and grabbed me by the arm.

*What the fuck?*

"Yo, that's our Boss, take it easy."

*Stand back, Marcus, the creases are sharp...*

"Yo. Respect," Marcus said, standing, arms up hands in the air as if he were resisting arrest.

I swear that I could see his heart beating through his skin. The protrusion in his pants was clear to me. Without a motorcycle, the angle was more like 90 degrees, or higher, even.

God, I was high.

Roger looked like a cartoon version of himself with tiny Valerie next to him, all sparkly and swirly.

"He's no good," Rog said to me.

"I know. I'm not looking for good," I laughed.

He stared at me a long while, uncharacteristic of Rog.

*Why is everybody looking at me?*

Marcus cut the tension by singing,

*"Cool on down,*
*Baby, I'm not jokin' around,*
*You need to go back to school,*
*Baby, I'm no fool.*
*I wanna give it to you,*
*Gonna give it to you."*

*Jesus fucking Christ.*

Marcus fucked up the lyrics big time, but he was right. I had to go back to school. I had to be Kennedy, the good girl. I had to be perfect.

But in the meantime, I needed it, whatever Marcus was wanting to give me, deep down in me. I couldn't wait for him to give me his Robert Plant imposter love.

*The bishop's love weapon?*

Aw fuck, I was going straight to hell.

I prayed the rosary that night, my fingers wrapped around Father Patrick Peyton's mission beads. I prayed for Dad. I prayed for Jesus-hope. I prayed to find the bishop's love weapon. I prayed for the poor souls in purgatory, namely Marcus's and mine, for we would be spending eternity there, or worse, in Mom-God hell.

*Father forgive us for what we are about to do.*

## CHAPTER 28

# The Chain

**January 1982**

After Christmas break, after Marcus, I decided that I needed to mend things with Jake. After all, Jake was just a guy full of lust for a girl who just happened to be Clarissa.

*Can't we be friends?*

I walked into homeroom, confident, and took a calculated risk.

*Math is abounding! God is abounding!*

"All you need is love," I said to him, thumbing at Mr. Meany's poster which remained hung.

Maybe that poster was Mr. Meany's reminder of hope.

"Who are you fucking now?" Jake asked, eyes glaring over his paperback.

"Jake, no one. I'm not having sex with anyone," I answered, hurt by his harsh accusation.

*Yet.*

"Kennedy, you are under the impression that you can do anything but intercourse and your virtue is still intact," he argued.

"You're the one having premarital sex, Jesus boy."

"I'm not the lying one. The sneaky one. The one who will make out with anyone," he said.

I wondered what Clarissa had told him. I'd been so comparatively chaste, no? I felt ashamed and dirty for about three seconds.

"You fucked my best friend behind my back and lied about it. You're still fucking behind my back and lying about it, both of you. Can't we just be friends like we used to be? Jake, we're graduating soon. I miss you," I said.

And then he kissed me. Full on, over the front of his desk, in front of everyone, not a peck—full out Jake—long and still, as if he was sealing our friendship with a kiss. His hands clenched my sweater's shoulder pads like a terrified kid clutching his mother.

Everyone in homeroom applauded as if we were a couple who had gotten back together. It made me want to cry. Not the clapping, but the kiss, his confusing olive branch. What was he trying to tell me? Why would he do this? I felt his urgency, but I wasn't sure for what.

Jake poured out like Niagara Falls, telling me everything. His brother moved away and his sister wanted to become a nun but his parents wouldn't allow it, which sounded like the opposite of Jesus camp, the ultimate irony. He told me that his mom got some new important position at a bank and how his dad was promoted to president of something, on and on. And then he told me about all of his college options thus far.

Although we had until May to decide, my collegiate decision had been made long ago.

"It's a ridiculous idea to spend all that money to go away to college when we have perfectly good ones right here in our back yard," Mom said repeatedly over the years to the older kids, when her lady parts were still implanted, planting her seed and burying my options.

I mean, that pretty much sealed the deal for me. I didn't even consider being ridiculous by applying to any college that wasn't in my backyard, and plus, what I made cashiering was barely going to cover the costs of tuition and textbooks, let alone room and board not in my own backyard.

I am not sure if Mom and Dad even remembered that it was time for me to be applying to colleges. And my main parent, recurrence, wasn't much help either.

But Jake? He had sights on far away schools, and it terrified me to think of losing him again.

"Give me your hand," he said.

Jake haiku-ed in my palm:

*Best friends forever.*
*Sorry about Clarissa.*
*All you need is love.*

*Humph.*
Time would tell.

I extended my inked palm and shook Jake's hand. I was willing to try. I needed all the help I could get.

*All you need is love.*

All I needed was love. Was that right? The bishop's love weapon? Jake's confusing give-and-take-away-memory-letter love, or maybe Marcus's sex-like love? The kind that Valerie and Roger had? The kind that supposedly the silent God had for all of us, no matter what we did as long as it was perfect yet He never even bothered to answer us? What was love anyway?

*What is love?*

## CHAPTER 29

# The Waiting

**February 1982**

*What do I always tell you, Schnapps?*

It became a ritual, or maybe just part of our normal Sunday routine: first mass, then home with one donut apiece (sometimes two for Dad); some sport on TV throughout the day; work or homework for me; early dinner. Afterwards, Dad showered, and we relaxed in the living room for dessert and *60 Minutes*, usually followed by more TV or parallel reading (or more homework) and knitting.

The first time that it happened, Dad called Mom into the bathroom, after his shower, which was just flat out kinky if you asked me. They mumbled behind the closed door, Dad's voice escalating until Mom opened the door uttering assurances like, "We'll see," "We'll find out," "No sense worrying until we know," "Probably just a gland."

She shot me a look filled with a decade of emotion, and I swear we shared a moment. If not, at least for me, I had, for once, seen a feeling harbor over Mom, and although I assumed it was a bad feeling, it thawed years of lemon-sucking coldness away. Mom was thawing back to the way we were before the ambulance swallowed her. Back to when she was Mom.

And then Dad appeared in just a towel wrapped around his waist, hair disheveled, wearing a look of horror that I never forgot.

*Like the peach shirt?*

"It's back."

"No," I used Mom's mumble, "it's just a gland."

"Well, if it's just a gland then it's two or three of them, and they're hard, and never before there. It's back."

And that was how recurrence became part of our Sunday ritual, nestled between Dad's shower and *60 Minutes*.

And so, on a consistently casual and progressively numbing basis, the almost familial lung surgeon cut out of Dad tumors the sizes of Atomic Fireballs and then sewed him back up like a hackneyed Raggedy Andy.

I started spending Sunday evenings away from recurrence, at the new fence, at Marcus's house getting high and felt up. It felt good to be wanted, and he was so damn good at it.

I was so pissed off at that Goddamn silent God for setting off bombs inside of Dad that I decided to fuck the rules. I'd show that motherfucker. I was so done. It didn't even matter what anyone said or did. You could be perfect and end up chopped up by a stranger wielding a scalpel.

Much to my dismay, and detrimental to my deflowering, Marcus always stopped short of going all the way, banging his fist against the wall or smoking another joint or another of his endless chain of coffin nails. He was the only guy that I ever let get so far, his fingers curling beneath and tugging at my Levi's waistband while his thumb pressed against that spot, that very identifiable spot, *my crass* where the funny feeling met serious rapture, and time after time I got crazed beneath it, only my jeans, sometimes my underwear, and sometimes nothing between us until he would once again stop and slam a wall or smoke.

I could barely wait to feel like everyone else, Mom's human hand puzzle in the flesh, Marcus's flesh, Marcus's real-life index finger between my peace sign.

*Recurrence, you motherfucker, you father kidnapper.*

## March 1982

The body butcher laid to rest his scalpel and ordered, in conjunction with another torture administrator called an oncologist, chemotherapy for Dad, to lessen the amount of fireballs.

*Turn the other cheek and pierce another vein...*

A perfervid elixir entered me too, surging through my blood like liquid fire. I became forever un-flinched.

I drove to Clarissa's, Tattoo Boy my copilot, where I found her buzzing like a bee about her mother's kitchen bragging about this and that.

I was hearing but I wasn't listening. Nothing she said could have possibly mattered. I answered and I acted. I was Hawaii, Goddamn it.

"Fuck you and your coming alive Frampton," I said in response to something I hadn't heard. Actually, it gave her pause, as they say, and she looked at me as if she were seeing me for the first time.

Oh, I'd been there before, that gaze had rested upon me many times. It didn't frighten me. It fueled me.

*Turn the other cheek, bitch...*

"Why did you laugh at me when I didn't make cheerleading? Why didn't you act like a best friend?" I asked.

"What are you talking about?"

She looked hurt.

I continued.

"Why do you call me Alcatraz?"

"Kennedy, my father died!"

"Everybody's father dies. And the scarf? The one you gave to that frosted teacher. How could you steal my work and give it away so...so...superciliously?"

I had found yet another proper SAT word.

"What? Kennedy, you're worrying me," she answered.

"Supercilious—arrogantly superior. It's an SAT word, or did you and Jake throw that away too?"

She smiled wryly, so fucking annoying.

*Like the Joker from Batman?* No, *I* was the one smiling like the fucking Joker from fucking *Batman.*

"You better worry about me," I said. "How long have you been fucking Jake?"

"What? Who?"

Clarissa fluttered unencumbered around the kitchen, less like a buzzing bee and more like a frail and flimsy—yet targeting and biting and blood sucking—mosquito, out to feed.

"You mean your little friend from school?" she asked.

I nodded. I smiled. Just like the Joker from *Batman.*

"Yup. Him. You damn near ruined my friendship and then you lied about it. You're still lying about it, you Jezebel. I Jesus-hope you end up in Mom-God hell for eternity."

I knew that she had no clue what I was talking about, how could she? She never ever took the time to hear me. I turned the other cheek, and my entire body, heart and soul, and walked away.

"Think of Easter!" I yelled over my shoulder.

Me and Tattoo Boy drove away.

## May 1982

"Move the lilacs!" Dooley yelled, as he and Mom and Dad entered the house.

I had cut them for Dad, and I suppose, for the Blessed Mother. It was Her month, it was May, and I thought their tribute, considering Dad's devotion for Her, would please him. Make him proud.

Dad disappeared into the bathroom to vomit.

"The smell will bother him," Mom said.

Mom was speaking more and more.

I nodded, and wrapped their stems in wet paper towels and aluminum foil. I set them outside, on the front steps, on the cold cement where I used to sit with Gina, waiting for Wayne.

I brought them into Mr. Meany the next day.

"All you need is love," I said, extending my arm and reciting his poster like a forgotten lament to Mary, the smell of the lilacs softening me, reminding me.

He hugged me.

*Weird.*

"Oh, Kennedy, these are beautiful. And in the month of Our Lady. Oh, aloha, Kennedy," he said.

He remembered my solitary word.

"Aloha," I said, and smiled, a real smile, one I hadn't felt in a long time.

By wind, waves, or wings, I had spread Sister Mary Evangeline's good news.

Chemotherapy was a carnivorous creature, a man-eating vulture. It fed on Dad from the get go.

*Stand back, everyone, the creases are so fucking sharp...*

Dad: "My hair is falling out."

Me: "Nah, it's CeCe's hair."

Dad: "I can't eat anything."

Me: "I'll make you milkshakes."

Dad: "I'm losing weight."

Me: "Your clothes stretched in the wash."

Sometimes Dad smiled. But mostly, Dad sat with a faraway look, trying not to barf.

I swept Dad's hair away and swapped out new smaller sized replicas of Dad's jeans and white tees that I bought and washed, Jesus-hoping that he didn't notice their difference.

I brought home from the store all of the ingredients that I needed to make milkshakes and cheese omelets, the other food that Dad was able to stomach, if even for a short time.

School and work went on, but when I was home, I sat with Dad, playing mostly Got a Minute, for he barely lasted more than a minute before rushing to the bathroom to throw up, or before feeling too sick to continue. I changed the TV channel for him, and adjusted the volume almost constantly. He teetered between not being able to hear it and it being too loud. I read parts of Father Patrick Peyton's book to him, especially the part where it told about when he came to Dad's high school to begin his mission to the Blessed Mother. I pretended to pray the rosary with him; if Dad prayed, he did so with his eyes closed. But instead of closing my own eyes and praying, I took those opportunities to study Dad, to calculate cancer, to figure out how much time I had to make Dad proud before it was too late.

CeCe lay by his side, playing the same waiting game.

CHAPTER 30

# You've Got Another Thing Comin'

**Still Fucking May 1982**

Finally, Marcus asked me if I wanted to take a ride with him. He had some business thing to do, and thought that maybe we could go to dinner and maybe get a room.

He drove a stupid-ass station wagon for whatever was his business, with weird supplies in the back, which I supposed he sold to wherever he drove. Or something like that. I couldn't have cared less about his stupid job.

I wanted to tell him that Robert Plant driving a paneled station wagon not unlike Mrs. Brady's was a turn off, but I kept my mouth shut.

I was excited about my deflowering, and wondered where we would "get a room," and what it would look like. I'd never been to a place with a room.

We got some coffee, which I thought was pretty cool, it was something that Roger might have done. But that day, I was a different kind of boss and copilot.

We drove for about an hour, east, maybe, to his place of business.

"Stay in the car," he said, *sit tight, Boss*, as he left, carrying a leather binder type of thing.

*God he looks stupid as fuck with his tan Dickies and striped Oxford and navy sports coat. Dad wouldn't be caught dead in those gauche clothes. Literally.*

Marcus's shoes were unkempt and his hair was in a rubber-banded ponytail tucked into his collar.

What a fucking buzz kill.

I didn't have to wait a long time in the car, *like a little girl?* and then we were off to the big event. It was noontime.

"Rooms aren't available this early in the day, Boss," he said.

*OK...*

The road was remote, resplendent with high reeds and pussy willow.

*Green grass and high tides?*

He pulled off in a clearing and got out of the car, removing both his jacket and his rubber band. His hair was loose, but his unkempt shoes bothered me to no end.

*Who goes to a business meeting with unpolished shoes?*

Anyway, once back inside the car, he shut off the engine, rolled down his window, and lit a joint.

"Glad that's over. Party time!" he said, passing the joint.

I sucked the smoke and wondered when we would be headed to "the room," or if we were going to have some lunch, or a romantic dinner with candles and flowers and maybe even rose petals and champagne.

*You mean champagne wishes and caviar dreams? Fantasy Island? Hail to the Mary, yes!*

He slid over to my side of the bucket seat, and in one fell swoop slid his hand behind my neck and his tongue into my mouth. He was a phenomenal kisser. I would always give him that much despite his shoes and other shortcomings. Marcus and I had developed a rhythm.

Spit and smoke drowned me in want for him once again, memories of his six pack and his dip stick and hot summer days and wedding dancing and smoky New Year's Eve and motorcycles and that writhing Jesus and it's the only cassette my car plays and I love you MK.

His fingers deftly undid my blouse's buttons, revealing a black teddy that seemed to fuel him into a different level of frenzy.

"Jesus fucking Christ, Boss. Get in the back," he said to me, "and lose the pants."

I had no clue what I was doing or why, and still wondered where we were going, but the high and his demands and his skills were masking my reason.

*He knows what he's doing, right?*

I slid out of my jeans and rolled over onto the spacious back seat, just like the one in Aunt Aileen's hand-me-down.

*It's got nice lines...*

Marcus exited the car a second time, took off his shoes, and half unbuttoned his shirt. He climbed into the backseat and covered my body with his, his fingers pinned into the small of my back.

I could feel it—IT—against me, and became a motorcycle on the stage, being ridden through clothes at maybe 12 degrees, sweat dripping onto me. And then his thumb was on it, the other IT, and it slid and I swirled until he sat up abruptly and announced, "There will be no love making here today."

*Yeah, no shit, buster, fuck my brains out...what's love got to do with it? I'm going to hell in a hand basket over you, under you. Now get your act together and fuck me.*

I put all of my parts back into my teddy, pulled my shirt from the floor, and half covered myself.

He re-fired a joint.

"What?" I asked. "What about the room?"

He sat there smoking his blunt, not offering it to me.

*He could have at least shotgunned me.*

So I did.

I straddled him, taking the near-spent joint from his fingers. I inhaled and then covered his mouth with mine. I was a big girl. I knew how to do it.

He put his hands in the air as if resisting arrest.

"OK, OK, I surrender," he said.

He pulled me to him and we made out some more, even more urgently, if that was possible, until he stopped as abruptly as he had the first time.

"Kennedy, I want your first time to be special. This isn't special."

He gave me a queer look, like the look that a guy gets when he wants to kiss you for the first time.

*Uh, what happened to him buying me dinner and sweeping me off my feet and whisking me away to a far-off paradise? Or maybe just fucking me? Huh? Huh? Huh?*

"Do you want to blow me?" he asked, pushing me back away from him and opening his shirt the rest of the way.

*There they are, one two three four five six, and there is Marcus beneath me with his muscles, me, little Mary Kennedy, and scary* muscle Marcus, in a car, in a field, high as fuck, hopefully fucking, but blowing? Oh, I don't know. I've never done that before.

I grabbed my pocketbook and removed a fifth of vodka I stole from the kitchen cabinet.

"Oh, look at you, little girl," he said.

It made me want to kill him.

I took a swig and passed it to him.

*Thou shalt not commit adultery.*

Sodomy was a mortal sin and potentially offended a handful of the seven deadlies as well: gluttony, if you swallow; greed if you want it; lust, because nobody doesn't want to fuck Robert Plant.

*But suck?*

I didn't want to seem like a little girl; Marcus was my man for the main event.

*All you need is love.*

He slid the back of his index finger, the dick in Mom's human hand puzzle, across my nipple until it answered him with hardness.

*Fuck.*

I swallowed more vodka, and slid to the floor between his legs onto the car's hump.

He pulled his Oxford out from his stupid-ass business pants, which he had already unzipped.

"Jesus fucking Christ, Kennedy..."

*Thou shalt not take the name of the Lord thy God in vain.*

I was so drunk, so high, so obliterated, so worried about Mom-God hell, all comingled with a strange hunger. Or was it something else? Was it power?

*I am Hawaii...*

I was terrified about seeing my first-ever dick, and thought of my posters and album covers, Andy Gibb and Joe Perry and well, Robert Plant, and looked down at what I was intending to eat, *swallow Jesus on Sunday*, at what appeared to be a mushroom of sorts hidden by an Oxford's flap, peeping out like a garden frog, staring at me.

*That's it? Mom's index finger was bigger...*

I didn't know what to do. I was confused, *get your wings Kennedy*, so I swallowed vodka and started to suck.

*Jesus never got a blow job.*

The mushroom got marginally bigger and harder as soon as it was in my mouth, and immediately, he started to moan, which annoyed the fuck out of me. Thank God and celibate Jesus that I was high and drunk or I would have bitten it off and walked home.

I made the huge mistake of looking at his face as I moved my mouth and tongue back and forth, and he was all contorted and screwy and didn't look like Robert Plant at all, but rather a has-been salesman with unkempt shoes.

*Death of a Salesman?*

"You're so beautiful. You're making me come like I have never come before," he said, pushing the back of my head onto the mushroom more and more, exponentially, making it nearly impossible for me to move.

*Spare the fairytale talk, Robert Plant imposter, let's get this show on the road.*

All it took was slightly more rigidity of my tongue for him to vice grip and suffocate me in the folds of his tacky striped Oxford. He grunted and yelled out some sound I never ever wanted to hear again as long as I live so help me God, and filled my mouth with his fungus's cum.

I swallowed because it seemed like nice manners, or maybe to save myself from choking to death, his grip around my head of fatal strength.

As soon as he released his death grip, he hopped out of the car and began tidying himself back together, zipping his cheap pants and sliding back into his shoddy shoes.

"What time do you have to be home, Boss?" he asked.

I looked down at my own unkempt self, my right tit half-in half-out of the teddy, reddened, the snaps along my crass wet and undone.

*Jezebel.*

I swished and swirled with vodka, resisting the urge to spit it at him, and got dressed.

"In time for supper," I said.

*He's no good, Boss...*

*Oh, Rog, if you only knew.*

I swallowed Jesus on Sunday even though it thrust me into a state of double mortal sin—one for the sodomy and another for eating Him with a tainted soul. I'd have to go to confession, but I wasn't sure if I could hide the blow job in the blanket of, "For these and all my sins I am heartly sorry." It was mortal.

Also, I wasn't sorry for the sin, I was sorry for the sin happening upon him—gross disgusting pedophile has-been salesman mushroom Marcus—and inside of my mouth.

Plus, I had to go to Communion or else Mom would have wondered why I hadn't. So I did.

In our final homeroom, I told Jake everything, and although he did not receive the information very well, he tried to be a good friend and helped me to figure out what to say in my last high school confession.

I told New Father that I had engaged in lascivious activity of potentially mortal and impure nature, and that I had subsequently taken Jesus in my mouth, and that seemed to both satisfy and silence everyone without further questioning.

New Father was OK. And Jake. Jake was OK too.

I didn't understand what had gone through Marcus's head, and why that day turned out the way that it did. But I was the one who was ashamed. I was the one who had fallen to my knees to that wolf with the weed and a six pack.

## CHAPTER 31

# Seasons of Wither

**May 1982**

Dad's condition worsened rapidly even though no one bothered to tell me anything at all. But it was plain to see.

The body butcher, or maybe it was the oncology mixologist, prescribed Ensure for Dad, which was a nutritional supplement for people who weren't taking in enough calories or nutrients. It was supposed to help Dad gain, or at least maintain, his weight.

Dad had grown suspicious of Mom, and rightly so.

"It's for dying people," Dad said to Mom, as she gave him a cheese glass full of Ensure. A shot.

It was.

Mom stored it on the counter in the kitchen, conspicuously, until Dad stopped eating everything altogether because he was convinced that she was adding it to everything that she gave him.

She was.

So Mom lied and told him that she threw it out, storing it in the bread drawer instead. We knew that Dad wouldn't find it there because he could no longer hold himself up with just one arm on his walker, he needed two arms. This prohibited him from being able to slide the steel covering of the bread drawer open.

*Like the confessional screen in the velvet closet?*

*Yes.*

Dad called me to his recliner.

"I don't trust your mother anymore. She puts that dead people shit in everything she makes for me. I want you to make everything for me from now on. Milkshakes and omelets," Dad instructed.

*Oh boy.*

"No dead people shit, you hear me, Schnapps? I trust you," he yelled, hoarsely.

*Hold up. He trusts me? Really?*

It wasn't love and it wasn't pride, but it was getting closer.

"Of course, Dad," I answered, straightening Coffin Nails on the wall above him.

So I did.

*One, two, how do you do? The Angels!*

But the thing was, Dad was withering away, and if Dad continued to wither, it would be hard for the chemotherapy to continue, and if the chemotherapy didn't continue, well...

*Three, four, guess who's gonna score? The Angels!*

I was visibly shaking the first time that I made the bogus milkshake, Mom behind me, whispering, reminding me where the hidden dead people potion was. I made Dad's milkshake the usual way—whole milk, Philadelphia vanilla bean ice cream, Dad's favorite, a hint of vanilla extract, and then, Ensure. I blended, and felt so small, like a spec, like Satan, and I worried that Dad would taste the death. So I added more extract and blended quickly, knowing that Dad would be timing the roar of the blender.

I didn't want to lose Dad's trust. It was all that I had left of him. I could not let Dad down. Plus, that was my chance to save Dad's life, to be his personal milkshake maker and savior. And maybe, just maybe, if I breached Dad's trust and added Ensure, Dad wouldn't die. Maybe I could save him.

*What do I always tell you, Schnapps?*

*Oh, shut the fuck up.*

## May All Day 1982

I used to tell Dad that by the time that I got married he'd be so old that I would have to push him down the aisle in a wheelchair.

He used to laugh.

I stood before him.

"I got a wheelchair for us. You're not going to argue with me. You're coming to graduation come hell or high water."

Dad stared at me with that look, the vacant one of non-recognition, like it was the first time that he had ever seen me.

I took Dad's silence as a yes, and laid beside him some new clothes that I bought for him, because his old ones only fit the former Dad, the one who weighed more than one-hundred pounds.

"Why these?" he asked.

"Because they're sharp."

Sharp was Dad's word for fancy, classy.

"They are," he agreed.

I was relieved that he hadn't argued about the pre-wedding wheelchair or the clothes.

I stole his belt from his closet and made new holes in it with his awl. I found it in the cellar, hanging from a silver hook on pegboard that hung over his workbench that had been silent for as long as recurrence first showed its face.

Dad bent to gather his hair from the floor around him, adding it to what had become a sizable, fluffy, white super ball...*when did Dad's hair turn completely white?*...which he kept alongside him in his chair, sometimes clutching and stroking it like a lucky rabbit's foot.

*Luck o' the Irish?*

Coffin Nails hung above him, a lonely, empty, resilient warrior.

We were a sight to behold. Me in full cap and gown, pushing Dad into the arena, wheelchair bound, donned with the extra graduation cap that I had ordered for him. Unbeknownst to me, he had decorated it himself with rick rack of maroon and gold, with the words "Kennedy's Dad, 1982" written in Elmer's glue and hardened with maroon glitter.

Dad's decorated cap milestone monument, and his effort to be there, made me prouder than any award I would be receiving with him there, my name glittering on his balding head.

No one had planned a graduation party, including me; it was implied that there would not be one. Having anybody or anything at the house was too much for Dad, too much noise, too many germs.

Dooley, to his credit, managed to deliver a cake, decorated in gold and maroon with "Congratulations, Kennedy" written in maroon piping.

But all I could see were the words "Kennedy's Dad, 1982." They seemed to haunt me.

I did appreciate Dooley's heroic cake gesture, and ate almost the whole cake alone in my room overnight with a maroon plastic fork (thanks Mom, appreciate the effort) after smoking the consolation joint Marcus gave to me after his fantabulous mush-room explosion.

Dad slept the entire next day, so much so that Mom and I took turns making sure that he was breathing, CeCe never leaving his side. I felt bad that our excursion had wiped him out so. His graduation cap rested on his chifforobe, hung over a statue of the Blessed Mother, fittingly drowning Her.

## Still May 1982

*Kennedy's Production*, that is, the adding of Ensure to everything, was successful for eons, or maybe it was weeks, or maybe it was just days or hours; it was all one big sickening blackening shadow of time, really.

Dad and I played Got a Minute less and less, and although I read to him, Dad mostly slept. I made sure that his rosary beads were in his hands where he liked them, and I turned the channel on every half hour or hour, dutifully. We all stopped pretending that his clothes were stretching, and even CeCe became annoyed by Dad's hair falling on her like unsuspecting feathers.

Unbeknownst to Dad, and only because I was the driver to chemotherapy that particular day, did I find out, that, despite the chemotherapy, the Atomic Fireballs were growing everywhere inside of Dad, faster than the chemotherapy could eat them. The oncology mixologist and the body butcher thought that it was best not to tell Dad, as his will to live would dwindle faster than the fireballs grew.

"The milkshakes are too cold, Schnapps."

"The omelets are too hot, Schnapps."

Even if Dad managed to get a swallow in here or there, he was hard pressed to make it to the bathroom in time to vomit because walking had become as difficult as swallowing.

The fireballs were making it difficult for Dad to walk, the chemotherapy was making it difficult for Dad to swallow, and the whole of it all was making it difficult for Dad to survive.

*Aw, fuck.*

*Hail Mary, full of grace, what the fuck are You doing here? You owe this poor guy after all of his devotion to You. You saved Father Patrick Peyton from death—what, Dad's not good enough? He prayed Your rosary ad nauseam, so fucking much, buying new ones for us all from Your mission man. Doesn't that count for anything? What about all those times we said Hail Marys when we heard a siren or felt scared or lonely? What about the way Dad said at bedtime, "Don't forget to say your rosary," instead of, "I love you or I am proud of you?" Huh? Huh? I said Your Goddamn rosary every time he told me to and a gazillion other times, because I was supposed to, because I wanted to, because Dad taught me to. Bitch. Remember how he called me a blessing from You? Oh, but it was Your holy card, Your virginal picture, not mine, in his wallet. Remember how he fell asleep each night holding Your beads laced between his fingers until they slipped away like unanswered prayers? And while I'm at it, what about the Goddamn lilacs I prayed over in Your name so that they would bloom so that I could pay homage to you? Remember those? Or did you whisper damnations into God's ear after all? You can't help this poor guy out? Make him drink make him swallow make him stop the fucking vomiting and the growing obscurity. So if You can't save him, Bitch, then maybe I can, because I'm here with him, I didn't abandon him. I'll keep using whole milk, Philadelphia vanilla bean ice cream, Ensure, and pure vanilla extract. Emphasis on pure, Bitch. Extra fucking pure. I'll add a straw and watch him drink trust and swallow betrayal. Watch him gain a pound and lose three. Watch him try to stand while I pull him up holding his jeans up with my fingers through his empty belt loops while he is between parallel and perpendicular to the floor. I'll watch the bathroom door close and listen to guts empty into sewers. Listen to him as he assures everyone around him that he is OK and add the Ensure to the next milkshake that he thinks he can keep down now that he threw the previous one up because he is starved since he vomited. Again. I'll pick up the hair on the floor around his recliner before he sees it or before I am forced to come to grips with its meaning or see it whisking away in circles of false hope and crumbled faith. But don't anyone make a milkshake or cheese omelet for him because that's my fucking gig and only I know how to make them the way that Dad likes them vestal embryos down his throat nothing but unadulterated love from a wannabe something daughter anything maybe even a hero to a dying dad. I can save him I can help him I can drive him to the doctor and I can tell him that it is all going to be OK but I can't tell him that I love him because I don't know how and we don't say that why don't we say that I am so unsure I add Ensure and I can keep it up for as long as I have to Hail Mary full of grace do something with him help him stop the lumps from coming and the vomit and the fluid and the shadows in his brain and the immobilized hip and that look of vacancy and fear in his eyes and save us because I think we are at the hour of our death.*

*Amen.*

## CHAPTER 32

# (Don't Fear) The Reaper

**May 1982**

It was never fun when a cop came looking for you, *click swirl tick-tock* especially when you were sitting on the hood of Aunt Aileen's hand-me-down with a Tattoo Boy between your legs.

"I'm out," he said, "unless you need me."

I smiled at him and head-nodded him away. Surely, his break was over.

The cop watched him run back into the store, and approached me slowly, as if I might bite.

*Funny.*

"Are you OK? Was he bothering you?"

This was a familiar cop. Dooley's best man friend. A fellow superhero.

"He's a friend," I said.

I watched him smirk.

"Oh yeah, I'm sure. He looked just like a friend. You better stay out of trouble."

The Tattoo Boy between my legs was not why he was there. I saw it in his eyes.

"Is he dead?" I asked, probably too bluntly.

"Not yet. He's asking for you."

Fellow Superhero asked me if I wanted a ride to the hospital, but I motioned with my thumb to Mom's classic.

"Follow me," he directed.

For seven miles I watched his lights swirl before me, trying to hear their click swirl tick-tock, and thought about what I was going to say to Dad when I saw him.

Dad was sleeping when I entered his room. Sort of. He was dreaming of CeCe the Cancer dog, asking for her, telling us to make sure that she was safe.

I refused to hold in my tears. I un-flinched.

There was no chest tube in Dad, just an IV. A hospital gown was draped over him, and a DNR was taped to the foot of the bed where the plastic lung fluid collector once hung.

I thought of the irony: once they had put a tube into Dad to remove excess fluid; and then they added fluid, slowly, over months, gallons and gallons of poison.

I watched even more irony drip drip from the IV, fluids to sustain him, to keep him alive, and fluids to anesthetize him from feeling death.

Dad was drowning.

I did the math and the percentages were wrong: 67 percent of one lung wasn't enough to pump out death.

"Why add more fluid if he has too much fluid in him already? Why not put a tube in him and suck it all out?" I asked.

Everyone answered like God, except for the body butcher.

"We will do our best to keep him as comfortable as possible," he said.

*What the fuck?*

Aunt Aileen was planted in the dying patient's family waiting room, sobbing, shaking her head no, and shooing me away with her tissue every time I tried to go near her. There were no Tabs, no cards, no puzzles.

I returned to Dad's room and watched the hospital bed sheet across his sunken chest rise and fall, rise and fall, wondering when it would be forever still.

Mom was like a statue—hard, gray, and silent.

I looked down at my own chest, secured safely in a sleeveless sailor shirt, a knot tied and begging to be lost in my cleavage. I watched the knot rise and fall, rise and fall, and thought about Tattoo Boy's finger tugging at it moments before the best man cop came.

He had seemingly lost his patience, his virtuous willpower waned, and backed me up until the backs of my thighs pressed into the front grill of the hand-me-down. Tattoo Boy lifted me onto the hood and slid his index finger *his dick finger* horizontally across my bare tummy.

I thawed into a puddle of missed opportunities.

"You would taste so sweet, I know it," he said.

He sniffed the hollow of my collarbone, his eyes grazing the knot of my shirt back and forth like a typewriter's return.

I was sweating, shaking, calculating our combined lust, knowing it was his desire to remain chaste until marriage. To that end, I tried to hop off of the car's hood, the temptation just way too much, but as I fumbled forward, he bent his knee up, keeping me locked on the hood. Our bodies melded tightly in the heat; parts of me were pressed and parts of me burned, sandwiched between the hardness of Mom's metal car and Tattoo Boy's steel flesh.

"I want to make love with you," he whispered, just as we both saw the police car approaching.

Man, it was a hot summer.

Dad's breaths were so labored, up and down, up and down.

We stayed at the hospital in Dad's room all night, Mom and I. It was unspoken. We never left.

I watched the morphine drip and Dad's sheet rise like a tennis match.

Just before dawn, a cacophony of sirens disquieted Dad who became oddly alert, looking for Dooley, asking if Dooley was on the fire truck putting out the fire.

"Of course he is, Dad. Superhero Dooley will be the one to save you," I said.

Dad went back into his delirium, but I could tell that the sirens were confusing him. He was drifting to somewhere else, and it seemed as if the reality of the sirens and the prison of his dream world were colliding and painful for him to endure.

There was commotion in the hallway followed by a nurse closing our door, whispering, "Fire! You must remain in the room."

I Hail Mary-ed once out of habit, even though I was furious with the Bitch.

It hadn't even occurred to me to be frightened of a fire. *Really, God? A fire?* I was more afraid of fireballs, the adenocarcinoma that ate Dad with a vengeance. I was even more afraid of his breaths, which were becoming increasingly strained and infrequent. I was frightened of what would happen when they stopped altogether. I was afraid that death would come here in the closed, locked, narrowing room; that he would arrive while I was locked with Dad in his delirious space of drift and reality.

Dad smiled and mumbled that CeCe was OK, Dooley had rescued her, and that Mom needed a ride on the motorcycle, and that the bread wasn't frozen enough. He asked for the Mary-babies and saw F-16s. He said he would not need a wheelchair for the wedding.

I gasped enough air for both of us because the sheet did not rise for way too long.

There was a bang that I believed wholeheartedly to be death arriving with his scythe, but it was only the nurse once again, who opened the locked door to Dad's room.

"All is safe! The fire is out!" she said, somehow happily.

*Breathe.*

The fire was out, and Dad was definitely dying.

I was seventeen and Dad was fifty-five and we were nowhere near safe.

The sheet rose.

The next day, we all stood around Dad's bed, a human hospital room perimeter.

I looked around. Mom. Dooley and Bea. Rog and Valerie. Gina and Wayne.

*Where the fuck have they been?*

Dad was awake, lucid and coherent. Spry, almost. He looked around, slowly, stopping to gaze at each of us, almost as if it was the last time he would ever do so.

He stopped at me and stared.

I attempted to lift the corners of my mouth.

"Well, now I *know* I'm dying. She called them all, right, Schnapps?" he asked me, attempting to head-nudge toward Mom.

I shrugged, openmouthed, but nothing came out. I tried to eye-speak Mom for help.

"This time it got to me, Schnapps. What do I always tell you?" Dad asked.

*If it seems too good to be true, it probably is.*

I hadn't the heart to answer.

His emptied eyes held the contact my young, sad, hopeful, blind eyes tried to sustain for him.

That was my job, to be hopeful for him. Jesus-fucking-hopeful. He clung to me for truths those days, not to doctors, not to Mom or to the older absentee kids.

*Is there Ensure in that milkshake? Am I losing my hair? Have I lost a lot of weight? Is Mom OK? Have they told you it reached my brain yet?*

*No Dad, we're OK, everything is going to be OK.*

I lied all the time—it was my way of keeping Dad alive for even one more day. I don't think that he knew that I lied. I Jesus-fucking-hoped not. I Jesus-fucking-hoped that I didn't break his trust.

So, as he stared, searching for final truth, I did the only thing that I knew to do, my best, and I stood before him one last time, and recited:

"Now the trumpet summons us again; not as a call to bear arms, though arms we need; not as a call to battle, though embattled we are; but a call to bear the burden of a long twilight struggle, year in and year out, rejoicing in hope, patient in tribulation; a struggle against the common enemies of man: tyranny, poverty, disease and war itself."

"Kennedy, what are you talking about?" Dooley asked.

I hadn't the energy to explain. If he didn't know by then, he'd never know.

Dad's spirit began to wander once again before me.

I watched the disappointment and the reality of his condition change his face from his forehead down, like a curtain of nauseating truth, a sentencing scroll.

"I have a date on Friday!" I said.

Dad smiled.

It worked. I lightened one more moment for him.

I exhaled.

The sheet rose.

## CHAPTER 33

# We're All Alone

### May 1982 Still

Atomic cancer
Adenocarcinoma
Assassination

I never realized that his eyes were so blue, like pellucid glass marbles with white striation. They looked so small and so clear, so peaceful and yet, so fake or frightened or void. They were such a pretty pale blue.

I was alarmed.

They were fixed not quite at the ceiling, but where the wall met the ceiling, the same point at which his angled toes stared. His arms were by his sides.

He was not wearing his glasses and maybe that was throwing me. But no. It was the eyes.

I had never seen those eyes before, those small, pale, oceanic crystals.

His hair was clean and looked like rabbit's hair of mostly white with silver. I could imagine its softness. I did not touch it. I thought that would have been bad.

I did not know what was good or what was bad at that particular time.

I knew that time froze in ocean crystals in the silence of death.

Did I really know him?

I did not really know death.

I did not know how I was supposed to act.

I said goodbye to him as if he were leaving for work because that was how I knew to say it.

I felt nearly nothing but astonishment and wonder at truly seeing the eyes of this man for the first time, and knowing that for eternity he would have pretty pale blue eyes that I had seen only once.

## CHAPTER 34

# Hells Bells

### Infinitely May 1982

Mom used an SAT word and said that limousines were "osten-tatious," so we drove in regular cars behind the huge tailgate monster-mouthed hearse. At least I was able to ride with Rog and Valerie.

There had been no wake at Dad's request—"If people want to look at me, then they should have done it while I was alive"—which was funny to me because he refused visitors at the house while he was still alive.

In church, I couldn't even sit near Roger and Valerie. I was last, alone, again, naturally, a pew to myself, behind even the Mary-babies who were somehow brutally allowed to attend Dad's funeral. I knew that they belonged there, I knew that we sat in birth order, but it seemed a slap in the face *turn the other cheek* to be relegated to last. I mean, I was the milkshake and omelet maker, and I was the one trying to be Dad's friend, and I was the one who played Got a Minute until there were no minutes left.

The only saving grace—*grace? Is there even such a thing anymore?*—was that Aunt Aileen moved up from her pew behind me, breaking protocol, and held my hand throughout the ceremony. I un-flinched and held on for dear life.

The church was packed. All of Dad's tavern and work friends were there as well as Aunt Aileen's other half and her pagan public school kids, and some distant relatives I don't think I ever even met. Roger's fence friends were there, including Mushroom Marcus, with their neighborhood families. A group of friends from my school was there along with Mr. Meany, Jake, and Clarissa. There were a ton of people there that I didn't even know, plus the entire police force.

I was devoid of faith, and hope felt more like despair, which made sense to me if Jesus gave it to us through death, through killing Dad. I mouthed the mass's rote responses so that no one would get mad at me for not participating. Silently, I chanted the only prayer that I could muster sans nauseam, the only way I could, *"O flock of heavenly cranes, cover my child with your wings."*

A week or so *who could even tell time anymore?* prior to Dead Dad's *Grand Finale Production*, the boy, the subject of my last hopeful sentence to Dad—*"I have a date on Friday!"*—began coming through my grocery line two or three times a day, buying one or two items at a time. I had decided mid-week, right before he asked me out, somewhere between his frozen chicken and ripe tomato, that I was going to marry him.

After the funeral, from the back seat of Aunt Aileen's hand-me-down, I saw my date, the floundering Funeral Boy of the newly reassigned daughter of Dead Dad, pacing on the sidewalk in front of church. I thought how chivalrous it was of him to come since we barely knew each other. I swear that I saw Clarissa extend an invisible claw out to bait him right there on that sidewalk, a target standing alone, but who also seemed to notice her not at all.

I watched Jake look around, maybe for me, maybe for no one.

"Yo, Rog—"

"Boss?" Rog asked the rearview mirror.

"See that guy on the sidewalk in the suit with the polished shoes? The one Clarissa is gawking at?"

"Affirmative, Boss."

"I'm going to nail him, and then marry him."

"Affirmative, Boss."

"Rog?"

"Yes, Boss?"

"What about hell?"

"Fuck hell."

We laughed the Christmas laugh, the happy laugh, the eat-too-many-cookies-because-we're-high-and-might-get-yelled-at laugh.

*Nah.*

If I went to hell for fucking Funeral Boy, then Roger would be right there, right next to me.

Roger was always there right next to me.

*Heaven can wait.*

The cemetery was hot and dry, but I was stone cold.

*Like Dead Dad?*

Yeah, I was stone cold like Dead Dad.

The priest mumbled his Catholic shit, but I have no idea what he said.

Roger and Valerie held me up by the elbows like a quintessen-tial prom queen, one on each side.

And at the end, all that was left of Dad was an American flag, folded into a pretty damn near perfect isosceles triangle, given to none other than Dooley.

We were finite.

*Fuck flags.*

CHAPTER 35

# Leather and Lace

**Forever May 1982**

The morning after my deflowering, I drove Mom and me to church in Aunt Aileen's hand-me-down, even though my soul was dead to God. I felt as if the score had finally been evened.

"How was your date?" Mom asked.

Mom had said more words to me since the funeral than the past *I don't know how many years* put together.

"Good," I said, "it was very grown up, with wine and candles and a bud vase with a single rose on the table. White tablecloths. Classy place."

"Nice," she said.

It *was* nice.

I swallowed Jesus even though I was in a state of mortal sin again, because I did not want to disappoint Mom. It was a bit like Santa Claus, the hypocrisy.

I couldn't even mouth the mass's rote responses that morning. I was riddled with shame, not because of my sin, but because all that I could think about was my sin, and how it felt when he danced inside of me, and how I needed to feel that feeling again.

Poor Mom. Out of her shell she came, whispering, "It's OK if you can't respond. I know it's hard to be here so soon."

*Ha! So soon after fucking, you're so right, Mom.*

So soon after all of the deaths. So soon after such revelation.

Hal-le-fucking-lujah.

Soon after, I went through Tattoo Boy's line with a shovel and a pack of cigarettes.

"Really, Kennedy? Do you need help?"

*Sometimes you have to mess things up before you can put them back together again, right, Schnapps?*

I shook my head no.

He walked around the register bay and hugged me. My third.

"I'm sorry about your father. May you find peace."

He kissed my forehead.

"Thanks. I mean, for everything."

"I know. You're welcome. Marry that boy that comes through your line. He loves you."

*Funny.*

I laughed and I left, shovel in hand.

## CHAPTER 36

# Goodbye to Innocence— Kennedy's Grand Finale Production

**May Queen 1982**

The sand was still loose and the shovel went in with more ease than I expected.

"So, hey Dad, what's going on? What's it like down there in the ground in that pretty nailed coffin of yours?"

*Father forgive them for they know not what they do...*

"Dad, I hope you will forgive me for what I am about to tell you. I know you will not be proud. I guess I never got there."

*Death be not proud...*

I dug.

"So, there's been a lot of goodbyes lately. A lot of death. A lot of little deaths, big deaths. I started off small. Bit off what I could chew, as you would have said. I showered for a gazillion days, or so it seemed. I said goodbye to the sweat of bearing the burden of our long twilight struggle, washed off so many tears, and rinsed and rinsed this damn cemetery sand that remained in my hair for days, until at last, it was gone.

"That day, the one I am about to tell you about, I showered again, extra long, said goodbye to the hair on my legs, my under-arms, my bikini line. Like usual. I said goodbye to baby powder and Soft and Dri, used and never to be seen again. Goodbye to perfume, diffused and evaporated. I said goodbye to my panty-hose before I even left the house, something I know that Mom found completely crass, because she told me so on my way out. Goodbye clean nose.

"All these little deaths added up to the main event—*Kenne-dy's Goodbye*. My dress was ironed, you would have been pleased, but it was goodbye pressed dress as it ended up in a wrinkled accordion around my waist. Goodbye to underwear on the floor. Goodbye to the bra that I left at home, like Gina, when she used to date Wayne. Goodbye to all of the untouched flesh that would become tenderly touched and eventually razor burned, gently grazed and brutally defiled.

"I had to say goodbye to Mom, what a big death, Dad, knowing I'd never return the same—I'd be changed, a sinner, tarnished, vanished. Her face showed some emotion I could not identify, one of a handful I'd ever seen on her. It was as if she knew how I had died already.

"I said goodbye to the house and to the gaping hole, the empty remains of a tree that used to mean something, now naked and devoid of life.

"And then I said goodbye to innocence. I said goodbye to Mary Kennedy.

"And now I have to say goodbye to you, Dad, because we shall never meet again. We are spending our time, earthly and eternally, in different places.

"You, Dad, you will be in heaven for sure, with Mom, and with all of the superheroes like Dooley, and maybe even the fake heroes too like Santa Claus and the Easter Bunny. Father Patrick Peyton will be there with you someday too. I mean, Dad, come on! With all of the good deeds you did and all of the Hail Marys you said and I said for you? It's simple math. It's unequivocal. You're in heaven.

"As for me? Well, I am in a state of mortal sin. I will be in hell, maybe even Mom-God hell, for eternity. I will not be repenting, because I am going to continue on my highway to hell as a motorcycle beneath Funeral Boy, over and over and over again, and I won't be sorry. Not ever. I am damned forever.

"I did it, Dad. I had sex. It was exactly like Mom's human hand peace sign puzzle, except for the fingers part. There was hard flesh and soft flesh, pulverized and mashed. Like Jell-O on a stick. And it all fit together, and like a puzzle, when it was finished, it was one.

"I was there. I was me.

"He was so focused, Funeral Boy, you'd like that about him— that and his shoes. They are kempt.

"Dad, there was life—there was living—inside of me. It was feeling and being felt at the same time. It got so quiet, Dad, the only sounds were the rustling of clothing and linens, mouths and moans. But then, the universe ebbed, the spinning stopped and the quiet resounded inside of me with every silent movement. I think I heard love. There were silent empty moments filled with sheer awareness of something OK. Something good. Acceptable. Yes. Lying back, lying under, the weight of feeling OK to be OK.

Feeling good to be good. Me being me. Just me. Inside. Outside. Filled. Empty. All at once. In and out. Blood surged to all of these new places and filled my heart with the sound of standing still. There was a voice telling me it was good, telling me that I was OK. I am OK. Kennedy is going to be fine. Kennedy can love. Kennedy will love. It began in flesh and it will continue with flesh because I am. Because I am. And I am OK."

I unloaded a box that I had packed and placed in the relic's trunk earlier that day.

"Dad, I loved God through my body, I let Him flow through me like a trade wind, just like Sister said to. It's sheer blasphemy, right? I want to do it over and over and over, infinitely for all eternity. That's bad, Dad, and you know it. To hell in a hand basket for me."

I finished digging a new grave next to the foot stone that tells everybody in perfect font that Dad is dead.

"Dad, I brought you something."

Into the ground, I laid to rest Coffin Nails, Dad's reminder of hope. Jesus-hope. My tears tapped tapped tapped its hard wood.

I scattered the one-thousand cranes, more tears dampening their folded memories.

I topped it all off with the graduation cap glittered with "Kennedy's Dad, 1982."

I buried our milestone monuments beneath the sandy death dirt.

I stuck cigarettes one by one into the ground like an earth birthday cake, lit them, and watched them burn into the dirt until only black filters were left staring from holes in a perfect line in front of Dad's gravestone.

I was eighteen and Dad was days, hours, minutes, moments and memories shy of fifty-six for eternity.

"Happy Birthday, Dad. I am sorry that I will never make you proud, my nose is dirty, my soul is stained, and my virtue has been thrust out of me over and over. Carved and incised like cancer.

"It's quiet at home without you, Dad. Your recliner sits still in the living room, CeCe dutifully alongside it looking up from her sound sleep every now and then to check on invisible you, to make sure you are still there. She looks, she sniffs, she raises her head, twists her neck until she sees what she thinks might be your movement, when it's really just me or Mom or the sun's dancing, and then she rests her head again, forever filled with Miss Turtle-neck's Jesus-hope.

"I watch her, wondering where she thinks you are or where you went. I wonder how long she will rest alongside your lingering smell and your constantly reappearing hair on the floor. I wonder when CeCe will give up her Jesus-hope, or give up her need to protect and be loyal, her need to be your friend. I wonder when CeCe the Cancer dog will need more than just being alongside someone who isn't even there."

*When will she surrender?*

I looked around, kicked the sand, spread new seed.

I thought about *Roger's Production, Goodbye to Innocence.* I remembered a little girl with a connection to, what? A tree? A brother?

I was alive, immersed, seen.

I danced around one of the six trunks that Dad said stood for each of us, twirling, showing off, flinging my hair. I looked free.

No one told me what to do. No one cried. No one stole. No one ignored me or told me to leave Mom alone. No one felt sad or alone. There was no fear. There was no pain. No one left.

There was no kidnapping or betrayal, no brutality, no cheeks turning. There was no lurch. There was no shatter. Only surrender.

I was seven.

The film was long lost, but I found that twirling seven-year-old beneath Funeral Boy. She was there and she is here, dancing freely, hand hugging life.

Maybe hope, simply, is love waiting to happen.

"Hey Dad, let's be seven."

## ⚡The End⚡

# Acknowledgments

Thank you, Keith, for our life together. You make our world possible. Thank you for the unimaginable amount of time you listen to me and read me. I still don't know how or why you do it. I love you.

Scott, Rebecca, Ethan, and Hannah: you give my life its purpose. Thank you for the privilege of growing up alongside you, walking in parallel footsteps, hand in hand. I love you and the families you are creating.

Parts of all of you are in this book, and I hope you smile when you read them.

To us—all of us—always the love and the hours.

rememberyoga

Thank you to my amazing agent, David Vigliano, who believed in me, and who provided invaluable editorial feedback throughout several drafts of this novel, over a decade, with patience and encouragement. I appreciate you.

Thank you to my editor, Madeline Sturgeon, and to everyone at Post Hill Press who launched *Kennedy's Goodbye*. Thank you for bringing my words to print. Thank you for saying yes.

For all of you who have been there for me, lending an ear or a hand or the silence I needed when I was a writing hermit, or a hermit in general, thank you. Each of you has contributed with your help and love. I am forever grateful.

Thank you, memory.

And to this faithful Trinity—The Blessed Mother, St. Ecanus, and St. Anthony (sometimes known as M, D, & T)—thanks. You know why.

# About the Author

Author Kati Rose has always said, "I just want to write a book."

*Little Women*, Laura Ingalls Wilder, one creative writing assignment, and a supportive teacher all inspired Kati to write—an outlet which provides her with a sense of belonging, a feeling of alignment, and the place where she turns real life into words with intimate candor.

Kati's novel, *Kennedy's Goodbye*, has arrived.

When she's not writing, Kati loves spending time with her children, grandchildren, her husband who doubles as best friend, and their movie star cats, Dakota (Fanning) and Tatum (O'Neal).

Author photo by Tom Wall Photography